FURY STORM

Sever Squad

Book 6

A.R. KNIGHT

ONE

Introductions

THE STRIP-MINED SYSTEM had little to recommend it. Their target, Aurum Three, came into focus on the *Prisa*'s windshield. A distant blue star shot its light past Sever Squad's ship as it flew in, catching the planet and making its yellow-brown surface clear. Darker, blurred lines moved along the land, like living smudges parading over paper.

"Massive storms," Eponi, sitting in the pilot's chair, noted. "Never fun to race in those."

"Or fight," Aurora, in the co-pilot's seat beside Eponi, replied.

Both had their brimming coffee cups, waking up to the first day in months that would really matter. Skinsuits—Eponi's a soft gold, Aurora's a blood red—snugged them, allowing quick access to power armor. Eponi's left arm no longer had its cast, the snapped bone having knit itself back into shape. The pilot's left hand drummed on Eponi's thigh, anxious.

Rusted nerves. A vacation's cost.

Not that Sever had many options. As much as Aurora may have wanted to chase the agent Vana all the way to this world, Sever left Gillane Four battered and exhausted. The fighters had hardly slept, had been strung out on adrenaline and whatever else could keep them functioning for days. Laser burns, concussions, knife cuts and worse all needed tending.

But, after more than a hundred days spent recuperating, repairing, and realigning her squad to its mission and its place in a galaxy that now saw Sever as a group to be detained or destroyed, Aurora felt they'd gone long enough.

More importantly, Aurora's maybe-more-than-friend and DefenseCorp admiral Deepak sent the message saying it was time.

Vana, the DefenseCorp agent masterminding a program designing near-invisible power armor suits coupled with genetically enhanced soldiers, had decided to stand up for her claims and bring DefenseCorp's leaders to a single spot. There, according to Deepak, Vana would convince the massive, galaxy-spanning company's leaders to go along with the plan, creating a new force that wouldn't so much handle contracts for help as drop an ironclad shroud over civilization.

After all, who could fight an enemy that could be anywhere?

"We could've stayed," Sai said, Sever's resident father and swordmaster. His voice came over the *Prisa*'s intercom, drifting in from the ship's right turret. "The cash was pretty good."

The station, a free-wheeling centerpoint in a large asteroid cluster, had offered Sever a standing contract to provide security. While Aurora would've been fine beating up drunk miners for steady pay on the galaxy's fringe, she'd already played that role once and watched as DefenseCorp swooped in and stole the work.

"How long you think we'd last before Vana's new toys took it from us?" Rovo, the squad's resident comms expert and a third cockpit occupant, spoke for Aurora. "We'd be bored, and then we'd be dead."

Rovo had his own motivations to hit Vana. All of Sever did. That tugging, burning feeling sat wrong inside Aurora: vengeance wasn't normally an issue, because Aurora's enemies tended to die long before they became a nagging problem. Vana, though, continued to escape, to twist the fights so they weren't clear-cut laser tags until one side lay smoking on the ground. Like blocks building up into an enraging tower, Aurora had spent the recovery time on the station assembling all the reasons why she needed to turn Vana to ash.

And now, they'd arrived.

"Tell me I'm seeing things," Eponi said, nodding towards the glass.

New imperfections crossed the planet's surface as the *Prisa* approached. What had looked like splotches, normal smears across a landscape seen from afar, resolved into sharper focus. Blurred lines became straight edges associated with man-made machines. One or two could've meant Vana's own forces, but as the *Prisa* came in closer, those dots kept appearing, and growing.

"They didn't just bring themselves," Aurora said, not wanting to believe it. "They actually brought their commands too."

"That's going to burn a lot of contracts," Rovo added, as if saying that, here, would convince all those admirals to jump back in their ships and return home.

"DefenseCorp must be losing so much cash for this," Eponi agreed. "Look at all these cruisers. I don't understand?"

Aurora simmered in the silence, putting together both

an answer and an inspiration, "They're here because they want a piece. Vana's advertising suits *and* a genetic upgrade. You can't get your soldiers a dose if they're across the galaxy. But it also means we have the audience we're looking for."

"The admirals?" Rovo asked. "Didn't we know they'd be here?"

"Not them. All the soldiers. The staffers. The pilots and the mechanics. If we can show them what Vana's planning, what this virus will actually do, DefenseCorp won't be able to hide it from this many people. Not like they did with Dynas."

That planet, with its secretive experiments, had escaped the galaxy's wider notice. Sever had been sent in on a botched rescue mission to the supposedly-empty world, only to find a festering project that turned its subjects into food for a ravenous disease. Angry, destructive food, but food nonetheless.

Only with severe cold had Sever been able to eradicate the disease before it claimed them all.

"Think you're missing a step, captain," Eponi said. "We're going to be popping up on a whole lotta sensors in a few minutes, and I can't imagine they're gonna be friendly."

"Are you saying people don't like us?" Rovo asked.

"I thought everyone loved the captain," Sai said.

Aurora grimaced. Sai's sarcasm had some truth in it. Aurora's name, Sever squad's name, would be known to plenty in that swarm up in front. As the *Prisa* popped on their scanners, all those cruisers, those frigates, those fighters would figure out who flew the ship. When they did, all the missions Sever spent crashing into the enemy's heart to save DefenseCorp assets and asses might be worth something.

Or, as the *Prisa*'s monitoring system sounded off a shrill chirp, not.

"Looks like the fun's over, kids," Eponi cracked. "We're getting hostile pings. Missile locks, radar range-finders, all the good stuff. Last chance to turn back, Aurora."

"You already know the answer."

"Diving in, guns blazing," Eponi affirmed. "That's what I love about this crew. No matter how dismal it all looks, we'll just keep shooting till the odds change."

"There's a motto in there somewhere," Sai said. "Eponi, what's our allocation?"

"You're getting just enough to play with," Eponi replied. "Engines and shields get everything else. This isn't a fight, it's a sprint."

Aurora sat back in the seat, looked out at all the ships arrayed around Vana's chosen world. Eponi angled the *Prisa* towards the loosest knot that'd still give them a straight run to the surface. The pilot had ample choices: this wasn't a cohesive DefenseCorp fleet expecting attack, but an officer stew, with every individual commander deciding where to park their vessels while they dropped to the rock.

Hmm. Aurora might be able to use that.

"Eponi, give me a broadcast channel," Aurora said.

"Feeling like a speech?"

"Something like that."

Aurora's console chirped, switching the small screen over to a broad green target list. Aurora could tap along the ship names to cut them off the transmission, but she wasn't going to play favorites.

The coffee had gone lukewarm, but the liquid salved her nervous throat. Aurora could lead a thousand troops into the enemy's teeth without flinching, but delivering a bold address to thousands, maybe millions? No thanks.

The things she did for Sever Squad.

"Hailing DefenseCorp ships," Aurora began, letting the bog standard beginning warm her way into the next piece. "This is Sever Squad and her commander, sending out a notice that we're passing through your perimeter en route to the surface." A breath. Here came the game. "Despite what your systems might be telling you, we've been granted one-time passage. Fire on us, and you fire upon yourselves."

Bold words, ridiculous words. An assertion that any competent officer would laugh away in one breath and order his soldiers to fire in the next.

Except every ship zeroing on the *Prisa* right now had its backups in charge. Leaders that didn't have all the details, that didn't have the rank or the responsibility to decide if a lone approaching ship should be a friend or a foe.

"Is it working?" Aurora asked in the silence.

"We're still target locked," Eponi replied, "but nobody's pulled the trigger yet."

"Voice like honey, I always say," Rovo added. "Everybody trusts you."

Aurora swiped away from the broadcast, looked at the scanners. The *Prisa* picked up velocity as Eponi used the hesitation, siphoning more energy away from the ship's weapons and feeding its hungry engines. The scanners displayed long orange oval frigates, red fighter dots, and fat cruiser circles. The bulk drifted towards the *Prisa*'s entry path, but they all kept their distance from each other too. No coordinated strategy.

"Look at all this," Eponi said. "The *Nautilus* always flies alone. Forgot who we work for."

"Used to work for," Aurora clarified, but she couldn't deny the sight.

Outside, running lights visible now, the hulks making

up DefenseCorp's arsenal cut into the view from every angle. Huge engines many times the *Prisa*'s size lit up in glows ranging from soft yellow to hot and feisty blue. The metal hulks went below and above, and Aurora could pick out swiveling turrets moving to track Sever's ship as it passed by.

"Friends left," said Gregor, Sever's own living hulk. Snared in the *Prisa*'s left turret, Gregor had been quieter since Gillane Four, choosing to use his limited words with care, as if each one risked betraying some emotion, some crack in the man's armor. "Fire?"

"Keep the fingers off the triggers," Aurora said, though she fought to hide a flinch when Gregor's friends, a fighter trio, blew by the cockpit. The wave-like craft, a thin edge frothing over with cannons, made sure the *Prisa* knew it would die in a thousand ways if anything changed. "We help nothing by engaging out here."

All those officers Aurora had heard would be checking, trying to confirm, with their commanders. Vana herself would probably catch word soon. One would come back, would order Sever destroyed.

The mystery would be when.

"Is Deepak coming?" Rovo asked.

"Why is that relevant right now?" Aurora replied.

"It's not, I guess, but we're flying here," Rovo said. "Not much I can do, so, uh, figured I'd ask a question?"

Aurora threw the rookie a raised eyebrow over her shoulder. Eponi, though, seemed zoned in on keeping the *Prisa* on its path—denoted by a translucent green arrow leading through the fleet and towards Aurum Three's surface—and neither Sai nor Gregor had another update coming through.

"I don't know," Aurora gave the only answer she had.

The conversation had been painful. The park on

Gillane Four, when Deepak said Sever would be targets forever barring a miracle. Aurora didn't mind getting shots fired her way, but beneath Deepak's warning came a second, harsher truth: the two of them had, in the short time between the *Nautilus* insurrection and the fighting on Gillane Four, rekindled lingering embers. Those sparks had been snuffed out in that park, and since then Deepak had sent along only cold advice.

"Might want to see if he's near," Rovo said. "because if this goes like we're hoping, I bet we won't have many friends in this bunch."

"He knows where we are," Aurora said.

"Good," Eponi interjected. "Those locks are starting to heat up—"

"Missiles fired!" Sai shouted. "Eponi, give me some power or we're done!"

Aurora leaned forward, swiping to the scanner as Eponi threw the ship into a corkscrew, angling towards the planet. Aurora wished she'd taken one of the turrets, wished she could do something beyond watch as death came for her ship and her crew.

But Aurora would have to wait till they landed.

Then, then she would get her fill.

TWO

Gunnery Games

ADMITTEDLY, the closing death did a lot to detract from the spectacular view. From his turret's windshield, Sai admired the clustered ships, their bulks mingling in strategically terrible, photographically beautiful ways as mismatched officers and bored pilots jockeyed for positioning. Massive cruisers larger than the *Nautilus* brushed smaller frigates and corvette clusters away like a stone rippling water. Lights in all colors broadcast intentions, putting dotted halos into the dark.

The whole scene turned jagged when the white-hot pops broke against those magnificent vessels. Rockets ignited, fuses telling batteries to go for broke and burn towards Sever and their ship.

The first volley emerged from a nearby corvette, a craft not all that much larger than the *Prisa* but bristling with weapons. Shaped like a coin, the corvette's missile launchers made a crown on its top side, each one spitting out a small projectile in turn. The ship's velocity left the puffs behind, a cloudy sign the attack was underway.

Sai tapped the console near his hands, swapping the

turret's settings to scatter shot. The corvette approached from his side, and, after shouting the incoming alarm into the comm, Sai wheeled the turret around and pressed the trigger, hoping Eponi gave him some energy to play with.

The pilot didn't let Sai down, and the *Prisa*'s turret burst like a cheap firework. Hot light exploded everywhere in the turret's direction, the focusing mirrors in the turret's barrels rotating at ludicrous speed to send bolts out in a wide field. They'd be far too weak to pierce any ship's hull, wouldn't do much against shields unless Eponi flew close enough for Sai to kiss the target. Against a paper-thin missile, though?

If the rockets puffed white smoke when they launched, the things blew up incandescent. Every missile came packed with different goals in mind, from crackling blue to nuke electronics to rosy red for heat and sunny yellow for sonic. DefenseCorp depended on overwhelming any resistance with a varied assault, and Sai checked off every color from the list in his head.

Twelve rockets in a volley, and Sai only breathed when he saw twelve explosions. The missiles had done what missiles did and flown right at the *Prisa*, right into the scattershot blasts.

"Like old times," Gregor called over the private turret-to-turret channel, meant to keep the gunners in sync without screwing the pilot.

"Little different scenery."

Sai and Gregor, along with Aurora, tended to take the gunnery positions on any drop ship dives towards war zones. The two had shot down more missiles than Sai could possibly count. The experience kept the butt-clenching fear from breaking Sai's concentration.

Didn't mean he wouldn't request something stiff that night.

Assuming there was a night after all this.

Eponi kicked the *Prisa* forward, sprinting towards the planet's atmosphere. Sai watched for more missiles, but the corvette changed its mind and held its launchers from a second volley.

"Are they scared?" Sai asked.

"Changing tactics," Gregor replied. "Fighters, both sides."

Swiping the turret back to its standard firing set, Sai frowned at the energy left to him. Eponi had the *Prisa* sending its power to the engines, with a bit left over for the shields, leaving a tiny concession for Gregor and Sai.

"Eponi," Sai said over the ship's general band, "you want us to play defense, you're going to have to give us something more."

"Can't have it," Eponi quipped back, as though Sai and Gregor were asking for candy.

"We're not firing at DefenseCorp ships," Aurora took over, her steel brooking no dissent.

But the captain wasn't in Sai's chair, didn't have Sai's view staring down six fighters lining up runs that, all together, would turn the *Prisa* to so much burning ash.

"Aurora, we're assaulting DefenseCorp's top brass on a planet they control," Sai said, taking up that dissent because nobody else could. Nobody had been serving with Aurora longer, nobody understood how she thought better than him. "They're going to be mad enough at us already."

"Not doing it. Distract them. Misdirect. Once we hit atmosphere, we'll be down before they can do damage."

Before Aurora finished speaking, the first lasers blitzed from the fighters towards the *Prisa*. Eponi jerked the ship around into another maneuver, one of an endless series that never seemed to repeat. The first shots splashed against the *Prisa*'s shields, fizzling out against the energy barrier. The following beams burned past, hitting precisely nothing.

Gregor's whistle carried over the comm as Eponi reversed the upward swing, cutting back just as the fighters pushed after her first move. Sai had to agree with the hammer man: Eponi's sharp flying bought them seconds, and in a game of minutes, that could make the difference.

"Close encounters?" Sai said, using the turret band.

"Only option," Gregor agreed.

Fingers on the triggers, Sai acted on Aurora's misdirect order. Sai fired, sending yellow bolts streaking at the fighters. He aimed wide, just off where the fighters would be, so the shots missed. The fighters reacted, splitting from their straight shootin' runs into dances and dives. The formation broke as Sai and Gregor sent their harmless fire into the cracks between the enemy, where the fighters had been instead of where they were going to be. So long as Sai's lasers didn't catch a shield or bounce off a hull, the fighters wouldn't know they weren't in real danger.

"They'll think we're the worst gunners ever," Sai said, laying a blistering trail through his target's blue ion exhaust.

Gregor's laugh carried back through, carefree and filled with manic joy. The man never found a battle he didn't love, no matter the stakes or the odds. A freedom that came with no attachments, maybe, as Sai had never seen Gregor talk about a family, a loved one. With nothing to lose, Gregor relished all this.

The console blinked, drawing Sai's attention. The *Prisa* hit atmosphere, and the system warned Sai that his shots might get bent, ever-so-slightly, by the heavy air. Not that Sai needed the console to tell him that: gravity's sudden re-appearance had Sai falling up, pressing against his restraints. Blood rushed to his head, only to flush away as Eponi rolled the *Prisa* into a better position.

"Sorry 'bout that," Eponi said. "Things are a little crazy right now."

But not as crazy as they might be. Gregor and Sai's bluff made the fighters cautious, with their approaches coming slow and from odd angles. The pilots had no way to know the *Prisa*'s turrets had about as much lethal energy as Sai's angry looks, and they flew careful. Why risk anything when the target seemed to be diving right into a death trap?

"Looks like we scared'em," Sai said.

"Too good," Gregor replied.

Through Sai's windshield, black space turned purple and orange, with flames licking the outside as the *Prisa* busted into the planet's atmosphere. The ship rattled and bucked, its structure adjusting as weight, heat, and all the laws of physics took their toll. Sai let up on the turret—he couldn't aim with all the bouncing anyway—and watched as the fighters kept their distance.

Hell, those pilots were cowards for sticking so far back.

"I'm getting an incoming hail," Aurora said. "Stay quiet."

Sai cocked his head at nobody, surprised. Aurora could've kept the transmission private, or just played it in the cockpit. If she wanted to broadcast it on the open channel, it must be from someone important.

"Aurora, I really wished that we would never see each other again," said a voice that twisted Sai's rather calm insides into angry knots. Vana, the DefenseCorp agent behind all this garbage. "Yet it seems you've come to spoil my party."

Sai pictured Vana's face in those flickering flames outside his window. The woman had taken Sai hostage, briefly, back on Gillane Four. The swordsman had spent a night in her terrible custody, endured her endless requests for him to ditch Sever squad and change sides. When he'd refused, Vana had instead probed for weaknesses, had fished around for what Sai feared most.

That night, for the first time in his life, Sai refused to think, to say anything about his family. Agents knew how to read a face, read eyes, and if Sai gave away the secret to his heart, he knew Vana would find them. She would reach across the entire galaxy and pull his wife, his children into her experiments.

Worst of all, Vana wouldn't laugh while she did it. She wouldn't promise some bold revolution like Renard, her dead partner. She wouldn't cackle like Anaskya, the scientist behind the disease Vana sought to spread, who obsessed over every opportunity to test her toys on new subjects.

No, Vana would kill Sai's family because it would make it harder for Sai to carry on. A calculation, made to boost Vana's position, and nothing more.

"Damn right," Aurora replied. "Why don't you make it easy on us and come say hello?"

"Unfortunately, I'm pre-occupied," Vana said. "You might have noticed I have some guests. They would prefer you don't crash our event, but I have a better idea."

"Dare I ask?"

"Oh, don't bother," Vana said. "I'm sure you understand that a demonstration makes a far better show than a speech. I'll open a bay for you. Please do fly safe."

The transmission cut. Outside, the fires died, replaced by a thick bronzed sky. The windshield caught golden dust, its specks sticking in the cracks and budding out over the glass. Sai sat back in the turret, letting his hands relax.

"She is making a mistake," Gregor said to the whole ship. "Letting us land is poor tactics."

"We're not the objective," Aurora answered. "She needs DefenseCorp to fall in behind her. What better way to do that than trashing one of their elite squads?"

"Back on Helix, I chopped up those infected monsters," Sai said. "They weren't all that bad. Neither were the agents on Gillane Four. I think we got this."

"Numbers, Sai," Rovo came in. "Your katana might be sharp and all, but look at this thing. It's huge. She's gotta have thousands in there."

Sai leaned forward, trying to look lower and seeing nothing but dust. He glanced at his console, the scanner showing the fighters had backed off all the way. No threats, then.

"I can't see anything from down here," Sai said. "Looks like they're pulling pursuit too. Mind if we cut in?"

"Swap with Rovo," Aurora said.

Smart move, and the rookie didn't object. As the *Prisa* slid lower and lower, Rovo showed up in Sai's turret nook, and the two switched spots. Passing through the narrow hall leading to the *Prisa*'s spine-like back half, Sai climbed through the small door into the ship's central chamber. Even though they were heading into a death trap, Sai could't kill a grin at what Sever had done to its ship.

In the hundred days spent on the fringe station, Eponi and Rovo, followed soon by the other three, had added their own touches to the *Prisa*. What'd been an efficient metal mix now sported souvenirs, painted on slogans for each Sever, and their carved names. Beneath Sai's sat his family's too, etched forever in the far wall.

Stairs to his right and straight ahead led down and up, to the boarding ramp and the crew quarters, respectively.

Sai didn't take either, instead going right and joining Eponi and Aurora in the cockpit.

Neither needed to point out where they were going. Neither needed to highlight a speck on the vast golden-brown desert below. Sprawling across the ground like an industrial spider, their target shimmered in the blue-washed daylight. A curved, solar-panel-coated structure sat central, with what seemed to be sloping tunnels diving into the dirt away from it. Those tunnels rose up to the surface again in all directions, bleeding into flattened fields covered with shimmering nets, modular buildings that seemed as though someone had dropped shiny steel blocks and left them where they lay, and where the spider's head ought to be, a vast landing pad with drop ships by the dozens.

Vana wasn't just playing with a few suits, a few diseased agents. She'd built a factory to make DefenseCorp a whole new army.

THREE

The Doomed

MUCH AS HE enjoyed spitting hot fire into space from his turret, Gregor relished the rush as his power armor snapped into place. The suit, plated over with energy sucking pads, knitted with mesh that could take a punch and send its absorbed kinetic energy to the suit's booster boots, cost cash Gregor and his hammer would earn back by breaking Vana's force into bits and pieces.

The big man stood in the *Prisa*'s center, appreciating the power amor's locking boots as they sealed Gregor to the floor. Eponi's landing dive had the ship curving left and right, making it a hard target. Vana didn't seem to be firing on them, but Aurora ordered the evasive moves anyway: it wouldn't be out of Vana's character to trick Sever into a placid approach only to blow them away with a sudden shot.

Next to him, Sai, also abandoning his turret, embraced his own armor. The pair, Gregor with his hammer and Sai with his diamond katana, would lead the assault off the *Prisa* and into whatever mess Vana had waiting for them. The two didn't exactly fit well—the hammer and the katana both had length that'd clip each other with their swings—but they'd break in opposite directions, clearing out any ambushing riffraff like deadly waves washing away encroaching sand.

Aurora and Rovo took the turrets instead, ready to handle any other surprises in the landing bay. Even at low power, the *Prisa*'s cannons held enough energy to torch a poor sap. Eponi, too, had the central cannon. Between them all, they could deliver fast devastation to any waiting force.

"They're opening a bay," Eponi said. "Far side of the base, not in the central compound. Their flight control's telling me to head that way. Do we?"

"Alternatives?" Aurora asked, the voices carrying through the speaker in Gregor's visor.

That visor, too, lit up with more than Aurora and Eponi's words. As the seal clamped down over Gregor's head, bars and graphs appeared and blitzed through statistics as the suit sprinted through Gregor's vitals and the armor's own functions and declared them all optimal. As a destructive machine, Gregor had the okay to obliterate.

"We could try blowing our own hole," Eponi said. "That might make Vana a little angry."

"All for that," Sai interjected.

"But on our terms." Aurora canceled the idea. "We don't know the layout, or where Vana's waiting. Once we know where she is, that's when we can take the initiative back. Follow the instructions Eponi, bring us in."

"As ordered, captain."

With the power armor closed over Gregor's arms and legs, the suit's various mechanisms tightening over Gregor's joints to ensure tight movement, he reached for his hammer. The meter-and-a-half long weapon ended in a large, cube-like head inscribed over with circuitry. Little circles linked by golden lines captured the energy spent in any swing and, as needed, delivered it back through an impact. Strong enough to shatter concrete, to bust through a wall.

To turn Vana into so much mush.

"Ready back there?" Eponi called. "Ten seconds to landing."

"I'm feeling sharp," Sai replied. "How about you?"

"Good," Gregor said.

The two went forward, almost into the cockpit. Gregor stood in front, with Sai bunching up close. Up ahead, past the cockpit's empty seats—save Eponi in the pilot's chair—Gregor saw their intended target. The *Prisa* took a long, lazy turn, shuddering as its primary engines shut down and swapped their power to the ship's maneuvering jets.

Their bay looked like a red maw sticking out from the golden-brown sand coating Aurum Three. The grains flowed over the opening, proving Vana's choice for Sever's docking bay hadn't been used in a long time. Darkness hid behind the red metal mouth.

Eponi flew right in.

"Energy's set for shields and guns," the pilot announced. "Rovo, Aurora, you should be good to send out all the death you need."

"Oh hurrah," Rovo said.

The *Prisa* cut in low, the blue daylight filtering in behind the ship as it went into the bay. The first look at Vana's base revealed not the expected hard metal, clean floors, and sterile efficiency, but, instead, unhinged madness.

The bay itself had been designed for ships far larger than the *Prisa*, the entry giving way to a huge circular expanse that looked like it might serve as a loading dock for troops embarking to hither and perhaps even yon. As the *Prisa* entered, as Eponi tried to figure out where to land, Sever took in a world as radical as they'd ever seen.

The bay's floors arced and swayed with debris, but not the junk of a world abandoned. Instead, the trash here had been piled into shapes. Towering constructs built with empty fuel canisters, rusted out pipes, and discarded shipping containers loomed in the giant space. The floor itself, too, looked like it had been used as a canvas by a thousand madcap painters, each one drawing with brushes of their own making. Lines in the purples and blacks of old-style fuels swirled beneath the *Prisa*'s lights, sometimes working themselves into faces, while often vanishing into indecipherable patterns.

Swishing between those darker colors came bright reds and blues, yellow splotches too. Gregor couldn't figure what chemicals had been sacrificed for these streaks, but the overall display offered up a confusing, disorienting feel. Gregor had seen too many planets, too many ships, and too many aliens to panic at the oddities, but the battle-ready urge to bash and bang smothered under the strange.

"I'm gonna guess nobody knows what we're looking at?" Rovo said. "I'm getting creeped out, honestly."

"Seen a lot of weirdness racing karts," Eponi echoed. "Nothing like this. Definitely not with DefenseCorp. It's like someone held a party at the end of the world."

"Land, Eponi," Aurora ordered. "Find a spot and get us down."

As if confirming Aurora's command, the maw behind them, Sever's only exit back into Aurum Three's skies, slid shut. No lights flickered on. Only the *Prisa* glimmered anything into the vast dark, those hollow hulks fighting the glow with tall shadows.

"Do we change our strategy?" Sai said. "Because this is not what I expected."

"Same plan," Aurora snapped back fast. "Vana's going to play with us. She said she needed to put on a show. This is all just a stage. Window dressing."

"Seems real old for window dressing," Eponi said. "Look at all the rust here. All these colors on the floor. No way Vana put all this together just in case we showed up."

Gregor played with that uncomfortable truth, tried to pair it with some tale he'd heard before, some explanation in all the DefenseCorp newsletters that'd come into his messages over the years and years. No way a company as focused on profit like DefenseCorp would let a base as big as this one just fade away, fall into this mess and leave it.

No way, unless, like Dynas, what happened here couldn't be salvaged.

"Let us down, Eponi," Gregor said.

"Sure you want to go into all that?" Eponi asked, and Gregor caught her crinkled nose, curled lip in the cockpit windshield's reflection.

"I am scarier than anything out there."

"Man's got a point," Rovo agreed. "I say let the hammer swing."

"Feeling like I'm getting no respect here," Sai muttered.

"I am glad you're standing with me." Gregor would've put his hand on the man's shoulder if he'd had the room.

"Isn't that just the cutest," Eponi said. "Good to go, captain?"

Aurora didn't answer, and Gregor could guess why. Like the rest of them, Aurora wanted a clue before venturing into the dark. Either a message from Vana taunting them into one direction or another, or maybe some light, some spark out beyond that would give Sever some hint at what waited for them.

When no call came, Aurora gave the order.

The *Prisa*'s secondary lift plummeted down. Meant for quick exits and entries without the vulnerability in lowering a long boarding ramp, the circular platform hit the painted floor before Gregor's body realized it was falling. Two poles connected the lift back into Sever's cockpit, but nothing else obstructed the ground-level view.

Nothing else interfered with the noises, either.

Living in space, in DefenseCorp bases, prepped Gregor for certain background sounds. The constant whirrs and churns as oxygen spun through recyclers, as heaters kept vacuum's icy clutches at bay. Echoing chatter bouncing down metal halls, or lifts dinging their arrivals and departures. Life's standard symphony.

Aurum Three, or at least this place, didn't conform.

The breeze hit Gregor first. Or rather, hit his power armor. The whistling wind rang through the hollowed constructs, rattling their tinny bones and swooping through their shambling bodies. Something tugged the air from one side of the room to the other, an unheard-of effect for a base like this one.

But, perhaps, there were no bases like this one.

"You hearing that?" Sai asked, the two power armor suits linking the swordsman with Gregor so their words went between them and nowhere else.

"The wind?"

"Beneath it. Like leaves, but heavier."

Gregor focused, dug beneath the whistling, and found what Sai meant. A deep rustle, almost like a hundred dogs growling low, their tones overlapping with one another. Unlike the wind, this sound came from all around.

Surrounded.

"Mind getting off that platform?" Eponi interrupted. "You two might be in power armor, but the rest of us are pretty, uh, naked up here."

"Sorry," Sai spoke for both of them, as they vacated the lift.

The *Prisa* sucked up the platform, leaving the two alone. The ship's running lights provided a halo, with its three landing struts serving as markers to the beyond. Gregor's visor stayed dark, detecting no threats. That, at least, meant rifles weren't aiming their way from the depths.

"Pick a direction?" Sai asked.

"Wait," Gregor said. "Be ready."

"Why?"

Gregor didn't answer. Instead, he hefted the hammer, stepped away from Sai, and then swung it down to the floor. The weapon struck the metal, flashing up sparks, old paint, and sending a clear ring reverberating through the wide room.

The rustle disappeared for a long moment.

"You scared'em away," Sai said.

"Wait," Gregor repeated, turning slow to see in every direction.

The howls started as one here, one there. Angry, confused. Others joined in the cry, some sounding clear, others hoarse, ending in hacking coughs. An animal pack, waiting to feast, this was not.

"Incoming," Aurora's voice came through. "Picking up motion on all sides."

"I told you," Gregor said to Sai.

"Yeah," said the swordsman, bringing up his katana in one hand, pistol in the other. "I hate it when you're right."

Gregor's visor caught the creature before he did. A scrambling thing, moving on all four, no, five limbs as it ran towards Gregor. Arms and legs like a human, but a fifth, a dark, fluid thing, pushed along with the man. Gregor couldn't, didn't suppress his own growl at the sight, at a nightmare returned.

Felix, on Dynas, had others with him like this. More virus than people. Back then, Gregor had burst a gas pipe, sent searing flame through the whole group. This time, he'd have to get personal.

Gregor took one step towards the creature before the enemy vanished in a laser blitz. Aurora's turret caught the monster, frying it to boiling tar in a blinding flash. Before Gregor could blink his way past the obliteration, Aurora's turret lit up again, finding and incinerating some other approaching creature in the dark.

"On your right!" Rovo called. "There's too many!"

Gregor spun, swinging his hammer with the turn. The hammer's head missed the target, but the haft caught the creature as it raked at Gregor's armor with hands sharpened to claws by the virus and its destructive designs. The hit sent the monster rolling to the right, but Gregor couldn't follow up as another took the creature's place.

Sever squad's hammer man let his left hand loose from the hammer, cocking back his elbow and delivering a crackling jab at the next, leaping fiend. As he struck, Gregor saw what had been a face, with half now devoured in that black, seeping gunk. Beneath and below, tattered clothes hung to the thing's remaining skin.

On them, hanging by a thread, was an identity badge that Gregor recognized: twin swirls climbing an invisible ladder. Helix, the company thrown together to control and supervise the Dynas experiments.

A flash burned over Gregor's shoulder, causing a yelp near Gregor's left ear.

"Pay attention, man!" Sai shouted, the swordsman whirling his katana in swift cuts, firing his pistol into the gaps.

Beyond, around the ship, the darkness disappeared into flashing lights as the *Prisa*'s twin turrets and Eponi's central cannon lit up. Fires broke out as bodies not meant for it absorbed superheated laser.

Gregor followed Sai's lead, grabbing his hammer and setting about around him as the creatures continued their assault, heedless of their own losses, their own lives.

Battles were supposed to be fun affairs, a chance to prove one's mettle in the purest competition remaining to humankind. Gregor wanted to relish every swing, every dodge and riposte that sent his enemies to the floor. He wanted to roar with delighted rage as he took apart his foes.

Instead, he kept silent, swinging and smashing and exterminating the people Sever had long ago left behind.

FOUR

Inside Out

FOR HER FIRST few Sever missions, Eponi couldn't get past the idea that she, now, starred in the action movies she'd watched as a child. With power armor on, rifle in hand, Eponi sprinted with Sever through one fight after another, pitching plasma and dealing death across planets at DefenseCorp's behest. Every time Eponi ducked a bolt and returned one of her own, or took a plunging leap off a crumbling building, only to land in the enemy's midst with guns blazing, her world seemed to zoom out, presenting the star at the climax.

Then, like sequels limping from one plot to the next, the flashy scenes began to run together. Aurora's mission briefings stopped juicing the adrenaline and kept Eponi's focus on the number at the end: the cash that'd be going into her account when all the slaughter ran out.

With that focus came the clinging need to survive, the understood thought that DefenseCorp wouldn't care one iota if Eponi caught a missile to the midsection, but Eponi herself would mind a whole helluva lot. How could Eponi spend all the cash she was earning torching people all across the stars if she wound up crisped herself?

The *Prisa*'s cannon whined, spitting fire ahead into the dark. The forms kept coming, and, without spending anything on shields or engines, the *Prisa* had the power to meet them. The cockpit's chosen cannon didn't have much flexibility, but the enemy didn't have much strategy. Eponi sat with her hand on the trigger, holding down the straight-ahead spray as it liquified the charging monsters one after another.

She wouldn't be getting any bonus pay for the body count, and sitting in a chair hardly made for a cinematic performance, but Eponi would live through this assault. That would have to be enough.

"Hanging in there?" Rovo, from the right turret, sent out on the broad band.

"It is a good workout," Gregor replied.

Eponi couldn't see the big man swinging his hammer, what with Gregor's position right beneath the *Prisa*'s middle. Evidence of his work, though, presented itself with bone-crunching frequency, as bodies flew out and vanished into the rubble. Sai's katana didn't quite have the same impact, but Eponi figured she'd get to witness that mess when the fighting finally stopped.

What a prize.

"We sticking this out?" Eponi asked, watching as the cannon's yellow bolts shredded another oncoming trio. "Is there an end, or did they get all the thousands on Dynas here for this horror show?"

"Vana wanted a display," Aurora replied. "She's getting one. And so is everyone else."

"They are?" Rovo asked.

"Recording." Eponi smirked. "So long as the *Prisa* doesn't get torched, we'll be beaming up this little event to the galaxy when we get out. Everyone's going to know what happened to Helix. It'll be a popcorn moment, for sure."

"The deaths of thousands by a horrible disease is a popcorn moment?"

"Rovo, we all have our own ways to cope, okay?" Eponi answered.

The reply shut the rookie up, and for more minutes than Eponi cared to count, the five dealt with the infected tide. When the rush slowed, though, Eponi did a double-take, then took another look to be sure. Despite the numbers, the casualties around the *Prisa* still seemed far less than the people living on Dynas.

Maybe some had escaped?

Maybe Vana had them waiting?

"Gregor, Sai," Aurora said when her turret turned its last target to ash, "take a look around. We'll get ready and meet you outside."

Saying goodbye to the *Prisa* always left Eponi with a twinge. She'd never owned a ship before, and despite having stolen the *Prisa*, Eponi had come to think of the big bird as her own. During Sever's respite, Eponi had scoured the craft, souped up what parts she could, and let her own personality bleed into the ship's settings. Eponi filled the *Prisa*'s memory banks with her favorite songs, movies, and games. She'd changed the themes on every console to her favorite colors, catching eye-rolls from the others.

Everything Eponi could claim on the ship, she had.

"Really?" Rovo asked as they waited for the boarding ramp to descend, the three now packed into their power armor.

Eponi had the *Prisa* blasting some ancient tune about a final countdown. It seemed appropriate.

"Do you just hate fun?" Eponi shot back as the boarding ramp hit the floor.

The cheery bang led the fighters down the ramp as the song hit its climax, putting a smile on Eponi's face.

Hitting the floor killed that smile fast. The power armor couldn't filter out the smell, the rotting stench from too many bodies too far gone, even though they'd been alive mere minutes ago. The visor picked out the stacks, the grim collections as the people that once were and now were not lay in their final places. A grim memorial for the *Prisa* to stand above, her struts forming a triangle around Gregor and Sai's ruthless efficiency.

Beyond the viscera, things didn't get much better. The turret duo and Eponi's cannon work provided their own unique take on the carnage: one blacker, often still burning, and blasted. Fragments lingered, collecting amid the rubble, telling short stories about lives ended with far more energy than a human body could ever handle.

Altogether, Eponi felt like vomiting. Altogether, she felt like running back into the *Prisa*, turning on the jets, and heading for the exit. Sure, Vana might have sealed them inside, but given enough time, the *Prisa*'s cannons could burrow them out.

And then what? Flee back through the entire Defense-Corp fleet?

"There's two exits," Sai said, his voice speaking right new Eponi's ear, driving a flinch. "Well, there's more than two, but Vana's only giving us two open doors."

"I could break in a third," Gregor added.

The two killers bounded away from the *Prisa* in the aftermath, tracing an outline around their apparent cell. The space, in the dark, seemed to stretch forever, but Sai claimed it did, in fact, have an end. A circular structure with at least seven exits, all positioned at random intervals, as if this bay had started as a hub for a base with rapid, unplanned expansion.

Both open exits looked like recent changes, with dust still lingering in the air where the large doors had shunted aside, so Sai said. Neither made its connection obvious, but Aurora broke down their respective directions in her methodical fashion.

"The first one leans to the north and towards the base's center," Aurora said. "The other docking bays are likely in that direction, based on what we caught during the landing. I'm betting Vana wouldn't want DefenseCorp's brass to go for a long walk after their trip here, so let's say she's that way."

"You think Vana would let you just walk right up to her?" Eponi asked.

The whole squad had come back together around the *Prisa*. Five power armor soldiers standing in a circle. Gregor had his hammer, Sai his katana, and Rovo carried the scythe thing he'd picked up on Wexer. Eponi had yet to collect on her bet with Aurora that Rovo would hurt himself with the weapon, but she figured it had to happen before long.

Eponi and the captain had their rifles, and all carried pistols, knives, and more grit than there were grains of golden sand on this cursed planet.

"I think Vana's going to let us prove ourselves a suitable threat before killing us," Aurora said. "At the same time we can clean up some of her messes."

"Like a few hundred Dynas refugees?" Sai said.

"We know she doesn't have a moral bone in her body," Aurora agreed. "We have to expect anything, particularly when her plan falls apart."

Oh, Aurora. Her endless confidence in Sever's sure

success always made Eponi grin, despite the ugly scene around them.

"So what's our plan, then?" Rovo asked. "Wander around and see what traps we can trigger?"

"Not quite," Aurora replied. "As much as I'd like to stick together, we can't put all our strength on one path. There are two exits, so we'll need to go in two groups."

"What if that's what Vana wants?" Eponi asked. "Wouldn't splitting us apart be, you know, a good way to get us killed?"

"It's a risk we're going to take." Aurora let her visored gaze swing across the squad, waiting for someone to speak up. "Right now, we're playing Vana's game. She expects us to lose. We won't."

Aurora's words gave little comfort as Eponi, Rovo, and Sai went into the tunnel off the westward exit. Gregor and Aurora went north, chasing after Vana. The two had so thoroughly destroyed the agent enclave at Gillane Four, Aurora figured they could handle anything Vana sought to throw their way.

"So we get, what, the leftovers?" Eponi asked as they left behind the bloody floor, the ramshackle rubble robots, and, thank all that was good, the decaying stench. "What if Vana gave us a long walk to, like, the base's septic system?"

"Then we'll find it, turn around, and tell Aurora," Sai said, leading the trio with his katana.

"You're just so much fun, Sai."

"Try me when I haven't just slaughtered a small town."

The tunnel, marked by an arched ceiling, shared one key quality with the bay they'd just left: a keen sense of style. Rather than the constant, dull metal found throughout civilization, the designers here delivered swirling designs. Symbols swept along the floors and walls, some even on the ceiling, in an interconnected dance Eponi couldn't decipher. Unlike the bay behind them, the symbols shimmered in golden yellows and brighter blues, as if the Sever trio had passed from a grim hollow to a pleasant meadow.

Adding to the impression were the lights. Straight, blue-white bars ran along just over head height, shearing away the dark as Sever went forward. Every meter or two, the next bar set would blink to life while the ones behind them shut off.

The breeze kept up its pressure, and Eponi figured this must've been the wind's target, because its whipping strength increased as Sever walked. The buffeting air pushed Eponi's legs ahead, tickled her joints.

"Feels like we're in our own world," Rovo muttered. "Dark behind, dark ahead. If we appear in some fantasy land, you all owe me cash."

"I'm not taking that bet," Eponi said.

"Quiet," Sai hissed, holding up a hand.

Ahead, there wasn't much to see. The tunnel continued, the bar lights shutting off not far ahead. And yet, Eponi caught the red on her visor. Something way down there had a sight on Sever, one clear enough to catch the power armor's detection.

"If the visor's catching it," Rovo said, "then they've gotta see us. And it's not like we're hard to pick out. The lights and all."

"It's almost like they didn't design these suits for stealth," Eponi added, but she aimed her rifle down the corridor anyway.

If the visors had a fault, it was in the machines failing to denote a threat's distance. Eponi couldn't tell if the red came from a meter away or a hundred. Thus, even though she figured something would be coming towards them,

Eponi was damn surprised when the lights ahead blinked on and showed . . . nothing.

"Invis suits," Sai said, taking a center-hall stance and putting his katana into a double grip. "Flush them out."

Eponi and Rovo took the order and ran with it, pulling their rifle triggers and sending red bolts, tuned hot enough to torch through most armor, searing down the hall. Without anything to aim at, Eponi went for the splatter approach, sending fire up, down, and everywhere across the tunnel.

The bolts hit home quick. Sparks flashed as Rovo and Eponi's shots caught objects sprinting down the corridor, ones closing fast. Hits left black marks in the air, floating as if made by magic as the suits charged.

"Not so hard to see now," Eponi said, aiming at the one coming right for her.

Her rifle exploded. One second, the weapon had itself primed and ready, and the next Eponi had her back on the ground. Her visor blared a warning that her power armor had taken a beating, and Eponi herself felt raw skin along her hands and arms. Tingling, torched.

Before she could come to terms with what the hell had just happened, Eponi felt a hand grab and lift her up. The invis suit had black marks all across its front, with sparks popping from a shoulder joint, but it still gave its wearer the strength to bring Eponi to her feet.

"Still alive?" A woman's voice, cocky and not at all concerned, asked.

"Sure, let's go with that," Eponi replied, taking in a strange scene.

Rovo, to Eponi's left, had his scythe out in two-weapon mode, dancing with what looked like a long, sharp cable whipping at him from another suit. Sai, further up the hall, kicked at what seemed to be air, only to connect and send his target banging to the floor.

"Good," the voice replied. "I'd hate to lose you so fast, after what you did to us last time."

Eponi's captor held up a pistol, waggling it in front of Eponi's eyes. Sever's pilot recognized the gun. She'd held it, had whipped its owner in the face with it.

Tarla?

Dammit.

FIVE

Rank and File

IF HE HADN'T SEEN the shot strike Eponi's rifle, a pinpoint laser from meters away that exploded the Sever pilot's weapon in her hands, Rovo wouldn't have had time to draw the scythe. The blue-tinged weapon, won by Sai on Wexer's black rock streets and donated to the rookie, had zero utility in the close tunnel until Rovo snapped the scythe in half.

The haft in his left hand, with a wrist flick, fanned out into a glistening small shield, while the right, bearing the scythe's long, hooked blade, swept up and out to catch the thing streaking towards Rovo.

A corded whip, unfurling over an invisible shoulder, corked at Rovo in a blink. Instinct more than skill helped Rovo catch the strike, to snare the whip in a swing. The whip's wielder tried to draw his weapon back, but Rovo's power armor gave him enough strength to do the opposite. The scythe blade worked itself against the cord, cutting through and snapping off the whip's last third.

"Guess you'll have to get closer," Rovo said, his words

washing out in ringing clangs as Sai's katana met another blade ahead and to Rovo's right.

The rookie wanted to spare a glance Eponi's way, make sure the pilot still lived. Power armor could absorb plenty, but the rifle had blown right in Eponi's hands. Even if the woman breathed, whomever had shot her weapon probably wouldn't pass up a chance to take advantage.

Before Rovo could move, the whip and its wielder returned. The enemy took Rovo's advice, closing until his damaged weapon could again lash out. The strike came in at Rovo's head, and the rookie moved the shield to block it. As the whip glanced off the circle in Rovo's hand, the rookie charged forward, giving a wordless roar. Two long steps went into a sudden forward chop with the scythe.

Either Rovo had picked up his close combat game, or his opponent really didn't expect a rapid attack from the hook. Rovo's blade struck home, digging into the suit's chest plate and drawing a sparking, rough scar down its front. The scythe found a hold and, with Rovo leaning into the swing, pulled the suit to the ground.

Rovo withdrew the scythe, brought it up for a killing blow, when a shout had him stop. Usually, someone yelling in a fight wouldn't take much attention—people tended to scream in combat for all kinds of terrible reasons—except this one shouted Sever's name.

"Stop, you Sever bastards!" The woman yelled again, and Rovo looked over to see Eponi, barely standing, with a pistol shoved right up into her chin. "Keep fighting and your pilot takes a shot to the head. One she won't survive."

"Are there many shots to the head that she would?" Rovo asked, flicking his left hand to return the scythe shield to a single bar.

At the same time, Rovo also moved his left foot. Planted the boot on his immediate enemy's chest, a wobbly move given Rovo couldn't see where the suited body really was. The power armor adjusted, though, and he managed the taunt without falling on his face.

A true power play.

"Only one way to find out," the woman replied. Her voice tugged at Rovo's memory, an itch there, but with the suit still vanishing the woman's face, the rookie couldn't place it. "But that's for later. For now, you can get off my friend. And your buddy there can put up the sword."

Sai looked like he'd done a number on his opponent too. The opposing suit had long gashes that now appeared to be floating, one leaking a thin, bloody line along the suit and down to the tunnel's floor, where it melded with the painted symbols.

"Don't you want to negotiate, Tarla?" Sai said, clicking it all together for Rovo.

The pistol shoved against Eponi's throat, the whip cracking at Rovo's scythe. Tarla and Javelin's weapons. Rovo didn't know who wielded a blade among the Twilight Rangers, that mercenary group that'd sparred with Sever back on Wexer, but given Perro's sniper affinities and Briana's fondness for giant guns, Rovo put good odds on Tarla's own pilot, Sanje, striking swords with Sai.

Putting an ID on his opponents only brought up another question: what the hell were the Twilight Rangers doing here?

"I've already negotiated," Tarla said. "Quite a spicy enemy you've found, Sever. Here we are, sitting on Wexer wondering whether we can wring enough cash from that coward Calico Max to get a new ship, and in comes a DefenseCorp agent. Care to guess what they offered?"

"More curious why they came to you at all?" Rovo asked.

With Sever up two to one in the fight, the rookie

caught Sai's hand signal as Rovo replied to Tarla's question. The swordsman wanted to play it slow. There were two other Twilight Ranger members somewhere, and figuring out if another ambush lay ahead would be worth doing. Not to mention Eponi's, you know, life hung at Tarla's pistol point.

At Rovo's feet, Javelin muttered a curse. Rovo dug his boot in, cutting off the words with a gasp.

"Wondered that myself," Tarla said, seemingly not giving one damn about her teammate's situation. "Until they started asking about you. Small cash for small info. I said you had too much heart to be a killer."

"His body count says otherwise," Sai said. "Telling Vana something she already knew doesn't get you here, Tarla."

"Oh, no. That was all me. I offered our services in exchange for a ride off that rock, and look at us now? New toys, same enemies."

"And no cash."

Tarla winced, shrugged, "Price of progress, I suppose."

"You kill us," Rovo said, "and then what? Vana gives you a big medal?"

"How about your ship and whatever's left on it?" Javelin said, voice tight, but still cocky beneath Rovo's press. "You took ours, right that we take yours, yeah?"

As Rovo went to clamp on Javelin again, Eponi shifted her hand and something clicked. Everyone's eyes went to the pilot, Rovo expecting Tarla to pull her trigger. Tarla, though, hesitated, and for good reason: Eponi's hand held a grenade, one of several everyone had on their power armor belts. In the tunnel's tight confines, the bomb would wreck them all.

Hard to claim a reward when you're in pieces.

"You're not taking my ship," Eponi said, jaw pressing against Tarla's pistol to get the words out. "Go—"

"See?" Tarla interrupted, nerves apparently unaffected by the certain death at her waist. "That's what I love about you all. Always willing to go full insane." She laughed, soft and delighted. "Oh, Eponi. What's your play? Explode and take us all with you?"

"Not even close," Eponi's eyes flicked Rovo's way. "Get your asses going, Rovo. If Tarla's parked herself here, Vana must be hiding something good down the hallway. They come after you, the bomb goes off."

"What?" Rovo said, while Sai stepped away from Sanje, his katana still in range for a quick, lethal strike. "We're not leaving you."

"Oh please," Eponi said. "I'll be fine. Go."

"She won't be fine," Tarla added. "But please, follow your pilot's instructions. I'd prefer not to die today."

Rovo hesitated while Javelin hacked out a laugh on the floor. Sanje, to this point, had kept quiet, not moving with Sai's blade so close. Leaving Eponi meant abandoning a squad member, one with a pistol at her face. Whatever lay down the hall, who knew if it mattered? Sai and Rovo could sprint away, leave Eponi to her death, and find all of nothing?

But Rovo didn't see another way out. Pulling his rifle trigger, snapping Javelin's bones beneath his boots wouldn't free Eponi either. Might get them all killed.

"You hurt her," Rovo started.

"And you won't live out the day," Sai finished. "That goes for all of you." The swordsman shuffled his fingers, and Rovo read the order. Time to go. "Eponi, stay alive."

"Sure," Eponi replied. "No problem."

Rovo dug one more power armor boot heel into Javelin as he stepped off. Sai, backpedaling, started down the hall until Rovo matched his stride. Together, without any taunts, without any shots, the pair kicked in their power armor and lumbered fast down the hall. The bar lights flickered on and off as they went, though every time Rovo looked back, in the growing distance, he could see the light where they'd left Eponi behind.

The tunnel ended with a door, as most tunnels did. The swirling symbols that'd followed Sai and Rovo along the tunnel's length came together for an end, coating the wide door slat in splashed decor. A single black scanner, searching for a wristlet to validate, waited on the door's right side. Sai, leading the rookie, stopped before the scanner.

"Bright ideas?" Rovo asked, coming up behind.

"I'm still thinking about Eponi," Sai replied. "If there was anything we could've done different."

"She made the call," Rovo replied, "and I don't think she did it lightly."

Whether Rovo honestly believed it or had convinced himself on the run to the door, the rookie figured Eponi was still alive. That she'd outsmarted Tarla and the other two. Maybe Eponi had dodged and ducked her way back to the *Prisa*, holding fast in her space-faring fort.

"I've tried to call her," Sai said. "No answer yet."

The visor hid Rovo's flush. For being a communications expert, he'd forgotten to send any squad-band queries out Eponi's way. Too much adrenaline, too much wondering what else waited down this line.

"Then we've gotta keep going." Rovo moved past Sai, brought up his wristlet to the scanner. It squawked an angry denial. "Guess that's not going to work."

"I could blow it open," Sai said, gesturing to the packs on either thigh. The demolition man had spent some of their restful holiday building bombs, and, now, Rovo fought off some unease at all that explosive power packed in right next to him. "But I don't think that'd do us any favors. If there's another few hundred behind that door, I'd rather not make myself an easy meal."

"As if," Rovo pointed at the katana. "You'd carve'em up."

Sai shook his head, brushed Rovo aside and went to the scanner. With Rovo giving him room, Sai took his katana, leveled the blade at the little thing, then stabbed it right in.

"What?" Rovo yelped as sparks burst and the scanner tried one sad, dying cry. "The hell are you doing?"

"Being desperate."

Sai drove the katana further into the wall and wiggled the blade as much as he could. Nothing seemed to happen aside from Rovo's growing disbelief that his friend, his very experienced Sever partner thought you could cut your way through a scanner.

The door shot open. A whisk that surprised Rovo and Sai almost as much as the Sever presence surprised the man on the other side. Frowning at his wristlet as he stepped away from the opposite scanner, the man looked up and saw the two power armor sporting soldiers. His mouth dropped, followed by the rest of him, when Rovo delivered a punch to the man's temple.

"Agent," Rovo said, kneeling to check the tag on the man's uniform, a dull crimson. Only unconscious, the man's wristlet stayed active, showcasing what the unfortunate soul had been doing a second before. "Responding to a broken door. Our broken door."

"See?" Sai replied, pulling his katana free. "Knew it would work."

Leaving the cold-cocked man behind, Rovo led Sai through the door and onto a ringing, rectangular walkway.

His visor adjusted to the brighter, blue lighting coming through a massive glass dome and its window to Aurum Three's sky. All that light fell into another huge space, larger than the landing bay the *Prisa* had scored for Sever. The walkway seemed to circle the entire outside, with red signs overhanging doors every so often.

The spiraling art continued, though the colors shifted between every door set, as if serving as a guide for what someone would find in the next passage. There were more agents wandering the walkway, eyes on their wristlets or, like Rovo's own, and Sai's, on what was happening below.

Sai cursed several times over, and Rovo matched it, because what else was there to say?

Hundreds, even thousands, stood in rows, straight and staring. Their clothes were often ragged, with little resembling a uniform. Some wore next to nothing at all, though nobody seemed to notice or mind. More agents walked the gaps in the rows, each followed by robots like the ones in the *Nautilus* med bay. As they stepped on the decorated metal floor, the agents inspected every body they passed, either nodded or shaking their heads.

Those poor souls that received a nod earned a shot, a swift stab by the nurse bot. Those who didn't were swept up by a second agent team. These duos grabbed the loser and dragged them from the line, pulling them to the room's side and out of Rovo and Sai's sight.

"The bay," Rovo said.

"The rejects get thrown aside," Sai agreed, his words heavy. "This, this is so far from right."

"It gets worse."

The front line had a different agent combo walking down the ranks. Followed not by a nurse bot, but by a long rack on a moving red-metal cart, the agents set the white-rimmed suits in front of every standing soul. Once the whole, several dozen long-line had its suit placed, the agents barked an order to commence. Almost as one, the captives accepted their gift, slipping on the power armor.

One by one, the rank vanished from clear sight. Only when the agents followed up their first order did Rovo understand.

"Make for the shuttles. Stay in your line," the agents setting the suits declared, while still more crimson-suited workers refilled the cart with more suits. "Our time is almost here, and with it, your chance to earn your freedom!"

If anyone gave two craps about the rallying cry, Rovo couldn't see it. He could, though, feel the sick winding its way around his stomach. Not fear, not quite. Fear would mean they stood a chance, fear would mean there was somewhere he could run.

But against this many suits, this many monsters, what could one squad do?

SIX

A Friendly Meeting

THE NORTHWARD EXIT led up to the surface. Or, rather, to an enclosed, two-way walkway sending Gregor and Aurora on a swift trip towards what appeared to be the base's center. The glass seemed new, and nothing bore the rubble or decorative paintings from the bay behind them. Simple, bland, and reassuring.

"I'm not getting anything," Aurora said as she and Gregor, rifle and hammer at the ready, started off down the black, zipping walkway. "Apparently Vana's not a radio fan."

"Or she has our frequencies," Gregor replied.

Jamming wouldn't be a surprise. Vana would know all that standard squad bands, having worked with Defense-Corp for so long. Sever still used their old frequency, and now Aurora cursed herself for not thinking to change it. Bravado and a belief in Sever's success wouldn't get her very far if it made her stupid.

"Then that's job one," Aurora said as Aurum Three's blue-lit, gold surface spread around them. "We find where she's jamming us from and take it out."

"Vana was job one."

"Job two, then."

Up above, Aurum Three's afternoon disguised all the artificial stars that'd show when night fell. DefenseCorp's patchwork fleet had to be wondering what'd happened to the *Prisa*, especially after Aurora's proclamation. How many would-be generals up there were sweating, thinking they'd let the enemy through their lines?

Would any decide to send some troops after, or were they all cowards, content to wait in their armored shells?

The walkway brought the pair to the tall, slope-sided structure Sever had seen during the landing. From the ground approach, the building's size took on a new significance: Aurum Three had nothing in the DefenseCorp logs about this place, including the cash cost or workers hired to build it. Scrubbing something this large, or hiding it, would take efforts and permission from the company's top personnel.

In other words, Vana might run the place now, but it'd been around long before she'd put her grubby agent hands on it.

The walkway ended with a spiral door, one that opened in time with a placid voice warning Aurora and Gregor against falling when the shifting slats came to an end. Neither did, stepping off and staring into a shallow entry. Hardly a grand entrance, the walkway spat the arrivals into a half-circle space, with three branches splitting off: a stair to the left, one to the right, and a lift in the middle with a red-glowing wristlet scanner next to it.

"For safety," came a voice, and Aurora had her rifle snapping to it before the two words closed out. Vana stood, arms down at her sides and empty handed, on the upper stair. She leaned on the stiff stone rail climbing the steps, looking bemused in over-done hair and a lean outfit. "You saw the bay, I presume? They couldn't trust who might come down this walkway."

Gregor shifted a step away from Aurora, giving them space to react, to dive away in case Vana had some trick. Aurora kept her rifle raised, finger on the trigger. She wanted to shoot Vana, but again, the agent had dropped a surprise. Vana wouldn't be out here unless she had something to gain, but what?

"Who's they?" Aurora asked, more to give herself time to puzzle out Vana's motive than anything.

"You've heard of the Raiders, of course?" Vana said, not moving, talking like a patient mother. "A little before your time, but I'm sure they teach you soldiers some history?"

The last botched infection endeavor. Create a slew of mindless soldiers, strong enough, numbed enough to pain and fear to push through any defense and accomplish the mission. Fun idea, until all the subjects decided they were done taking orders, were all for destroying everything they could.

"Guessing this was their home?" Aurora said.

"Left alone for years and years." Vana nodded. "Everything Renard needed, right here and ready. Lab space, weapons manufacturing, and no curious passers-by. The man thought he and Anaskya could bring the Raiders back, and better than ever."

"That worked out well for him," Gregor muttered.

"Renard's dead, and you're about to be," Aurora said. "The only reason I'm not pulling this trigger is I'm trying to figure out your play. What is it?"

"For that, you'll have to follow me," Vana replied, then threw a look up the stairs. "Not far. There's some people I'd like you to meet. Maybe they'll persuade you that I'm not your enemy."

"Not likely," Aurora said. She had questions to ask, ones Aurora Vana might not answer, but the agent seemed so calm, so in control, so why lie? "Who were those back in the bay, the ones you left to die?"

Vana frowned, her eyes flipping floorboard. Was that actual sadness?

"Casualties," Vana said. "Thank you for ending their pain."

The agent turned, started up the stairs. Aurora pulled the trigger. A red bolt shot past Vana, scorched into the wall on her left. The agent froze, turned back.

"I'm not finished yet," Aurora said.

"Then talk," Vana replied. "But be quick. I don't want to keep our other guests waiting."

"I don't give a damn about your other guests. There was another exit from the bay. Where does it go?"

"Didn't you send your others that way?"

"We did, but you're jamming our communications. I can't contact them," Aurora said. "Either you stop, or you answer my question."

Vana shook her head, "Kill me if you like, but I'm not going to ruin the surprise. You'll have to trust in your friends."

"Vana, does it look like I care about your surprise?"

That, at least, had Vana fully turning back, putting her hands on the rail and gripping it, "If you persist, Aurora, I will ensure your entire squad dies, one by one, before your eyes. Now, please, follow me and we can dispense with this whole ugly business."

This time, when Vana moved to continue up the stairs, Aurora didn't fire. She kept her finger on the trigger, kept the barrel on the agent until she disappeared along the curving steps.

"You didn't shoot," Gregor said. "She was right there."

"Let's go," Aurora replied.

She moved past Gregor, heading for the stairs. Made it two steps before she felt Gregor's hand on her shoulder, pulling hard.

"What?" Aurora said as she looked at the big soldier.

The visors did a lot to hide expressions, to make people difficult to read, but up close, Gregor's face showed through the translucent barrier. It was, in a word, angry.

"We agreed Vana was number one," Gregor said. "I am not here for games."

"Do you think I am?"

Those words, from a commander to a squaddie, should've forced a flinch. Maybe a *no sir* and a back down. Whether Gregor took Aurora's long ago words to heart, about Sever no longer having DefenseCorp's command structure, or because the big guy simply didn't care, Gregor stood his ground.

"I am not sure," Gregor said. "Sai, Rovo, and Eponi are in trouble. Every minute spent here risks them further."

"If I shot Vana now, we would never make it off this planet alive," Aurora replied. "She isn't trying to kill us, and I want to know why. Maybe, if there's a reason we can exploit, there's a chance we'll survive this."

"Or we will die failing."

Aurora nodded, "I'm asking you, Gregor, to trust me. One more time."

Gregor hesitated, then took his hand away. Returned it to his hammer's haft. "One more time."

The stairs led up, the railing giving way to solid metal and entrenching the steps between two windowless, gray walls. So little personality etched itself into the scene that Aurora missed the bloody, interesting ruin back in the *Prisa*'s bay. Eventually, the steps came to another door, one reinforced with extra bars across its middle and a laser shield's humming sound.

Vana had said this long entry had been built for defense, and she wasn't kidding.

The wristlet scanner gave Aurora and Gregor, who'd climbed single-file on the thin stair, a green light. Aurora held up her left wrist, the power armor sliding back a slit to reveal the computer to the scanner's eyes. Even with the green, Aurora still felt a shock when the door opened. Somehow, for some reason, Vana wasn't taking every opportunity to kill them.

Beyond, a wide, rounded room with a double doorway greeted them. What looked like makeshift barriers leaned against the right wall, ready to be pulled down in case of an attack. To the left, a room-length window showcased Aurum Three's golden dunes. Mixed in the room, watching and waiting, were people Aurora had only known from pictures.

Specifically, the pictures on the drive Sai said Vana had given him, back on the *Nautilus*. Renard's web, all present to take in their apparent success.

Many of DefenseCorp's top brass, its financial, military, and diplomatic masters, stood in their varied crimson getups. Some held weapons, but most looked, in all their finery, with all their poise and assurance of invincibility, at Aurora and Gregor with zero concern. As if a polite conversation had been interrupted by servers with finger food.

"I was starting to get worried," Vana said, standing just inside. "Here I was, telling all of my guests that they were about to meet DefenseCorp's finest squad commander, and then you didn't show up."

Aurora couldn't think of anything to say. She'd pulled

the trigger on a thousand or more enemies, survived count-less deals with death, but no part of Sever's role, of Sever's plan for Aurum Three, discussed meeting the people who'd sent her on one mission after another for so many years.

"You can lower your rifle, captain," said an older man to Aurora's right, one she recognized as a top admiral serving on the galaxy's opposite side. "There's no need for violence here."

"Or anywhere else," Vana added, waving Aurora and Gregor inside. "All of you understand, as I mentioned when Aurora and her squad arrived at our gathering, that she believes our work here is a disaster. We must convince her otherwise."

Aurora, pointing her rifle at the floor but not moving her finger from the trigger, stepped inside the room. The move was less about following Vana's direction than giving Gregor a clear view, because so far as Aurora saw it, everyone in this room had considered Sever, like every other DefenseCorp squad, expendable in the face of cash. Nobody here would hesitate to put a laser into her back if it meant guaranteeing DefenseCorp's profits, and Aurora wouldn't even blame'em.

She'd been doing much the same her entire career.

The assembled group, Aurora's quick count put the number at fifteen, broke into what appeared to be a pre-planned speaking order. Each one, introduced by Vana, laid out how the invisible suits, how soldiers enhanced by the virus, would benefit their position. Less turnover, better control. Endless threats to those who might refuse Defense-Corp's generous contracts. Commanders like Aurora would have squads without personal squabbles, ready to fight at a moment's notice.

And, with the virus serving as a steward, DefenseCorp

could recruit from anywhere. No vagrant, no lost soul would be without a place. At last, anyone could receive the injections, give up their tortured existence to DefenseCorp's murderous comforts.

Aurora's trigger finger grew numb at the speeches, at the grins growing on the faces around her as they pitched what seemed so blatantly wrong. To her left, she saw Gregor's hands tightening around the hammer. Neither had said a word so far, neither had been asked for their position. And they wouldn't be: the only choice Aurora and Gregor had here was to accept the inevitable, or die trying to prevent it.

"See, Aurora? Gregor?" Vana said when the last man had finished his rousing vision of a galaxy under DefenseCorp's well-meaning rule. "That is what we are doing here. Giving our civilization a better, brighter future. What do you say, will you join us?"

Aurora had seen tempting offers all her life. Sever squad targets offered ludicrous bribes at her rifle's end, while other squads tried to buy Sever's help, or her own self, to join their missions or their ranks. Smaller outfits had asked Aurora to remain in luxury on various planets, providing special security to some VIP or celebrity. She'd said no to all of those, declaring the eventual DefenseCorp payout would be worth more in the end.

But knowing, really, that she stayed for her squad.

"Where are the others?" Aurora said into that vacuum. "Rovo, Sai, and Eponi? You let them go a different way."

The admirals, the politicians, the executives in the room turned to Vana, who shook her head.

"The wrong way," Vana said. "They stumbled into a place they should not have gone, Aurora. I'm sorry, but Sever Squad is down to only two. The best, most important two. If you agree, however, then I'm sure we can scrounge up their bodies for you."

"Liar," Gregor growled while Aurora tried, again, with the squad band.

The hail, kicked out across their frequency, met nothing but a jammed signal's fuzzy silence. Vana could very well be lying, or she could be, as she had below on the stair, telling the terrible truth.

"Believe what you wish," Vana said, replying to Gregor. "Nonetheless, I need an answer. Now."

The agent, backing away towards the room's rear, raised her wristlet. The others gave Aurora and Gregor space, retreating towards the walls, the window. Did Vana have some trap set? Some laser that would shoot from the featureless ceiling, or perhaps a pit that would swallow Gregor and Aurora whole, crushing them in the dark?

Aurora didn't need to use the fingers, didn't need to send the silent code. She'd come to Aurum Three to take Vana out, believing, hoping that would be the end. Now, that wouldn't be enough. Without Vana, one of the people here would take up her mantel. They all saw the same thing Renard did, wanted the same thing he did.

And that, Aurora could not allow.

Snapping up her rifle, Aurora aimed at Vana. As Aurora pulled the trigger, Vana slipped back while pulling another hapless soul in the way. Aurora's rifle spat, the yellow-red bolt lancing out and taking its target. Vana kept retreating, ducking into the crush as the gathered officials realized their time had run out.

Gregor took the signal and ran with it, leaping forward and laying waste with the hammer. The first swing took two, the second another three. Those few still holding weapons didn't attempt to fight the armored squaddies, but fled.

They didn't make it far.

Deadly seconds passed, ending with Aurora and Gregor standing amid a ruin. People that'd conquered planetary systems lay around them, side by side with others who'd masterminded DefenseCorp's cash accounts to buy the giant vessels giving the company its power. In a few heartbeats, the galaxy's most powerful had been destroyed.

On their ships, these people would've had guards. Loyal soldiers. Vana had brought them here, stripped them of their protection through greed. Aurora would've pitied the bastards, except she had no pity left to give.

"Some escaped," Gregor said, not even breathing hard. "Follow?"

"Vana didn't even try to stop us," Aurora said. "She just ran."

"Agents are cowards."

"Then let's catch a coward."

Aurora took the lead, ditching the bodies behind them. Her rifle would work better in the hallway beyond, a narrow stretch continuing the windowed view on the left with one scanner-sealed room after another. There was a chance, of course, that Vana had slipped into any of these, along with the officials that'd escaped.

The sounds coming from up ahead, though, made that course unlikely.

Shouts, demands rang back through to the Sever pair as Vana's remaining guests ordered her to take some action, to get them out. The words were heated, and while Aurora wanted to pull the final trigger on Vana herself, she wouldn't be too upset if someone shot the agent first.

The hallway bent, creasing inward, with a sealed door preventing further straight on walking. As Aurora neared the bend, the arguing grew louder, more determined and then, like a flipping switch, more panicked. Flashes marred

Aurum Three's afternoon light, and when Aurora rounded the bend, rifle ready, the source made itself clear.

Another five bodies, burning holes in their chests, lay on the floor. No Vana among them.

"She's not running," Aurora said, watching the smoke rise from the victims. "Vana's taking control."

Swordplay

THE MOMENT WATCHING the agents at work, equipping the marching ranks with suits, lasted both too long and not long enough. The ringing walkway Sai and Rovo stood on gave little cover, so Sai wasn't all that surprised when his visor flared red as the other agents patrolling sighted the armored duo.

"Time to go," Sai said, sheathing his katana and drawing his pistols instead. The sword wouldn't be much use at this range.

"Go where?" Rovo replied as the two slipped down, as much as they could in the bulky armor, behind the ring's railing. "Tarla and friends are behind us. In front, there's a few thousand enemies."

"Then think of something."

Sai, looking back towards the tunnel they'd exited, waited for the visor to tell him when the approaching agents neared. The red halo crawled from his visor's bottom to its left and right edges. Close, now.

"I'm going left," Sai said.

Rovo didn't reply, and they both moved with snapshot

experience as the red hit the right level. Sai rose, turning left as the agent, her own weapons drawn, came around the corner. Sai squeezed off a shot, but the agent apparently expected it, because she came around in a sudden dash. Sai's bolts trailed her, scoring black marks in the painted metal behind.

The agent's right wrist flicked as she sprinted, two bright silver orbs bouncing out Sai's way.

"Grenades!" Sai shouted.

If he had free hands, Sai might've tried to throw them back. If he had his katana, he might've tried slicing them apart, defusing the blast before it could start. Instead, he kicked in the power armor's boosted boots, launching Sai forward. He flew over the grenades in a wild jump, crashing into the agent, who had used the wall to catch her run and start a retreat from her own bombs.

Sai hit the woman, coated in slimmer, DefenseCorp standard crimson body armor. Together, they smashed into the far side, with Sai's weight driving the agent into the metal. Sai felt her body go limp—agents always seemed to think helmets weren't cool—as he backed off. The agent slumped to the floor, unconscious.

One down, a million more to go.

Sai's visor flashed a new red threat on his left, but the Sever swordsman didn't see anything along the walkway.

The suited fighter revealed himself with a hot blue bolt fired from distance, followed by another. The swordsman flinched away from the shots, staying low. One bolt clipped Sai's right shoulder, the armor taking the hit with alarm as the heat burned through half its protection. Sai brought his pistols up, hoping to lay down some covering fire for an approach, to make the shooter blink and buy some time.

The grenades went off.

Two rippling pops echoed off the walls as fire shredded

the catwalk. Sai tilted sideways as his footing disappeared, the metal folding beneath him or burning away. The power armor took the fire as it took the laser, caring not at all. Sai, though, yelled as he fell, striking the floor below as debris rained around him. The knock fuzzed Sai's head for a second, and his pistols weren't in his hands anymore.

"You there?" Rovo's words came in Sai's ear. "Please say you're there."

"Here," Sai replied, feeling blood in his mouth where he'd bit his tongue on the impact. "Been better."

"I've heard it's smarter to run *away* from the grenades, rather than towards them."

"You're not wrong."

Sai rolled over, blinked at the scene before him. Those citizens, the injected many from Dynas awaiting their chance at the suits, stood level with him. Stood, and didn't seem to react. The agents passing out the suits continued their process, laying out new hardware and helping each new line embrace their armor.

Didn't they care that two grenades had just destroyed one end of the room? Didn't they care that two soldiers, in power armor, had invaded their operation?

The next rank began their near-silent, invisible march, and Sai saw why. The new suits went to Sai's right, heading towards a large opening. Patched to the portal's sides declared the destination as landing zones, those broad patches Sever had seen during the approach. The agents kept yelling for every new set to get to the shuttles, prepping for a trip off-world.

Where would those shuttles go? Would they scatter all these maniacs across the galaxy, or was it a targeted invasion?

"So, uh, help?" Rovo's voice crashed into Sai's thoughts. "I'm surrounded up here!"

Sai pushed to his feet, reaching for his katana. Around him, light filtered in pieces through the walkway's remnants. The suited enemy that'd been shooting his way hadn't followed up. Maybe he thought Sai dead. His mistake.

"I can't get up to you," Sai said. "My boosters don't have the energy yet."

"What a help you are," Rovo replied. "I've taken down two, but there's another five surrounding me."

A couple choices, then. Sai could charge out from the rubble, draw attention and maybe find a way to connect with the rookie before agents overwhelmed him. But they were already outnumbered. The Sever pair couldn't fight every agent in this place, not without cover, without surprise on their side. But there was another option.

"Run," Sai said. "Get out and away. They're taking these suits to shuttles, and I don't know why, but we can't let them leave."

"Yeah, uh, I'm not gonna care about those soldiers if I'm dead."

"Then don't be," Sai repeated. "Go. Find a door, leave, and get a message up there. Someone in DefenseCorp has to care, has to believe letting these monsters go free is a problem."

Sai followed laser flashes above as they streaked from around the second level towards its left side. The bolts hit the rail, struck the wall above, and a few blazed right over the top. Sai couldn't make out Rovo's form, but he hoped the rookie took his words to heart.

Another newly-suited line broke the ranks and started their march towards the long opening and the landing pads beyond. The motion drew Sai back to the point, to the ranks before him that, as yet, hadn't bothered to investigate the rubble and the power armor rising from it. Sai still couldn't believe none of the agents working the suits had made a move his way.

They had to see him, had to know a fall like that wouldn't kill someone in power armor. Even if they had to get all these placid people suited up and gone, it seemed ridiculous not to . . .

The visor's red flare pushed Sai to dive forward. Behind him, debris shrieked as something sliced through. Catching his roll on his shoulder, Sai balanced himself with his left hand, raising his katana with his right to block any follow-through.

The invisible suits did what they could to shield weapons attached or covered by the suit's compartments. The damn knives Vana tended to use had a similar light-bending coating, making them hard to track. This guy, though, had a curved, buzzing red-steel blade that did nothing to hide itself. Looking like it hovered in the air, the sword waved back and forth, its owner showing off.

"Round two?" said the suit, though Sai couldn't see the man speaking.

Round two?

Sai didn't give a crap about any rounds. What mattered was that the guy, standing there swinging the sword, gave Sai a chance to get back to his feet. To get the katana into a comfortable grip. Maybe a duelist would consider that a rite, an honor given to an opponent, but in a place like this? A fight like this?

Honor would have to wait.

Sai drove forward, bringing the katana up into an overhead swing. Leaving his chest open for a strike, Sai baited the suit, and the man took it. The red blade pulled up into a straight stab, leveling itself towards Sai's stomach.

Normally, a katana would be too heavy to single-hand a chop like Sai's, would be too unwieldy and liable to wobble out of harm's way. Normally, a swordsman didn't have a suit of strength-amplifying armor keeping his grip where it needed to be.

Sai dropped his left hand, sweeping his protected arm down ahead of the katana to bat the red blade. The buzzing proved its meaning as the energy surrounding the sword fizzled white-hot sparks off the power armor, but Sai redirected the deadly point down and away. Instead of stabbing through Sai's ribcage, the sword glanced off Sai's leg, leaving its owner open, vulnerable.

The katana sliced across the man's shoulder, cutting away the invisible suit and the clothes beneath. Only by dropping the blade and falling back did the man survive, a deep cut in his shoulder nonetheless. Sai flipped the katana's grip, angling its point into a fatal stab, when the suit shunted off its invisible energy, showing the cloaked man beneath.

"Perro?" Sai said, kicking away the red blade and staring at the wounded man. "Why?"

"Is cash a good answer?"

"We already met Tarla," Sai said. He didn't have time for this, but the man might be useful. Once the agents saw Sai had dealt with their protection, the Sever swordsman figured he'd be swarmed. "She explained your deal. I'm asking why you didn't shoot me."

"Didn't seem fair." Perro winced as he threw on a loose grin. "Besides, wanted to try out my new toy. They've got all kinds of cool weapons here."

"I bet."

Sai glanced over his shoulder, up towards the walkway. Lasers weren't crossing anymore, suggesting Rovo was either dead or gone. That Rovo hadn't sent any word didn't answer the question either, as the whole base seemed to block any communications once they'd left near-field range.

"You're not going to live long, you know," Perro said. "Killing me doesn't matter. Look at'em all. They're gonna be everywhere in the galaxy before long, answering to that agent's orders."

Sai leveled the katana at Perro's throat, "Tell me how that helps you. Won't be much work for a mercenary if everyone's already dead."

"Guess we hoped someone like you would stop her, after we collected, of course."

"You know a way? To stop them?"

Perro laughed, winced again, "Kill'em all?"

Not happening, much as Sai might want to. Perro's suggestion, though, put together a different track to follow. Sai and Gregor, along with Sever on the *Prisa*, had taken care of the Helix creatures without too much effort. The suits were what made them deadly, what gave Vana's motley force a chance to disrupt the galaxy.

Get rid of the suits, and maybe there was a chance.

"How long have you been here?" Sai asked Perro.

"Few weeks," Perro said. "Vana wasn't sure when you'd arrive."

"So you know the base."

Now Perro sat up, grimacing, "Might be I do. Why?"

"Can you show me where they make the suits?"

"Think you're forgetting what side I'm on."

The katana moved, rested its tip against Perro's neck.

"I think you're forgetting how desperate I am," Sai said. "Show me, and maybe you'll live to collect all that cash."

"We only get paid if you're dead."

Sai wanted to strangle the man. Perro wouldn't get a damn dime if Sever died. Vana would probably kill them, or cash itself would be meaningless once Vana's invisible, unthinking army bent the galaxy to her will.

"Perro, I'm going to say this to you slowly," Sai said. "You're going to take me to where they make the suits. We're going to destroy the production. Then we can discuss your payment." Perro opened his mouth and Sai pressed the blade closer. "If you say anything else except yes, I'm going to kill you now and take my chances."

Perro blinked, offered up an icy grin.

"You got it, boss."

EIGHT

Bait, Switch

TWICE TODAY, he'd wielded the hammer. Twice today he'd used the weapon's awesome power to smash and mash helpless enemies. The first time, they'd charged Gregor with the reckless abandon suited to ones who'd untied their rope to reality. The second had been an act of defense against a foe that couldn't attack.

Like Aurora, Gregor had seen the names and faces on Sai's drive. Each one, tied into the scheme Sever had found itself trying to stop. Each one guilty of, if nothing else, an attempted crime against civilization. Regret should not be felt when dealing with ones such as these.

And yet, Gregor didn't find himself flushed with victorious glory. This wasn't combat that made legends, this wasn't heroism.

Slaughter fit the description.

Worse, Vana, the only one that really mattered, kept getting away. Gregor stood with Aurora at the hallway's end, red-blinking scanners blocking rooms all around them. Vana's most recent victims lay behind, smoking as their corpses cooled. With the way forward locked, and the way back a fast journey to nowhere, Gregor had to find something to hit that would hit him back.

"Or I will lose it," Gregor said the last part out loud, drawing Aurora's look from the scanner, one continuing to reject her wristlet.

"You'll lose what?" Aurora straightened.

Sever's commander had put up her rifle, kept her pistols holstered. Her power armor appeared unblemished, while evidence coated Gregor's own. Their weapons telling a story.

"We are trapped, and now we are clear criminals to our former company," Gregor said. "Even if we destroy Vana, nobody will see us as heroes."

"Were we ever that?"

"Perhaps not, but I dislike being the villain."

"Never knew you cared."

"Do you not?" Gregor asked.

Aurora turned back to the door, gestured at it, "I care about getting through here. I care about finding Vana. I care about stopping all this."

"And then what?"

"We'll learn the future when it arrives. I'm not much for predictions."

"A bold stance from our commander."

Now Aurora faced Gregor head on, "What's wrong with you? You're questioning me, getting philosophical. This isn't the Gregor I know."

"The Gregor you knew did not murder the helpless."

"Any of them would have killed you if they could." Aurora put a hand on Gregor's shoulder, heavy. "This isn't the time to get sentimental, my friend. You have a chance, still, to fight for the galaxy. Don't forget that."

Push away the internal debates for another time. How exactly like Aurora, like Sever. Gregor frowned, tried to do what Aurora asked. There were concerns, moral quandaries to puzzle over, but those could be done after, when Gregor was either dead or locked in a cell for his remaining centuries.

For now, he would have to silence the voices the way Gregor always had.

"Stand back," Gregor said and Aurora complied.

Free from collateral damage, Gregor twisted the hammer's base. Stored kinetic energy, maxed out through the swings in the bay and then back in the preceding room, charged the hammer's head. With a strong overhead swing, Gregor smashed the door's top-center head on.

Vana's comment about the Raiders did a lot to explain the base's layout, with the *Prisa*'s bay marking the discordant, mad shambles as soldiers twisted inside and out were forced into service. Much like Gregor's own family and friends, working the comet mines, had been kept separate from the administrators, the shareholders, the corporate owners.

So far, this central building demonstrated a protected core. All the scanner-locked doors, the narrow corridors and rooms built to funnel an attacking force through one chokepoint after another. The Raiders couldn't be controlled, but they could be eliminated, wiped out and then restarted with a new batch.

Gregor knew a slaughterhouse when he saw one.

Through the door, humanity returned. The plain walls vanished, replaced with hung artwork, with DefenseCorp's corporate slogans plastered on suddenly smoothed, soft-gold walls matching Aurum Three's dunes. The collapsing door, folding beneath Gregor's hammer, let in a filtered, warm breeze modulated to match optimal humidity and temperature for sustained human health.

"The ones at the top always have it better," Aurora grumbled, taking in the difference.

"And the ones at the bottom never see," Gregor agreed.

Aurora let Gregor, being the one with the giant hammer, take the lead. Leaving all the other locked doors behind them, Gregor climbed over his own wreckage and clomped into a strange place. As much as it looked like a posh office and lab—walls had windows in here, giving view to spacious work rooms and meeting spaces—the eerie silence, coupled with the dustless, perfect spaces, made it feel like Sever moved through a museum display.

Vana either ran a very tight operation, or she'd wanted a pretty show to serve the visiting brass.

"Deserted?" Gregor said as they continued down the carpeted hall, rooms on both sides.

"Or evacuated. Maybe we scared them away."

"Then they had the least panicked evacuation I have ever seen."

Choices came when the hallway hit other options. Going right, continuing straight, the dilemma would've been hard to parse in the building maze. Would have, if Vana's boots hadn't left a clear track everywhere she stepped. The depressions in the carpet, marred by golden dirt and bits of things Vana must've picked up while stepping on bodies her guests had left behind, were easy enough to pick out.

"She is being sloppy," Gregor said after the second intersection again had a clear path marked.

"We're underestimating her," Aurora replied, turning in the space, keeping her rifle looking back and front and to the side. "She led us to all those VIPs, and she has to know we're following."

"We have seen her surprises, and they are weak," Gregor replied, and resumed walking.

The lonely labs and offices bled away as the two reached the hallway's end, this time with an open door, green-lit scanner staying unlocked. Gregor glanced at Aurora, who shrugged and nodded him on through. If Vana wanted to spare her doors the pain of Gregor's hammer, Sever could oblige.

The whisked-away door led to a broad, flat space. At the far end, an open side let Aurum Three's natural air in. Meters higher than the standard floors they'd been walking through, shuttles filled the obvious docking bay. These were specialty ships, blazed over with insignias, gaudy paint jobs, and names declaring themselves property of the bodies Aurora and Gregor had left behind.

More concerning were all the guards lingering around those same ships. The security that'd been missing from Vana's private bloodbath apparently all waited here, armed and turning, now, in Sever's direction. Gregor's visor tallied up the potential threats, splashing his vision with red, and estimated close to fifty.

"Not good," Gregor said, standing there in the entry with his hammer ready.

"Agreed," Aurora replied. "We go back. Take cover in the hallway. Limit their numbers."

A fifty against two advantage would take more than a hallway and some closed rooms to even out, but Gregor would take a chance over the zero odds they'd get fighting in the open bay. Aurora started to retreat and Gregor followed while the guards watched.

"Everyone," Vana's voice boomed from intercoms, echoing through the hallways behind and the bay before Gregor. "I'm speaking to you scared and hurt. Two DefenseCorp deserters have attacked, under a peaceful flag, your charges and left their bodies behind. They must be destroyed before we can recover, before DefenseCorp's bright future can be defined. As your commanding officer now, I'm ordering you to eliminate these two immediately."

A sloppy order, devoid of strategy and substance, but Gregor saw the splashy results as he back-stepped: the ship closest to the entrance, a green-and-silver transport, spat its guards into the bay via a boarding ramp. The Defense-Corp special forces badge, blazed over the green-black armor, shown clear as the squad raised their rifles Gregor's way. Other squads would follow as they checked in with their leaders and found them unresponsive.

"Time to go," Aurora said, and Gregor had to agree.

Sever's commander led an active retreat, popping windows as she went with precise blasts from the rifle. The big glass panes were more than large enough for someone to climb over and through, and each opening offered an ambush any pursuit would have to investigate. The trail would be slowed, however little bit it could.

They broke left at the first intersection, hoping nobody saw the sudden turn. Aurora swapped with Gregor, breaking back towards the hallway split to cover while Gregor dealt with the door in the only way he could: another bash.

The hammer hadn't hit enough things to recharge its kinetic burst, so the first strike only dented the door. The scanner squealed, triggering an alarm.

"Sorry," Gregor said, hefting the hammer for another blow.

"And after I shot all those windows," Aurora said. "What a waste."

The captain shed her sarcasm with a curse, drawing Gregor's glance as Aurora dropped to a crouch and squeezed off shots. Gregor turned back to the door, swung again and shattered the portal. Beyond sat a broad lab, where half-made suit prototypes hung from hooks. Glass-ware coated tables, some still filled with various polymers waiting for their chance to be formed for murderous purpose.

More doors offered exits on the lab's right and opposite side, while to Gregor's left, at the end of the lab equipment, a yellow-painted door declared the room beyond a freezer. An idea took shape as Gregor went into the space, prompted more by games he'd played on the floating rocks as a child. The most effective hiding places were the ones that were both possible and ridiculous, too risky to be allowed.

But if you wanted to truly win a game, to send the seekers home without their prize, then you had to work as a team. A decoy coupled with a well-chosen spot would lead to a chance, would lead to victory.

"Go in there," Gregor said, pointing at the freezer. "Now."

"The freezer?"

"I'll lead them away. They won't check."

There were commanders that would deny Gregor's move, that would take stock of their squaddie's offer and wonder whether they could trust the intentions. Whether the squaddie wanted to offer up the commander as bait.

Aurora looked at Gregor, offered a simple nod. She reached, took off a grenade from her belt, and launched it back down the hallway. Nobody would run towards the bomb, and it might delay the followers enough for her to hide.

"Get going then," Aurora said.

"See to Vana."

Aurora didn't need to say anything. The way she tightened her grip on the rifle was all the answer Gregor needed. She'd waffled before, curious about a way out, but that line fled when Sever took out the brass in the other room. Survival wasn't the goal anymore.

Gregor whipped around and ran towards the right-side door. As he ran, he again twisted his hammer's haft, charging the swings from the first door into a metal-mashing blow into the next. The thin thing blew apart, its two halves scattering into the next hallway and gashing the walls in their flight.

The hammer man didn't bother taking one last look behind, didn't bother seeing if Aurora made it to safety. Instead, he ran on, letting the hammer make its mark on the walls around him, letting its noise trail his footsteps.

The dogs would follow, and when they caught him, Gregor would finally find his fight.

Tour Interrupted

THE PAIN KILLED HER COWARDICE. Any urge to run, to cry, to give up never made it past the ache in her palms where the power armor hadn't been able to cope with her exploding rifle. The burn sang now, with Eponi cupping the grenade in her left hand. Sai and Rovo had run off, leaving a fun three on one stalemate.

"I said give me a minute," Tarla snapped at Javelin, who'd picked himself off the ground. The cocky whip-wielder had patched up Sanje's katana wound and now both glowered Tarla's way, complaining about lost cash. "She's not going to blow us up, but she might get scared if you get stupid."

"Seems likely," Eponi added, the words stiff as her jaw pushed against the pistol barrel. "I'm a crazy pilot. Might blow us up for no reason."

"Don't doubt that," Javelin muttered.

"Now, now," Tarla went for the smooth-over. "I pegged you as the smartest in your squad way back on Wexer, remember? Bought you those drinks and we went on a grand adventure together?"

"You tried to kill me."

"Oh, every story has its turning points," Tarla continued without a hitch. "Disagreements are bound to happen in our profession. So much violence, so much cash." Tarla leaned in, her eyes glittering. "Speaking of, how much is ol' Aurora paying you to come along on this suicide mission?"

Eponi had nothing to say. She'd known, and Aurora had made it plenty clear, that Sever's role in coming to Aurum Three wasn't a short-term play. This was about keeping the galactic order and its various cash avenues open and intact. Oh, and Aurora added something about saving humanity in there too, if you wanted candy beyond the bottom line.

"Nothing?" Tarla answered for herself when Eponi didn't speak. "Hear that, you two? Aurora has her squad operating on a pro bono basis. Bunch of heroes, here."

"Not heroes," Eponi goosed up a reply. "We just hate Vana."

Tarla blinked, "Well, on that, at least, we can all agree."

Now Eponi's own eyes popped. "But you're working for her?"

"Sure as shit we are," Javelin said, "but just because she's the one puttin' in the deposits doesn't mean we can't see she's rotten. Perro did some digging after we got the offer, and she's got a grim history, that one."

"Safe to say," Tarla bounced off Javelin's words, "after this gig's up, we're out. Working for her means a quick trip to the grave."

"Bet I can make it quicker," Eponi said, shaking the grenade. "Unless you get this pistol outta my face."

Javelin's remark about Vana's past bit Eponi's brain,

but any investigation needed to wait until her proximity to fiery laser death was gone.

"Then what happens?" Tarla said. "You take off? Shoot us?"

"How about I take you to the *Prisa* for a tour? That way you can see the ship you're fighting so hard to get." Eponi developed the play as she made it, putting the pieces into place as they formed. "You won't be able to get in without my codes anyway."

Tarla glanced towards Javelin and Sanje, the latter of whom hadn't done anything save grimace and keep a hand on the bandages covering his chest slash, "What do you think, Rangers? Do we trust the Sever stick jockey?"

"You're offerin' me a choice between exploding or getting a ship, I'm gonna choose the ship," Javelin said.

Sanje nodded towards the other man, "What he said."

Tarla swept her pistol away quick, stepping back from Eponi. She raised the pistol again, keeping it centered on Eponi's face, the only place in her power armor that a direct shot might do damage. Before Tarla could talk, though, Eponi decided to double down.

"Oh, guess what?" Eponi said, holding out the grenade. "My friends might be in trouble, and it's all your fault I can't help them. So how about you two go make sure my buddies are safe, and I'll give Tarla the tour. That way you know you're getting something good, and I have a reason not to blow you all up right here and now."

Javelin started a cursing insult, but Tarla shut him up with a pistol shot to the tunnel's ceiling. The bright flash had Eponi wince and she nearly took her hand off the grenade's trigger. The only thing stopping her? Tarla's infectious grin.

"This one, this one." Tarla shook her head. "You're special, know that?"

Eponi didn't know about special, but she did know going from three to one into an even match-up made a lotta sense. Rovo and Sai had enough of a head start by now that, unless they were the slowest Severs ever, Javelin and Sanje wouldn't find'em.

She didn't want to blow the grenade, but Eponi had gone this far. Might as well maximize the benefit.

"Javelin, Sanje, do what she's asking," Tarla said.

"And the contract?" Javelin replied. "We just ditching that, then?"

"Vana paid us to stop Sever," Tarla said. "There's still time to do that. Way I see it, whether Sever lives or dies, we're getting ourselves a ship today."

Sure. If that's what Tarla wanted to think.

"Your call, boss," Javelin said. "Ready, Sanje?"

The pilot didn't look ready, but with Javelin helping him stand, the two started off down the tunnel. Tarla kept one pistol aimed at Eponi, waved the other in the direction of her two squad mates.

"There you go, Eponi," Tarla said. "Just what you wanted. Now let's put the bomb away, shall we?"

The trick had played itself out. Eponi thumbed the detonator back to its safe spot and slid the grenade into its holster. The move lanced loose pain through her palms, a reminder that bravado didn't cure all that ailed her.

"Hey," Tarla, nodding at Eponi's peace-making move, shouted down the tunnel towards the retreating pair. "Whatever you find they're doing, don't risk yourselves. This place, this deal isn't worth it."

"Some mercenaries you are," Eponi said.

"I'm betting DefenseCorp's sent you on some crap missions too," Tarla shot back. "No contract is worth dying over."

"That, we can agree on."

"Good, then let's get going. I want to see my prize."

Her prize. Eponi turned away, killed her frown. She'd be damned before letting Tarla take the *Prisa*, but letting the woman ride that belief until Sever finished its job here wouldn't kill Eponi. She'd just have to shut up and let Tarla win for a while.

The two marched back through the tunnel towards the bay, Tarla peppering Eponi with questions about what'd happened after Wexer. Recounting Gillane Four and the long rest at the fringe station took more time than Eponi expected, and she fell into the moments. The long run through Gillane Four's streets, shooters at her back, torched off her tongue, littered with curses, and for a while Eponi forgot it was Tarla she spoke to.

Sever was Eponi's family, but they'd heard all her stories, had been right alongside her for most. Tarla, though, took in the tale with a fresh perspective, and probed every other moment to prove she'd been listening the whole way.

"Have to say, I gave Aurora a crap back in DC," Tarla said. "But she's turned you all into a damned good machine."

"She didn't do it all," Eponi countered as they reached the open door back to that dark, bloody bay. "We started strong."

"Of course you did," Tarla replied. "I wouldn't take babies into the Rangers either."

Tarla's words faded as she looked at the bay. Eponi watched the captain's expression as the power armor's baked in lights turned up to reveal the bloody paint, the stacked rubble, the obvious struggles that'd played out in this horrible place.

"You know," Tarla whispered, all the cockiness gone. "You go around the galaxy enough, you see places like this.

You try to forget, try to get over all the awful things that we do to each other, but you never really do. Each one of these adds another bad memory I need to suppress."

"Vana did this. It's on her."

Tarla didn't say anything to that, but waved Eponi on.

With Eponi leading, the two made their way towards the *Prisa*. The ship's running lights gave a clear beacon to follow in the dark, that breeze pushing against them the entire way. Tarla didn't come up with any quips and Eponi didn't object to the quiet: the atmosphere seemed wrong for stories, for jokes, for threats.

The *Prisa* required codes to unlock, sent via a wristlet or a keypad on the ship's front strut. Eponi had those codes, the trick was how to get into the *Prisa* without Tarla following her. Or, Eponi could take her chances in straight combat. Even with a pistol drawn on her, Eponi's armor could take the hit and let her buy time to get away, draw another weapon and fire back.

All those ideas circled one uncomfortable truth: Eponi didn't really *want* to kill, hell, hurt Tarla. Maybe it was being faced with a more dire enemy in Vana or the scurrying, infected things that'd attacked after landing here, but a cocky mercenary with character? The galaxy could use a few more of those.

The quandary hadn't resolved itself by the time they reached the *Prisa*. Tarla whistled, the sound carrying through her suit visor. She'd put herself back under the invisibility cloak and the suit's full protection, apparently figuring Eponi just might pull something. Instead, both looked at the remnants from the earlier fighting, still there in all their grisly leavings.

"I like the ship," Tarla said. "Could use a wash and a change of scenery, though."

Eponi just nodded. The visor pinged and she focused

in towards the rear struts. Beyond the twin, slanted pillars was where Sever had piled the bodies that hadn't been burned to ash by the turrets. The visor seemed to think something moved back there, beyond the running light's reach.

"I'd like nothing better," Eponi replied. "But I'm not leaving without my squad."

"Or mine."

"Sure," Eponi said, starting forward. The visor kept pinging movement alerts, though it couldn't define what it saw as a threat. Eponi wanted to draw a weapon, but Tarla still had hers out, and getting shot in the back fell pretty far down the list of what Eponi wanted. "You getting this?"

"Getting what?"

Maybe those suits weren't so fancy after all. Down-graded the visor tech to get all that reflective trickery going?

"I'm picking up movement behind the ship," Eponi said. "We didn't exactly scour the bay after they stopped coming. Maybe one's left."

"You going to fight it with your bare hands?"

"Just didn't want you to plug me."

"Eponi, I know when to shoot," Tarla said. Her voice came from Eponi's left, and if the pilot concentrated, she could pick out the telltale blurs the suits left in the light. "Get yourself a weapon, please."

Okay then. Eponi drew the spare pistol, held it in her right hand. Put a combat knife in her left, extracted from a storage slot in the power armor's thigh. Not exactly a high powered offense, but enough to handle one of the diseased wrecks.

"You take point," Tarla said.

"Scared?"

"Smart."

Eponi snorted, but went forward anyway. Closing in on the *Prisa*'s back, the visor finally found its lock, highlighting at least fifteen sections in Eponi's sight with orange squares. Her armor had found motion in those spots, but wasn't sure if it signaled a threat, or what. A new sound came into play too, a cooking skillet's popping, bubbling churn.

With the *Prisa*'s engines above her, Eponi brought up her power armor lights to their brightest level. They erupted from the spots on her shoulder, lancing out and coating what should've been a moldering, awful pile in bright yellow-orange light.

"What the . . . " Tarla said.

The mass moved, all right. It quivered and shook in its rippling darkness. Fuzzy, snaking growths roped over the pile, bubbling up and dying down over and over again. At its base, the inky form spilled out, growing ever-so-slowly like a pond filling with water. A strange smell, like fertilizer from the crop-filled planets Eponi used to race over, filtered through her visor.

"It's the virus," Eponi said. "From Dynas."

"Where?"

"Doesn't matter." Eponi raised her pistol towards the mass. "We can kill it with fire."

Tarla didn't need a second order. The mercenary brought up her pistols and started laying into the mass. Eponi followed suit, their bolts lacing into the hulking pile and doing precisely nothing. After exhausting their power packs, and backing up several steps to avoid the pile's creeping edge, Eponi figured they needed a new strategy.

One that meant letting Tarla inside the *Prisa*.

"Follow me," Eponi said, opening her wristlet and tapping in the code. "We're not killing this thing out here."

"I'm getting that idea. Mind telling me what it is, and whether I need to be scared of it?"

"That's what's going into the soldiers," Eponi said as the *Prisa*'s ramp sank to the floor. "Or some version of it, anyway. It'll make them real strong before it makes'em real crazy. Then, they get to looking like that."

"Vana's murdering her whole force? That doesn't make sense."

Eponi led the way up the ramp, the two suited soldiers pounding into the *Prisa*. Tarla didn't even crack a joke, or marvel at the ship, a sign that maybe, just maybe, the mercenary understood the stakes here.

"She's not killing them," Eponi replied as they hit the ship's center. "On Gillane Four, they had some suppressing dose that kept the virus in check. She's not empowering all these people—"

"She's enslaving them," Tarla said. "That's, that's some seriously evil business."

"Now you get why we're here." Eponi locked visor stares with Tarla, the woman's blur standing out this close. "This isn't just a job for us. In a second, I'm going to get out of my armor and do what needs doing. You get to choose whose side you're on."

Racing karts, Eponi had to make bets all the time. Had to predict where the racer ahead would go, whether the one behind would try to rush up and nudge her off course. Making the wrong play could cost the race, even the kart. This wasn't much different, and at least, if Tarla shot her in the back, Eponi wouldn't have to worry long.

Turning her back on Tarla, Eponi told her power armor to let her out. The suit popped, split, and loosened so that the pilot could extract herself. Stepping away, heading towards the cockpit, Eponi closed her eyes for a long second, waiting for the bolt to come. One shot, and Tarla would have her ship, would have a good start at taking Vana's contract.

The smile came when Eponi slid into the pilot's seat, tapping awake the *Prisa*'s jets. The big ship hummed to life, the boarding ramp retracting. Gently, oh-so-gently, Eponi eased the craft off the ground without raising the struts. Twisting the flight stick, Eponi fired the *Prisa*'s maneuvering jets and sent the ship on a slow spin. Out front, the rubble statues and paint-splattered floors gradually turned into the growing, churning virus pool.

"You talk a good game," Tarla said, sitting in the copilot's seat. Without the invisible suit, Tarla didn't look half as deadly, but twice as cocky. Her grin wasn't clipped by the visor, and her large eyes sparkled. "I sent the message out back there. The Twilight Rangers don't take contracts from anyone that would do this."

Eponi's lips curled up towards her eyes, hiding the relief she felt. She couldn't quite kill the sigh that came with all the tension flooding away, though, and Tarla laughed.

"You thought I was gonna plug you? After all that?" Tarla said.

"Never know," Eponi replied, then took another look outside the windshield. Dialed up the energy to the turrets. "Ready to fry this thing?"

"Show me what my ship can do, pilot."

The *Prisa* didn't disappoint.

TEN

Out The Hatch

WHEN SAI BROKE LEFT, Rovo took the obvious other option. Leaving his scythe in its holsters, the rookie flared right, bringing up his rifle and burning cover shots across the vast, domed chamber towards approaching enemies. The visor helped, highlighting the agents against the blue-gold light coming in above.

DefenseCorp standard body armor could take a bolt, maybe two before burning through. The agents seemed to know this, because they treated Rovo's advance like a screaming notice to dive. Rovo had four targets as he sprinted along the long straight to the room's corner. He nailed the closest one, trading bolts to the shoulder that his power armor shrugged off and the agent's defenses . . . didn't.

Rovo couldn't tell if he dropped number one or the man dove, but by the rookie's third stride he'd swiveled his aim to number two. This agent staked things out safer, crouching near the railing and popping up to hit the bigger, wider, bulkier-in-every-way power armor. Her rifle laced white-hot laser towards Rovo's chest, but the rookie kicked in his kinetic boosters, leaping forward and firing all the while.

A ludicrous move that should've had Rovo's fire spraying across the room instead turned into a dangerous assault thanks to the power armor keeping his aim adjusted. Rovo felt the gentle pressures on his wrists and arms as the armor put his rifle where it needed to be. The agent found herself exposed as Rovo's leap carried him to the corner.

Give Rovo a straight-line shot and he'd hit it.

After confirming the first agent had indeed gone down, Rovo slimmed the odds in half. The latter two agents, farther along the rectangular walkway than the first duo, took what happened to their friends and turned it into caution. Slipping into doorways, the two offered potshots Rovo's way, ones Rovo countered with a rifle stream.

What could've been a drag-out fight ended when the grenades went off. The thundering blast shook the agents into deeper cover and pushed Rovo forward as the walkway's back section crumpled to the bottom level. The rookie didn't see Sai fall, didn't see his partner at all in the mix.

On his left, Rovo's run-up hit another door, this one red-locked like the others. Using the shallow recess to put himself on even footing with the agents further up the walkway, Rovo tried to get his bearings. He reached out to Sai with his comm, caught the man and felt the relief knowing the swordsman hadn't bit it in the blast.

Being alone in an enemy nest, as Rovo had learned on Dynas, tended to suck.

New fire broke Rovo's chat with Sai, blue bolts streaking from across the chamber. At the far range, the shots missed by millimeters as Rovo crouched back inside the doorway. Now he had two agents to his left and one across the way, a combination that stressed any possible strategy.

Then Sai told Rovo to run.

The idea felt wrong from the start. You didn't flee with Sever, you made calculated changes in position to turn tables, to flip the odds. Sai, though, didn't add in any of those details. Instead, Rovo needed to get his ass out of there as fast as possible.

Spraying some fire at the agent across the chamber, the wild volley bought Rovo time to look at the door behind him. A red scanner meant he wouldn't be getting inside, unless he found a working wristlet with access.

"Does this ever get easier?" Rovo muttered to himself.

Taking a breath, setting his rifle, Rovo lanced a few more bolts across the way to keep that agent suppressed. He followed up his shots with a turning run, clomping along the walkway towards the other two agents advancing towards him. Rovo's charge caught the agents, who probably assumed Rovo pinned, by surprise, sending them stumbling backward.

The rookie's power armor took a couple stray hits, the heat washing into Rovo's left knee and ribcage as rifle fire did its damage. The stumbling retreat didn't do much else for the agents, and Rovo caught them after three long strides. Aiming with his right hand, Rovo pulled the trigger and took out the one on that side. With his left, Rovo did something he'd only ever seen in movies: he grabbed the agent's arm and flung the enemy into the left wall.

Dazed, the agent dropped his rifle, put his hands on the ground to catch himself. Rovo caught him instead, helping the man up and guiding him right on to the next door in line.

"Keep still and you don't die today," Rovo said, letting the words spring from the power armor's speaker.

The agent laughed, that wicked, strange chuckle Rovo remembered from Gillane Four. The man had been injected, then.

"You think I care about dying?" The agent said, though he didn't resist Rovo's tugging. "We're all going that way soon. Only question is whether it's you or me that goes first."

"Then I'm hoping it's you," Rovo said.

Before the agent could reply, they'd reached the next recess. There, again, stood another spiral doorway with another locked scanner. Slapping the agent and his wrist against that black box, Rovo hoped he'd picked a hostage with a high clearance.

The scanner beeped its cheery sound, cascading more than a little relief. Despite their continued ignorance of the fighting around them, Rovo had to figure all those suited bastards below would get called into action eventually. Fighting the Twilight Rangers, Vana, even normal agents in those suits was bad enough—Rovo didn't need to try battling people who'd lost all sanity.

Beyond the door, a narrow pathway sloped up, with notches serving as steps paired with handrails on either side. The appearance was strange enough that Rovo did a double take even as fresh fire came in from behind. A blazing bright red sign on the door and both inside and out labeled the portal as an emergency exit.

Because, of course.

"Do I suck at this?" Rovo asked the hostage as he dragged the agent along, slapping the scanner on the way to shut the door. "Like, how did I choose this one?"

"All the exits on this side are emergencies," the agent replied between bouts of yipping glee. "You're at the edge of the base, where'd you think these would go?"

"What?" Rovo started up the steps, dragging the agent

along. It didn't seem like a good idea to hang around back there. "I saw the doors. There were at least four along this side?"

"Is this your first day here?" The agent asked. "Did you not watch the orientation?"

"The orientation? Who the hell do you think I am?"

"Someone who missed their dose?" The agent chuckled. "Like I'm going to if this goes on much longer. We get'em all the time. Some people don't have the tolerance to meet the schedule."

This place kept on getting worse. Rovo couldn't come up with another question after the agent's revelation. No wonder the suits down below, the other agents didn't stop their work. Sever wasn't an enemy force, just some sick people who'd laid their hands on some gear.

No need to reveal the truth to the agent. Instead, Rovo flipped the suit's communications to beam out on Sever's band. Finding silence, Rovo cursed his way through the agent's story, embracing the catharsis and waiting, maybe, for Eponi, Gregor, or Aurora to chime in and ask just what in hell's name was going on.

Nobody answered. Only fuzzy quiet.

That disturbing situation aside, the upward slope ended in another sealed door. This one didn't have a scanner, didn't have the fancy spiraling gate. Instead, offering a turning latch, the door operated through the age-old muscle method.

"Mind doing the honors?" Rovo asked the agent, who blinked at him.

The rookie aimed his rifle, and the agent understood. Rovo didn't want a hostage, didn't really want to kill the agent—not out of kindness, mind, but the agent seemed to know where to go—but, most of all, Rovo didn't want the agent to break off running while the rookie opened up the door.

With a totally expected loud, creaking squeak, the agent forced the doorway open. As the man did, golden sand coated his crimson armor, flooding into the tube from above. The agent coughed, Rovo listened as his suit confirmed Aurum Three's atmosphere was breathable, if not necessarily pleasant. The agent eventually found his lungs, looking over at Rovo with eyes that asked *now what?*

"We head out," Rovo said.

Sai's order told Rovo to find some way to get a message up to all those monsters in orbit that'd tried to blast Sever from the sky during their approach. For some reason, the swordsman felt those ships didn't deserve to have their insides ripped apart by a horde of invisible, bloodthirsty maniacs. Leave it to the squad's dad to have an ounce of empathy.

"You know what's out there, right?" The agent asked. "Because it's nothing. Nothing's out there."

"I'll take nothing over death by laser."

The agent couldn't fight that logic, and with Rovo's rifle continuing to prod, the agent climbed up and out. Rovo followed, leaving the soft blue light inside for the dimming afternoon and a sky filled with roaring engines.

Those suited ranks had been ordered to shuttles, and it sounded like those shuttles were getting ready to go. Electric ion jets didn't have the same rippling thunder-rumble older rocket fuels, like the ones Rovo rode on growing up back home, but they kicked up enough noise with their crackling energy. The sound came over the dunes like a shriek on the wind.

Beyond the noise, Rovo found himself disoriented to be in such a wide open space. After so long on a space station, in its tight corridors and then on the *Prisa*, with its tighter cabins—particularly Rovo's, which he shared with Gregor, the view stretching towards the horizon all around made the rookie dizzy.

Until he saw the big base's center, a silver-gray mass rising up from the sand. Its lights, a purple-yellow scheme, blinked on as daylight started to dwindle, making the structure shimmer from the ground like some cosmic treasure. Around it, stretching away like metal arms, were overland walkways leading to places Rovo didn't know.

And to the right, less impressive but still present as an ugly disc on the sand, sat the bay holding the *Prisa* amid its horrors.

"Where's the comm center?" Rovo asked the agent.

"Comm center? Why?"

"Need to tell my mom I love her," Rovo snapped back. "Doesn't matter why. Show me."

"What if I say no?" The agent giggled.

"With all this blowing sand, it'll be a long time before anyone finds your body."

The agent flipped away the laughter, maintaining, for a second, the composure due a moment where his life was very much at stake.

"There's three comm centers here," the agent said. "You want the main one, you gotta go to the big place in the middle. You want somewhere with less attention, you can head that way." The agent pointed behind Rovo, off to the central structure's left. "That's the barracks. Normally I'd say you're toast heading there, but we're emptied out."

"Can't imagine why," Rovo muttered. "Barracks sound like a good play. Let's go."

"Don't want to cover your tracks?" The agent pointed at the open hatch. "They'll know where you went."

"They saw us leave. They saw me smash you into a wall. I'm confident I'm being followed."

The agent waffled, kneeling over the open hatch, "Maybe, but there's a lot going on down there." A soft laugh. "Could be they'll forget about you."

Rovo rolled his eyes. If he didn't need this agent to get through any other scanners, the rookie would've roasted or knocked the man out by now.

"Fine, shut the hatch if it'll make you feel so much better."

The agent leaned down, reached for the hatch. Rovo watched, hand idly on his rifle. The agent had a pistol, but Rovo figured he could blast the man before the agent could draw the weapon.

The move happened fast. The agent slid on the sand, slipping over the hatch lip and back inside the tunnel. Rovo brought up his rifle, but the agent pulled the hatch down. The latch clicked, shut and sealed.

"Somehow, in all our fights, I forgot you all actually have training," Rovo said, clomping over to the hatch.

Meant for exits, not entrances, a smooth surface greeted him. No obvious way to open it. Rovo was all alone on Aurum Three, with a general direction and nothing else to go on. Sighing, the rookie started off, stomping through the sand and cursing his own idiocy.

As he walked, the first shuttles rose into view, tilting their forms star-ward, bringing their doomed cargo up to an unsuspecting fleet.

The Run

You don't work your way up to lead an outfit like Sever Squad and imagine finding yourself in a chilled lab freezer. Nonetheless, Aurora followed Gregor's words, and slipped —as much as one could in power armor—into the frosted confines, crunching back among the shelves stocked with crates, vials, and labeled stuff Aurora neither had the time or temperament to read.

Instead, she listened. First, the grenade she'd tossed back down the hallway went off, its muffled thump heading through the freezer's doors, followed by the steady crinkle as glass cracked beneath the approaching boots.

Orders swept in next, barked calls and pushback as officers, soldiers from mismatched outfits tried to find a chain of command when none existed. Rogue gunners, running around and hunting. Aurora smiled beneath her visor.

Even if it came to a fight, the response would be scattered. Loose. Vana couldn't control these bastards anymore than Aurora could.

Vana's name spun the smile away. What was the agent

doing? She'd brought Aurora and Gregor deep into her base, almost without trying to stop them—Aurora didn't feel for a second the dying mob in the *Prisa*'s bay had any chance at killing Sever— so what was the real game?

Deepak's theory leading into the mission, the idea that brought Sever to their rest-and-relaxation station and now to here, had all been predicated on blowing up Vana's supposed conference. Take out Vana or destroy her experiments before she sold DefenseCorp on their merits. Then, with nothing left, and so much cash wasted bringing their ships and their personal selves all this way, the brass would turn on Vana, ending her if Sever hadn't already and giving the squad a free ticket off world.

And, finally, clearing Sever's name to go their own way.

Instead, DefenseCorp's leaders left their blood back there. They wouldn't help Sever from beyond the grave, and neither would any seconds-in-command staking out their own positions in a roiling company that would, if Aurora had it right, be looking for scapegoats. Always easier to blame the opposition instead of looking inward.

Which, again, brought Aurora back to Vana. The Sever commander swept her eyes along the frozen lab, trying to parse the agent's plan. All these orders, the vials, and the crates had dates plastered on them. Stickers showing they'd been shipped here years ago. That tracked with Renard's slow plan, with the whole Helix operation.

All that took place before Vana, according to her own words on the *Nautilus*, had been involved. So Renard reclaimed this base and recruited Vana after?

Why? And why would Vana join?

The silence jarred Aurora's thoughts: no breaking glass, no orders, no clomps as armed soldiers moved on through. None bothered to check the freezer. An oversight, one any normal DefenseCorp squad should've accounted for, except these weren't normal squads on normal missions.

Bodyguards who'd lost the bodies they were supposed to guard, and now they wanted vengeance.

Aurora approached the freezer's exit, waited another long moment and listened. Her visor didn't pick up on anything the Sever commander missed, so with her rifle drawn, Aurora unlatched the door and eased it open with her foot.

The lab had been trashed, in part by Gregor and in part by the swarm passing through. Without the muffling door, their calls came back down the hallway, shouts suggesting their prey had gone this or that way. Another yell declaring a broken room clear.

Aurora nodded to herself: Gregor, keeping up the fundamentals even as the man ran.

Breaking right, Aurora retraced her steps back towards the bay. Getting to the threshold, Aurora looked around the end to see at least seven soldiers hanging around the bay's center. All seemed to be wearing rank patches on their crimson armor, along with their respective ship's badge. The leaders, then. Hanging back to measure their team's progress.

Aurora felt her rifle trigger at her fingers. She could wrap around, lay down some lightning fire, and take out most before any reacted. Deliver laser-filled justice . . . except these fools weren't here under some malevolent motive. They didn't land here expecting to see a super soldier demonstration, or to witness the next wave in DefenseCorp domination. They were doing a job, and getting paid for it. Aurora might've gone on missions with any number of these people, might've had her back covered by their rifles, their starfighters.

These weren't agents, these were DefenseCorp soldiers, and they didn't deserve this.

Reaching into another slot in her armor, Aurora pulled out her last grenade. The small silver ball looked pretty in the dimming light, glinting as it caught the blue from the base's overhead beams. The closest ship to her, where those special forces fighters had poured from, had its ramp down. The cockpit looked clear.

There might still be collateral damage, but Aurora had done her best to limit it.

The Sever captain threw the grenade, arcing it up and into the bay. The blue ball hit the ship's cockpit with a loud clank and bounced up, nestling on its second impact into the gap between the ship's cockpit and its mid-mounted engines. Aurora couldn't see the group, but she could hear their questions, their concerned calls.

"Here we go," Aurora said to herself, missing, yet again, the squad band that'd normally bring Sever together on a mission like this.

The grenade blew. The tiny explosive found juicy targets inside the ship's midsection, catching flammable opportunities and lighting them up into a fiery chain spilling over both sides, as if the craft were a chrysalis splitting in the middle, about to announce some beautiful new star.

Shrapnel rained, and Aurora looked around the edge to see the gathered soldiers breaking for their own ships or diving for cover behind stacked provisions, fuel, or tools. Snapping pops echoed around as wires superheated and oxygen pockets vanished as the ship fell apart. Enough chaos, Aurora had to figure, for an attempt.

Clomping around the corner, Aurora brought up her rifle as she ran. She couldn't keep much attention on her aim in the busy bay, though, because Aurora had no idea where she was running. Vana had come this way, gone through the bay, so the exit had to be somewhere, the trail had to exist.

Hope wasn't something Aurora preferred to rely on, but today there weren't many other options.

The docked ships sat ten to their line, an impressive number, though some had to carry more than one VIP down from above. Aurora's grenade torched the first one, bringing all remaining eyes that way as its demise roared along. Along the bay's left side, the twilight gave the ship inferno a pretty back drop, while the bay's right side served to hold equipment clusters, loading carts, and supply caches clumped in gray mounds.

No exits there.

Aurora made it a dozen steps, near the second ship, before the first laser came her way. An orange bolt zipping by Aurora's face and burying itself into the wall on her right, the shot had a hasty feel, a shooter compensating for their target's faster and faster speed. Lowering the rifle—Aurora gave up on the gunning idea after she started sprinting—the Sever commander poured all her suit's energy into those boots.

A person in power armor was nobody's idea of a ballerina, a smooth and svelte dancer. But the suit was a train, building up speed as Aurora kept herself pointed in one direction, sinking the kinetic impact from every stride into the next.

The grenade and its damage bought Aurora enough time to get going, and while other bolts followed the orange one, most went far off the mark. Only a couple struck home, their lingering heat fading through Aurora's back. The visor showed no critical damage, and Aurora kept her focus on what lay ahead, beyond those ships.

The visor did pick up one thing, though: outside to

Aurora's left, their lights shining bright in the dark. Shuttles with flaring engines. More and more lifting off. Transports? DefenseCorp ships returning to their homes in orbit?

Aurora would've pondered the idea more, except her sprint had brought her to the ship line's end. If speeding up the power armor's lumbering kilos took time, slowing them came faster. The docking bay ended in a thick wall, which would turn Aurora into so much paste if she kept charging right into it. Instead, she turned off the kinetic boosts, nearly tripping as the strides lost their easy, floating gait.

Holding her breath, Aurora jumped forward, bringing her feet together over the short distance. Bringing up her knees as much as she could, Aurora hit the floor at an angle that should've sent her rolling head-over-heels into a collapse, where the following fighters would fill her full of laser.

Instead, triggering the kinetic boosts not spent for several strides, Aurora launched herself upwards. The impact and its momentum spun Aurora forward and she curled herself with the loop, swinging her feel all the way around until those thick, armored boots slammed into the bay's end wall first. The metal slats crunched, sparks showered as her boots latched into the wall, suspending Aurora several meters over the floor.

"Anyone impressed?" Aurora said, looking up along the bay she'd ran.

The answer came in more bolts, fired from afar and off-target. Aurora killed the latches, letting herself fall towards the ground and rolling to the side when she hit it. Lasers cascaded in as Aurora pulled out of the roll, caught a quick look around.

The docking bay's only exit mirrored Aurora's entrance

on her left. A large door leading who knew where, but also Vana's only escape option. Scrambling to her feet, suffering a few hits to her side and legs in the process, strikes that singed her muscles and burned away the suit's protection, Aurora went back on the run.

She could've shot them all. Could've wasted the soldiers as they came on, trying to dodge from cover to cover in the crowded bay.

"You all owe me your lives," Aurora muttered, clanking over to the door with its blinking red scanner.

With a quipped command, Aurora had the visor start a countdown. Thirty seconds to get the door open before Aurora would have to deal with the group charging her position. She didn't have Gregor's hammer, didn't have Sai's sword.

But she did have one weapon. One idea.

Aurora kicked the door. Hard. Switched feet and did it again. The impacts dented the plain gray slat not meant to hold off anything more than a disgruntled landing crew. A third kick, and a fourth.

The visor beeped. Someone behind her shouted for Aurora to stand down.

"I'm surrendering," Aurora said, broadcasting the words and raising her hands as she crouched.

Anything to buy another second.

The same voice called for Aurora to leave the suit. That one, the Sever squad captain wasn't doing.

"You might want to stand back," Aurora said. "This isn't about you."

Who was there, who heard her words, Aurora didn't know and didn't really care. The confusion bought Aurora one more second, enough time to kick in those charged up boosters. Between catching Aurora's run and getting topped off with the kicks to the door, her power armor had kinetic energy to burn.

Feeling like she'd strapped herself into a launching drop ship, Aurora burst from the crouch, blitzing at the weakened door like a human-sized missile. She didn't have time to rotate her shoulder, to duck in her head. Her helmet struck first, a jolt that stopped nothing. Aurora saw, felt the door peel apart as she burst through, the armor shredding the barrier only to bounce off the ceiling on the other side and send Aurora into a tumbling roll.

A roll that sounded hard, that felt stiff and bruising. As she slid to a stop, Aurora realized this half, this section wasn't carpeted and clean like its opposite partner. Instead, Aurora looked at hardened walls bordering cells. Languishing between sizzling energy barriers, split only by a meter or two, were hapless people or worse.

Like the ones on Dynas, deep in the Helix complex, experiments swirled around Aurora. Some bore the dark virus hallmarks, while others evinced new traits, like a white scaly skin or a blue tint to their bodies. What purposes those might have, what additional concoctions the scientist Anaskya might be throwing into her mix, Aurora couldn't know.

The shock died as her faculties returned, body aching from the fall and now staring into a larger, motley squad pouring in from the bay. Armed and angry, the batch came after Aurora into the hallway. Initially, their weapons pointed right at Aurora and her power armor.

Initially.

It's hard to hold a focus when you're surrounded by things that don't match your reality. The squad captains, the special forces commanders faltered as they grasped that they weren't in some dull installation for some Defense-Corp summit.

"The hell is this?" one asked, his green bands marking him among the deadlier specialties in DefenseCorp's arsenal.

"This?" Aurora said, staying planted on the floor. She saw her chance, and keeping sudden movements to a minimum might let Aurora make it. "This is the truth."

TWELVE

Electric Heart

WITH PERRO'S buzzing blade out and Sai's katana put away, the agents and their glazed soldier ranks ignored the two as they walked towards the chamber's rear. What, towards the front, operated as a clean suit'em up and ship'em out game trended darker towards the back. There the line dwindled to a single-file row coming from a wide tunnel. Agents flanked the entry, and makeshift electrical barriers corralled the Helix hopeless into a steady file.

As each one left the tunnel, a nursing robot sat, its many arms whirling from a case containing vial after black vial. The robot sucked each substance into a syringe, whirled around and jabbed it into the next person. The line moved forward a step and the process repeated, each stab hitting its target in their upper forearm.

The victims barely winced. Their faces slack, their eyes distant.

"Drugged," Perro said as they walked. "Creepy, isn't it? Vana says they'll all go insane if they're left without the sedative."

"And that's what's in those vials? A sedative?"

"Hell no. That's the cause. The secret sauce all these poor saps have been getting since the start. Supposed to turn'em into fighting machines."

"Spoiler: it doesn't."

Perro shrugged as they approached. Finally, an agent seemed to notice that Perro and his chosen captive weren't part of the normal order. Waving for the injections to continue, the woman left her post and came a few meters off the line to look Sai in the visored-eye.

"This the one that caused the mess?" The agent asked.

"He's the one. Withdrawal," Perro replied. "Need to take him down below and get him outta this thing."

The agent looked at Sai, noticed the sword and the pistols. The power armor itself.

"Didn't think we had any models like this here," the agent said. "This is DefenseCorp standard. Where'd you get it?"

Sai didn't move. Kept to the simple plan. Perro could turn on him here, could give Sai up and put him in a very difficult position. Perro claimed that he'd never do that, with his honor.

For some people, Sai might take the honor line. Perro, though, had tried to sneak a strike in while invisible. Had pushed Sai into a duel on Wexer's streets, and then laid an ambush to snipe from a distance. Honor played no part in the shooter's game.

So Sai made sure the mercenary would stay true.

"Few old ones down below," Perro spoke fast. "Guy somehow dug way deep to find'em. Made it all the way out another tunnel. Almost broke the real bad guys loose."

The agent paled, "Then you're taking him to medical?"

"You know what Vana said," Perro nodded, "get every body that can fight worth a damn and throw'em in line."

"Today's the day," the agent agreed. "Get him back here fast, then. We're loading up everyone we can fit, and we're not keeping leftovers."

At the agent's direction, two others opened a gap in the Helix line, letting Perro and Sai through to the chamber's other side.

"Medical?" Sai said. "I'm not going to medical."

"Don't worry about it," Perro replied. "You wanna see where they're building the suits? It's right by the doctor. There's no real medical here, man."

That, Sai could believe.

On Sai's right, the next suited batch clomped. Invisible in their armor, they made noise nonetheless. Ahead, glowing shuttles took on the marching recruits, full ships popping up into the air. They'd have the clearances, they'd dock at the fleet in orbit and tear through DefenseCorp's core. Rip it apart and leave a vacuum at the head of the galaxy's largest, strongest company.

"They'll never make it out alive, will they?" Sai said as Perro veered them left across the wide shuttle landing pad. On the pad's left side sat what looked like a bunker, with fortified walls and a single double door opening their way. "Even if these suits win up there, Vana's not coming to get them, is she?"

"You're asking questions mates like me don't know the answers to," Perro said, though the cocky vibe in his voice faded.

Useless, this one.

"That's where we're going?" Sai said as Perro marched him to the new structure.

"You wanted to see where the suits are made? That's where they're made," Perro said.

As if on cue, that double-door opened and a new rack filled with hanging suits wheeled out on another cart.

Beside Sai, an empty cart sped past in the opposite direction, its steering agents wheeling it along fast. Seeing those two agents working so hard to get the suits moving sprung up a different question, one that Perro might actually know.

"Why're all these agents running the lines?" Sai asked. "Doing the manual work? Is there nobody else?"

"Not even many of them," Perro said. "Don't know why, but we're talking less than a hundred of Vana's shadows here. Maybe that's why they brought us in. Provide that extra security."

"Which you definitely did."

"Hey."

Approaching the double doors, Perro pulled Sai aside while they waited for the next cart swap. Aurum Three's night approached, making the shuttle launches look like shooting stars as they went towards orbit. It would've been beautiful under any other circumstance.

"So when we get inside, you take this off, yeah?" Perro said.

"I'll take it off when we're done here," Sai replied. "Just don't let anyone shoot you in your thigh and you'll be fine."

Both glanced at the mercenary's leg, visible while the man had the suit's refraction turned off. A close eye could see the bulge where Sai had dropped the grenade, triggered this time to detonate off Sai's short range transmission. One wrong move, one wrong look, and Perro's suit wouldn't save him.

With a whirring click, the fresh cart ran out. The agents pushing it spared the slightest glance at Perro and Sai, not stopping at all as the two slipped in behind them and entered the suit's production center.

"Security seems lax," Sai said as they moved.

"Today's the big day, and it's already on," Perro replied. "There's nothing you can do to stop it, my man. They're already shipping out so many suits."

"That's your opinion."

Getting inside the building and its raucous cacophony, though, threatened Sai's optimism. The entry opened into a rolling, rambling line arcing from the building's ceiling all the way to the floor. To the right, a molten pump at one end shot up the raw, hot metals that cascaded through the long sequence until, nearly at Sai's feet, the end product came out for a bot to scoop and hang onto the next cart in line. A few agents hung near the line's end, ready to shift the next cart and looking not the least concerned.

Perro didn't give Sai long to watch, steering the swordsman off to the left where a lift sat waiting with a green-blinking scanner.

"Impressive, right?" Perro said as they moved.

"Vana built this over the last few months?"

"Faster, mate. This was up and running by the time we got here."

"Then we have to destroy it."

"Hold on." Perro dropped his voice. "I know you've got your suicide wish and all, but me? I'd rather make it outta this one alive. You want to take out this thing, let's find a way to do it quietly."

"Is that why you're taking me over to the elevator?"

"If we stood there, someone would ask what the hell we're doing. I'm buying time, but that's gonna run out soon so I'm hoping you can find a better idea."

Sai swirled one more look at the massive line. He could throw some grenades in there, wreck things, but that would bring down the house and more. Worse, there seemed every opportunity that Vana could reconstruct any damaged line quick. Perro kept saying today was the day, but tomorrow could be worse.

Aurora brought Sever here to try and end Vana's threat. Sai owed it to her, to his own family, to keep these suits from coming back.

"How deep does this lift go?" Sai asked.

"Now that's a tone I'm looking for," Perro replied. "And I've got no idea, boss. We've been around the main base, this spot, and not much else. Vana didn't exactly give us the tour."

"Then let's find out."

The scanner took Perro's command without complaint. The lift popped open, offering a nice option set. At the very bottom, Sai saw what he wanted.

Power Management.

Perro whistled when Sai picked the option.

"Starting to get what you're thinking," Perro said as the lift lurched into motion. The shaking threw Sai for a minute until he remembered this wasn't a new base, but something Vana had stolen, converted to her own taste. "Just make sure you give us enough time."

"We'll have time," Sai replied, "if we do it right."

The lift doors opened, showing Sai what *right* really meant. Overloading something's energy, be it a starship's batteries or a building's tap into its planet's super hot core tended to take an amount of computer savvy Sai didn't have. He wasn't going to go hacking into some system, change some values, then sit back with a smile and watch the world burn.

No, Sai would do the destruction himself, and Vana had done what she could to keep things easy for him.

Superheating enough metal to make that many suits, and the power armor or whatever else had come before, meant the DefenseCorp mastermind that had built this thing long ago had tapped into Aurum Three's deep crust and below. The drill's structure and its siphon filled the room Sai and Perro stepped into. A monitor wall greeted them first, displaying where all that energy happened to be going, and behind it, the great blackened beast with its converters sucking heat up and churning it into charge.

Looking at those monitors told Sai they hadn't come to the power source for the suits, they'd found the energy supply for the whole base.

"I'd call it beautiful, but then I'd feel bad killing it," Perro said.

"Don't," Sai replied. "It's a machine, nothing more."

While a scanner sat below the monitors, Sai didn't try to log himself in. An alarm might trigger, and that wasn't the point of this exercise. Instead, he went around the screens while Perro followed. The drill's end bulged out like a sphere getting smashed by a giant, black-steel brick. That brick, sitting several meters over Sai's head, would be doing the hard work turning the heat to power.

It'd also be the most vulnerable part of this whole operation. Disrupt it, and the base would fall apart.

"Boost me," Sai said.

"Boost you? Like if we were kids?"

"Not a question. Do it."

"Okay man. You could laugh a little."

Sai clenched his fists, gave Perro a glower that the visor hid, "My squad mates are fighting for their lives out there. My DefenseCorp friends, here through no fault of their own, are about to get killed by murderous invisible maniacs. Excuse me if I'm not grinning just yet."

Perro, for once, kept his mouth shut and helped Sai lift up towards that metal brick. The man's hands weren't the most stable, so Sai attached his grapple to the brick's side for some stability. Sai's hands went next to the small discs attached to his lower back.

It'd been a while since Sai had been able to play with his favorite tools: mines. The tiny explosives packed a big punch, and he'd built up a new set during Sever's vacation on the station. These, using tiny teeth, snatched into the brick's surface and beeped their readiness to detonate.

"These'll go off when I tell them to," Sai said after Perro let him back down. "We get up top, get clear, and we'll shut this place down."

Or at least, that's what Sai would've done. Instead, both he and Perro froze as the lift doors opened back towards the entrance. Several boot pairs came into the room.

"We know you're down here!" The voice calling sounded not the least bit scared. "There's many of us, two of you. Shut your suits down and surrender, and maybe Vana will be kind."

Sure she would.

Keeping quiet, wishing Perro knew how to read Sever's hand signals, Sai drew his katana and made his way opposite the route they'd taken. The agents, though, didn't follow their footsteps exactly, but split apart, their voices calling commands giving them away. Sai and Perro rolled their feet, muffling the soft clanks with the drill's constant rumble.

Coming around the bend, Sai caught a breath and swung the katana before he could even see his target. The agent, proving again that Vana's fighters weren't to be underestimated, darted back. The katana's edge caught the agent's arm, drawing a cut but nothing more. The agent shouted, tried to bring up a rifle as Sai charged, putting an end to the draw before it began.

Perro dashed around Sai's right, engaging the agent there before she could get off a pistol blast into Sai's side.

"Time to run," Sai said, breaking through the next two agents in line as their weapons came up. "Too many for us!"

Not really, maybe, given the close quarters, but Sai couldn't risk it. Getting shot here could ruin everything for Sever, and those mines needed to blow. Waving the katana, he cut at one of the pipes, slicing it clean and roaring out a simmering hot blast. Sai's power armor kept him safe, but the two agents fell away, trying to protect themselves.

Perro fell in line as Sai ran, the two wrapping around towards the lift. Six more agents waited there, rifles drawn and beads centering on the two suited soldiers. Not good.

"Hold on!" Sai grabbed Perro with his left hand, held the katana in his right, and triggered the power armor's boost jump.

Together, the pair flew into, over a laser flurry. Sai felt new burns add to old ones as his visor popped up one alarm after another, but the agents dodged away from the armored bodies, letting the two roll, smoking, into the open lift.

"Gotcha," Sai whispered, using his katana to stab the upward button while he sent the signal.

The lift doors juddered as the agents ran his way, as, behind them, that black steel brick lit up in luminous flame.

Tactical Retreat

THE HAMMER SWUNG, the boots pounded hard floor, and Gregor rumbled his way through the halls. Windows shattered behind and around him, both from his wild swings and the occasional cracked shot. He met intersections with selective randomness, picking directions gradually leading Gregor back towards the walkway returning to the *Prisa*'s bay. A plan, beyond distracting the enemy, hadn't formed, but if the forces after him kept up the chase, at least Sever's ship might give him some cover.

Gregor, on a normal mission, would've sent out a call for help. He would've showered DefenseCorp airwaves with his location and his pursuit, calling in airstrikes or reinforcements. Instead, now, he ran in silence, his own breathing the only sound giving him any company on the journey.

If you could call the laboratories, offices, and conference rooms a journey: Their staid decor and functional purpose brought repetition with every turn, so much so that Gregor would've lost his place many rooms ago if his visor didn't keep the *Prisa*'s general direction projected.

He'd deviate from the golden arrow laid out on the ground every few turns to keep his pursuit guessing, and so far, Gregor still lived.

Smashing through the next door—Gregor charged the hammer between those sealed portals by banging in walls and windows—brought the Sever soldier into a familiar room, albeit not quite the same. Clear concrete walls on either side buttressed with slats made to be pulled down, nothing on the floor, and another door on the far end. No window here into Aurum Three's night, but Gregor recognized a twin when he saw it.

The room might've been dull, but its sole occupant had Gregor stopping one step into the space. Briana stood hulking in her suit, not in the least invisible with her giant cannon held in both her hands. She had her helmet flipped up, a fiery grin matching her blue-tinted hair.

Gregor had nowhere to jump, no pistol handy to shoot, and he had no doubt Briana's cannon would shred his power armor like confetti. But knowing you were going to die and letting it happen were two different things.

Raising his hammer, ready to blaze out fighting, Gregor started forward.

"Get outta the way," Briana said, flicking her head to the right.

Not one to question orders in the moment, Gregor did as she asked, diving right as Briana opened up with the cannon. Rather than turning Gregor into so much ash, Briana's lasers blazed behind Gregor's back, down the hallway he'd been wrecking. Panicked shouts poured back, calling to retreat, to find another way around.

Watching her shoot as he steadied himself, Gregor caught the hot light as it blanched Briana's face, saw the burn marks on her gauntlets darken as the cannon reached terrible temps. She held herself steady, keeping the aim level as the battery packs on her back sent energy coursing over her shoulders into the big weapon.

A damn beautiful sight.

Gregor hated to end such a wonder, but those retreating forces would find the other way soon. Once they had Gregor and Briana trapped, the end would come fast, and it would hurt.

"We must leave," Gregor said, heading towards the far door and bashing it down with two hard hammer swings. "Now."

Briana, backing up towards Gregor without stopping the laser stream, finally shut off the burn at Gregor's second shout.

"You want to run?" Briana asked. "I didn't think you were a coward."

"Changing the battlefield," Gregor replied. "They will cheat."

Briana started to counter, but they didn't have time to banter, so Gregor took off. Clomping through the door to the stairs, Gregor hopped the railing and plummeted to the floor below. Landing with enough force to crack the metal tile, Gregor grunted as the power armor informed him that the suit's kinetic boosters were now overcharged.

Always good to have another weapon in the arsenal.

Briana came slower, grinding down the stairs in an awkward walk.

"They didn't make my gun for this," Briana said after Gregor called for her to go faster. "You want to leave me, you can. I'll take'em on all by myself."

That wouldn't answer the thousand questions Gregor had, starting with why the hell Briana happened to be standing in a random corridor on a random planet like this one. Instead, Gregor looked right, then launched his hammer at the ceiling over the other stair. With its energy burst activated, the hammer struck the overhead slats, shattering lights and breaking the supports. The heavy bang shot the hammer back the way it came, landing the big weapon not far from Gregor's feet.

And the stair? The stair now had a giant rubble pile blocking its upper steps.

"Nice throw," Briana said as she made it down.

"Easy," Gregor replied. "Come on."

With Gregor leading, the two went back to the moving walkway heading over the long expanse towards the *Prisa*'s bay. Briana couldn't walk fast, so once they hit the walkway itself, Gregor moved aside, letting the walkway's electric drive carry them on while Briana set herself to spray anything that came after them.

In Aurum Three's approaching night, the white lights lacing the walkway's central arc illuminated the journey. Outside, brighter engines flared as craft lifted up towards space. Drop shuttles? Gregor couldn't be sure, but he figured whatever it was, the launches didn't mean anything good.

"Thank you," Gregor said when nobody appeared after the first few seconds.

"For saving your ass after you dumped us back on Wexer?" Briana replied. "Don't thank me. Thank Tarla. I was going to roast you till she switched the game."

"What?"

"Vana hired us to torch you all if her people failed." Briana spoke without throwing her gaze from the enemy's direction. "From what I saw back there, you had them beat. I was supposed to wait, keep you from leaving."

"You were supposed to wait?"

Now Briana shrugged, "Vana's paying, she's the one that gave us the orders. Once you made it into the base, we were supposed to keep you in there or kill you. I had central, Tarla and the others had the real prize."

"What real prize?"

"All those lights out there, I'm guessing," Briana said. "Something about setting off a human bomb today. If we had to kill you, we were supposed to. Otherwise, delay, delay, delay."

More questions that Gregor couldn't swat with his hammer.

"We killed the traitors in there," Gregor said, looking back down the walkway with Briana. "The ones that wanted this. They're gone."

"Cool," Briana said. "Those people didn't sign the contract with us. Vana did."

"You could have attacked in there. Stopped us."

"Torn you apart? Yeah, I could have. Vana had me holding up that other stairway after you all landed." Briana laughed. "Sounds like she's been playing you all."

"She will lose."

"Sure looks like she's winning." Briana squinted. "Game time, Gregor."

Raising her cannon, Briana loosed a white-bolt volley along the walkway. Shapes scattered away from the entrance, getting ever farther behind. Gregor slotted his hammer into its sheath, pulled out his pistols. Between the two of them, nothing would get—

The walkway stopped, the lights flickered as the ground shook. Gregor pitched forward, catching himself on the walkway's railing. Briana fell backward, the cannon taking up her hands. Gregor heard the crunch as her battery packs caught the fall, and when he looked her way, he saw sparks spraying from her weapon.

The lights died. Everywhere.

From a glistening base sprawling across a golden desert

to a black expanse lit by the afterglow from rising shuttle engines in split second. And in the second after, lasers cut through the black, streaming towards Gregor and Briana from the walkway entrance.

"They're not even calling for a surrender," Briana said, pain edging her voice. "You must've really made them mad."

Gregor snapped off two pathetic pistol shots back towards the oncoming fire. The visor blanketed the whole tunnel with potential threats, and his two cracks did nothing to diminish the assault. His power armor took hits, burning away his left shoulder and weakening his chest plate to little more than flimsy plastic.

"We cannot stay here," Gregor said.

"Great, I can't run," Briana replied. "Cost of having this thing."

"Then I will carry you."

Briana started some protest, but Gregor crouched as lasers filled the gap overhead. Hooking his gloves beneath her shoulders, Gregor kicked in his kinetic boosters and jumped. Carrying Briana kept Gregor's height from hitting its usual apex, but the walkway wasn't tall, and the Sever fighter remembered the glass ceiling when he smashed into it.

Perhaps the walkway had been designed to resist Aurum Three's continual wind, but it certainly wasn't made to block a hard-charging power armor suit. Gregor's head broke through with a bone-rattling crash, splintering the glass and splitting the walkway's central bar, along with all the now-dead lights embedded inside. As Gregor's jump died, and with Briana shouting curses the whole way, the pair fell back through the shattering glass, cascading the total failure up and down the walkway.

Aurum Three rushed to fill its new gap, blowing in

sand. The whipsaw wind picked up glass shards and swirled them back and forth through the passageway as the two mercenaries landed. Gregor's leap gave them a few meters, and bought them a giant distraction.

Ignoring Briana's complaints and his own sudden headache, Gregor pulled the Twilight Ranger back. The lasers had stopped, and while Gregor didn't know why, he sure as hell wasn't going to take the bonus for granted.

"They can't see us, the morons," Briana laughed as Gregor finally helped her up. Her backpack seemed to have shorted itself out, the sparks dying away as the batteries fizzled. "This is why you have to get up close. Can't miss that way."

"Do not give them ideas," Gregor said. "Go ahead."

"Letting a lady lead? How polite."

"Never seen a lady like you."

"And you never will again."

Briana took the offered place, turning her back to the enemy and breaking into an awkward run. The walkway's end neared, and with it, some cover as they descended into the bay. Calls to advance came over the air now, rising above the wind. The DefenseCorp force hadn't given up yet.

Never before had Gregor returned to a space as disturbing, bloodied, and ruined as the *Prisa* bay and felt relief. Without the lights, without the power, he had to draw his hammer and smash in the door, but beyond, Gregor saw hope: the *Prisa* remained, and its running lights had power. Whatever had damaged the base itself had left the Sever ship alone.

"She looks nice," Briana said as they picked their way through the rubble and around the strange sculptures. "Everything else in here is real weird."

"You missed the fun."

"I bet."

Behind them, closing sounds signaled their pursuit had gained ground. Operating on impulse, Gregor flipped his comm from the squad band to the near-field broadcast. Sending out the signal would give them away to the chasers, but if someone was on the *Prisa*, then . . .

"Gregor, buddy, that you crashing around out there?" Eponi's sweet, snarky voice replied to his hail first. "I'd say I'm shocked, but who else would make so much noise?"

"Lower the ramp," Gregor replied, not bothering to engage. "Cover behind, we are being pursued."

"On it." Eponi might be suffused with humor, but the pilot knew when business took priority. "Stand by for annihilation. Tarla, head to the starboard turret."

Tarla?

The name threw Gregor nearly too long before he remembered the second, important part of the request.

"Scare them only," Gregor added as he swept away a rubble pile with the hammer, clearing the way for Briana. "No deaths."

"Why?"

"Because he doesn't want to hurt his old pals," Tarla, this time, joining in from her turret. "You're all softies."

"No deaths," Gregor repeated.

"I hear you," Tarla said as the first shots came whizzing over Gregor's shoulder. "Shade those peepers, people."

The *Prisa* lit up the black bay, streaking low-powered orange volleys from its turret over Gregor and Briana's head. Rubble, sculptures burst into flame or melted away, the hissing and pops giving way to calls to retreat, to run.

"Gregor, wait till you get in here," Eponi said. "I've one helluva story to tell you. But first, I gotta ask, where's Aurora?"

FOURTEEN

Exit Strategy

GREGOR AND BRIANA timed their entry to perfection. After the whole base shook and all the lights went out, Eponi and Tarla had burned the minutes getting the *Prisa* ready to fly. As the hammer man and cannon lady, as Eponi called them, burst in through the trash and the bloody paint, Eponi had been sending the *Prisa*'s power to the engines.

The idea? Get real close to the exit and use the ship's concentrated power to melt a hole.

Then they'd go find whomever they could, scoop up the squaddies into the *Prisa*'s bay and make a break for it.

"You would leave the mission incomplete?" Gregor said as he popped free from his power armor in the *Prisa*'s central chamber. The man's suit bore black marks, holes, and all the good scratches that came from a job well done. "You would let Vana live?"

"Not for long," Tarla said, catching Gregor's suspicious look and tossing it back with a smile. "Your pilot here has all the recordings we could ever want on the ship. Once we hit orbit, we can broadcast them out. Not even Defense-Corp can go against the entire galaxy united."

"See?" Eponi added. "I'm pretty much the best."

"You are, but this will take too long," Gregor replied. "Vana will run, or attack."

"She already is," Briana said, following Gregor out of her suit.

Eponi eyed the big gun on the floor, next to its damaged battery packs. If that thing exploded, the whole ship could go with it. Which would, uh, not be good. Maybe, if Eponi could stuff the cannon inside a weapons locker, that might keep the blast from—

"Then we have to stop the shuttles," Tarla responded to something Briana had said. "I'm not a hero, but I want my cash and my contracts. Those invisible monsters aren't taking them from us."

"Uh, what?" Eponi asked when all the eyes turned her way.

"Get the ship moving," Gregor said. "We have targets to down."

Ah, well, Eponi could do that.

The *Prisa* hovered to life not long after, floating in that dark-as-dead bay while Gregor and Briana took their spots in the two turrets. Eponi couldn't shake the weird feeling seeing Tarla in the co-pilot's chair next to her, where Aurora ought to be sitting. The two captains couldn't look more different: Aurora always seemed either ready to fight or getting ready for one, straight and stern. Tarla leaned back in the seat and picked at her teeth with one hand, swiped at her console with the other.

"So we're shooting our way out?" Tarla asked as the *Prisa* juddered off the ground.

"Unless you have a code that'll open the door?"

"Have to get the power back on first." Tarla saw

Eponi's questioning look—if the captain really did have a code, getting the power on might be a better option. "Sorry, Vana didn't hand over all her secrets."

"And you didn't take them?"

"Didn't think I'd need'em to beat you all."

Eponi guessed Tarla's Twilight Rangers hadn't torched a single Sever yet, but the pilot figured she'd keep Tarla's ire down while Eponi needed her hands on the *Prisa*'s flight stick. As the ship rose over the rubble and the still-burning slag that'd been the virus's remains, Eponi flared the lights bright and zeroed in on the gray-metal line closing the bay from Aurum Three's starry night.

"You want to shoot through that?" Gregor's voice came over the intercom, crisp and clear. "We don't have time."

"Nope," Eponi said. "We're taking a different way."

DefenseCorp built the bay into Aurum Three's sandy landscape, stuffed in a thick gateway and surrounded the whole platform with metal. While the gate came standard, thick and strong, Eponi figured the bay's other areas didn't get the same treatment. With the *Prisa*'s lights shining, grooves etched from the bay's walls by those trapped souls laid clear that the foundation didn't exist to defend against an attack.

Because who would attack DefenseCorp, the most dangerous company in the galaxy?

"Everything's sand around us, right?" Eponi said into the silence left by her last comment. "It's not a stable foundation. We shoot out the supports beneath that gate, and it's all going to slide down, giving us an opening."

More silence. Long enough that Eponi started wondering if she'd missed something obvious. Tarla glanced at her like Eponi had gone insane.

"All for being brave," Tarla said when she saw Eponi

looking, "but collapsing a bay down on our heads doesn't seem like a good play, even for you."

"It's not going to," Eponi shot back. "We won't touch the other sides. They'll keep the roof up long enough for us to fly out."

"Better have perfect timing," Briana added from her turret. "It'll be a close shave."

"I've had closer," Eponi said.

She had, too. At least a dozen kart races where a centimeter's gap had proved the difference between a successful finish and a disastrous collision.

"Okay." Tarla shook her head. "I don't have a better idea, and unless either of you two numbskulls has something buried in your noggins, I think we go with our pilot and get shooting. Every second we burn here, more shuttles lift off."

Gregor and Briana didn't offer up any more dissent, so Eponi nosed the *Prisa* forward until it hovered two ship lengths back from the gate. Using her pilot's console, Eponi painted the sections she wanted shot, giving the two turrets and her central cannon options. Dwindling the energy going to the ship's shields and engines, Eponi maximized the blast power.

"Ready?" Eponi said.

"Ready," Gregor and Briana replied together.

"Then go," Tarla said.

Eponi squeezed the trigger, and the bay became a spastic light show as the *Prisa*'s weapons bit hard into the bay's wall. The metal beneath the gate took the hits, glowing more and more orange as the fusillade continued. The three centers grew white with heat, the metal edges peeling back under the assault before dropping, as ashes, to the floor.

Gregor and Briana worked from the outside in, while Eponi used her central cannon's more limited range to dissolve a larger hole directly beneath the gate's center. The destruction came quiet, with the lasers emitting a whine, the metal creaking and cracking, but no explosions rocked the bay, no screams from enemies giving up their last.

Eponi would've called it a meditation, would've fallen into a trance, if Tarla hadn't started pointing and shouting like a little girl.

"There's the sand! It's coming through!" Tarla sat up and pointed below Eponi's burning hole. "I can't believe your stupid plan is working!"

"Stupid? You thought it was stupid?"

"It still is stupid!" Tarla laughed. "I'll keep saying that till we make it outta this alive, but that's freaking sand right there. Amazing."

Tarla's delight proved infectious, and Eponi couldn't keep herself from laughing right along with the Twilight Ranger captain as the three lasers worked themselves together. Aurum Three's grains filtered through in several places now, rushing against the weakening foundation. Success brought its own complications, though, as Eponi dialed back the laser power, particularly for her center cannon, so the *Prisa* would have the energy to launch forward at a moment's notice.

"The gate's juddering," Briana said. "Look at that thing shake."

The clamps holding the gate's sides, holding the thing from above, no longer had any real support from below. Sand continued rushing in, the force breaking away metal at the edges already weakened by laser fire.

"When it happens, it will happen fast," Gregor said. "Be ready."

"Oh, you know, I'm watchin' a movie," Eponi replied. "Just let me finish the scene and I'll be right back."

At least Tarla chuckled.

The break came with a rending warning. With a slicing shriek they could all hear in the *Prisa*, the gate's side supports broke away. The massive door dropped into the flowing sand beneath, tearing its top attachments with it. Metal broke, splintered, shattered and rained all around the *Prisa* as Eponi goosed those jets.

In front, the gate's former spot held an open view of the night sky. Well, not quite open. Isolated wires, girders, and plating hung in the way. Gregor and Briana shot what they could, immolating debris as Eponi pushed the *Prisa*, with a couple wince-inducing scratches and bangs, into the open air.

She might've pumped a fist. Might've cheered.

The *Prisa* took to the night sky like a bird to a summer breeze, lofting up over the dead-dark base as Eponi brought the ship around to get a better look at the long shuttle line lifting towards orbit.

"So we're flying into all that?" Eponi said. "Rather than looking for Aurora, Rovo and Sai?"

"Aurora is busy," Gregor said.

"Sai and Rovo have the other Rangers looking after them," Tarla said. "We'll come back for a pick-up. Let's go."

Just saying the words didn't make anything happen, though. Eponi still needed to pick a target. They could write off the shuttles already up in the air and try to stop any new ones from lifting off, or Eponi could shoot the *Prisa* towards the fleet and try to keep as many from docking . . .

Vana could only win by crossing the finish line.

"Buckle up," Eponi said, pushing power to the *Prisa's* engines and shooting the craft star-ward.

Eponi's flight path looked like a triangle's side, burning into an ascent that would intercept shuttles right near their atmospheric exit. Their targets rose with the steady non-urgency given to automated pilots. None reacted as the *Prisa* drew close, none bothered to take evasive maneuvers. Each one kept on their rise, going right for their targets.

"Okay kids," Tarla said. "Let's light'em up."

No reason to wait till they'd reached the front of the line. While Eponi kept passing the shuttles, Gregor and Briana opened up with their turrets, delivering scorching volleys. Shields absorbed some hits, while others broke through, blasting away armor plating or blowing holes. Drop shuttles like these were meant to survive a crash landing under fire, but a concentrated assault with no cover?

They'd go down quick.

The *Prisa's* windshield flashed white for a hard second, followed by a squealing alarm. Eponi swiped off the sound while throwing the *Prisa* into a corkscrew. Other shots followed, their lasers filling the air around the Sever ship.

"Those shuttles have teeth," Tarla said, staring at her console. "Not very good teeth, but teeth nonetheless."

"They're automating everything," Eponi said. "I'll dance, you all keep on the lasers."

She'd have to sap a bit more power from the turrets to give the *Prisa* some shields to soak the inevitable hits, but Eponi would pit her piloting against a computer's guns any time. Though, as Eponi looped back towards the rising shuttle line and saw the four turrets-per-shuttle taking their potshots towards her, she felt a queasy flurry in her gut.

"Take'em down fast," Eponi said, lining up the *Prisa* so

all three guns could find a shot, "because if you don't, we'll be next."

"I just got this ship," Tarla added. "I don't want to see it damaged."

If incoming lasers weren't filling Eponi's windshield, she'd have said something. As it was, the pilot leaned forward, gripped the flight stick, and tried to keep them all alive.

FIFTEEN

Messaging

___

An already dire quest to find the comm center became an impossible one when the lights went out. Trudging across the sand as fast as his power armor could move him —which, given the slippery grains, was less than swift— Rovo had been aiming for the lit-up, squat destination his former hostage had pointed him towards.

Then the ground shook, the dunes rattled, and all went dark.

Well, not all: the shuttle engines glowed plenty bright in their flaring takeoffs, and DefenseCorp's massive fleet looked like a condensed constellation up in the sky. Combined, their silver light gave the dunes a ghostly cast, as if Rovo had fallen into some nightmare.

"That'd fit," Rovo muttered, standing near a dune's crest and looking into the dark.

He wasn't all that far from the barracks, but if the doors didn't have power, Rovo would have to bash them down. Possible, maybe, with the power armor and its boosters, but the idea didn't catch any momentum as his eyes returned to all those shuttles lifting off. Some would be hitting the DefenseCorp fleet soon, probably well into their docking procedures.

If a message would have any effect, the rookie would have to send it now. Or, preferably, a few minutes ago.

Flashes up above kept Rovo's eye skyward. One bright engine wash, a larger ship than those drop shuttles, seemed to be darting between Vana's onslaught. Yellow and orange bolts blitzed from both shuttles and the looping craft, looking like flickers from Rovo's far down vantage. Maybe one of the DefenseCorp ships had realized the truth, had sent someone down to stop the shuttles.

One ship, though, wasn't going to cut it against all those rising vessels. The stilted, coordinated response from the shuttles said their flight computers were handling the fire, but the sheer volume speckling greenish flares around the fighting ship. Still, the way the craft twisted, dove, and cut back while maintaining its turret's firing lines drew a whistle from the rookie's lips.

"Eponi, you should get a look at this thing," Rovo said, broadcasting it on the squad band, expecting the message to go nowhere. "There's a ship out here flying like you."

"That's because it is her, you moron," Tarla's voice came back over the band, and Rovo nearly fell over into the sand. "She's up here saving your dumb ass. Where are you? Somewhere useless doing useless things?"

Rovo decided not to consider Tarla's question.

"How are you on—" Rovo started, only for Tarla to cut him off again.

"We're in the *Prisa,* doing what needs doing," Tarla said. "Maybe you should shut up and clear this channel for important information."

Rovo did shut up, if only because he took a harder look at the ship dancing through the laser streams. The dots started connecting themselves: he could send transmissions because the base's power had died for some reason, and now their signals weren't being jammed. Eponi must've taken the *Prisa* out before that happened in some deal with Tarla.

Tarla, who'd now decided to switch sides?

This mission just kept getting stranger and stranger.

Overhead, the *Prisa* swooped into another pass. Orange flashes lit towards a shuttle, one that sparked, then burst into open flame. Like a blooming flower, the shuttle's wound grew as the craft listed, then turned back towards Aurum Three's surface in a blazing dive. Rovo watched, breeze whipping around him with its attendant sands, as the falling shuttle grew larger and larger.

For a long moment, Rovo thought the crashing ship would hit him, but the thing's engines kept sputtering enough to turn its plummet into a descending glide. The burning ship passed over Rovo's head, carrying with it heat and a shrapnel wave that bounced off the Sever fighter's power armor as if he'd been pelted with small rocks.

Rovo stepped around, watching the shuttle crash into and through the next dune over, stopping to rest not all that far away. A close call, but one that might also present an opportunity.

Drop shuttles didn't have much, but they could talk.

Breaking into long strides, Rovo half ran, half tumbled down his dune and up the next. He'd always been thankful power armor could handle vacuum, but now Rovo applauded the engineers for that airtight seal and its ability to keep out all the damn sand. Fighting against a sinister agent and her invisible suits was bad enough, doing it with grit getting in everywhere would be the worst.

Cresting the next dune, Rovo looked down on the ruined shuttle and confirmed his hopes: the thing's cockpit looked to be dented up, but otherwise intact. The shuttle's back, where all those drugged up troops were, looked to be in dismal shape. The engines still glowed, but with so little light and thrust that they couldn't shift their ship against the grain.

Rovo hadn't seen anything so beautiful in a long time.

"Show you useless," Rovo muttered as he clomped down the dune to his prize.

Up close, the burning shuttle certainly looked like hell. Having been on the ships before, Rovo couldn't repress a little sorrow at the thing. It hadn't asked to get drafted into an evil scheme. The drop shuttle should've been used on a giant raid against some poor population targeted by wealthier, powerful groups that could afford DefenseCorp's prices.

Maybe it was good Sever had ditched out of Defense-Corp's ranks. Rovo's soul might be better for it.

Rovo accessed the shuttle's cockpit through the only way open to him: smashing the windshield with a strong, kinetic-boosted kick. Crunching in over the glass into the cramped space, Rovo found the pilot's console still working. Tapping off the panicking autopilot, Rovo swiped—a tricky gestured with thick, gloved fingers—over to the shuttle's broadcast program.

Another few taps opened up a simultaneous transmission on every DefenseCorp channel, more or less ensuring any ship with its ears open would hear what he had to say. Rovo cleared his throat, reached to open his line, and felt a hand on his shoulder.

The hand gripped and pulled, yanking Rovo back from his transmission and sending him past his attacker in a fall towards the drop shuttle's burning half. Heat washed through the suit, the crackle snaps of a burning ship filled Rovo's ears, but none of that meant anything compared to what he saw.

Looming over him like a patchwork terror stood one of Vana's horror-shows. Protected by his invisible suit, the man had made it through the laser assault with his body intact, though the armor had pieces missing, showing the cheap uniform beneath had burned away. The man's helmet, broken off, revealed an ash-coated face, a mouth in a permanent grimace, and eyes as red as any Rovo had ever seen.

"Hey, buddy," Rovo said, but the man didn't seem like he heard the words.

Instead, issuing something between a growl and a scream, the man wrenched a heat-warped knife from a suit holster and stabbed it towards Rovo's chest. The rookie deflected, reaching across and grabbing the man's suited wrist before he could connect. With the power armor, Rovo should've been able to throw the man around like a rag doll.

Instead, as Rovo's visor sounded an alarm, the man continued to push down. The knife edged closer.

"That shouldn't be possible," Rovo said, reaching with his right hand and drawing a pistol. "Impressive, but I'm not gonna let you stab me."

Rovo snapped the pistol up and shot the man in the chest. Vana's soldier stumbled back a meter into the shuttle's side, letting Rovo pick himself up. With the spare distance, Rovo raised the pistol, finger on the trigger to deliver a few more fatal answers to the question of whether the soldier would survive the crash.

Another body slammed him from behind, knocking Rovo ahead. The rookie barely had time to turn before another poor soul, this one actively on fire, ran through howling all the way and tackled Rovo through the cockpit remnants and out into the sand beyond. Hitting the ground, Rovo tried to get his arms up, tried to get his pistol in a spot to fire, but his original enemy returned, grabbing the gun and ripping it away.

The burning, burned, and utterly roasted trio dove on Rovo, punching at his power armor, reaching for their knives and stabbing at his arms, his chest, his legs. The rookie punched, kicked, deflected, but every time he knocked one of the monsters away, they'd jump right back in, oblivious to pain.

For the first time since Gillane Four, Rovo believed he was going to die.

The fear attacked the rookie as much as the soldiers did, throwing his moves into a panic. Nothing in Defense-Corp's training covered a suicidal assault like this, nothing covered failed science experiments coming at you with murderous intent.

Nothing prepared Rovo for being so utterly alone.

"Would you stop the screamin', man?" The words came in hot, loud, and Rovo realized he was, in fact, screaming. "I'm almost to ya, but I can't think with you yelling like that you know?"

Rovo blinked, felt a sharp sting as one of the soldiers slipped a blade into his shoulder. No sooner had the monster withdrawn the attack to make another did a long cable fly out, circle around the soldier's neck and yank the thing off Rovo. The next one over took a pistol shot to his confused face, and Rovo himself managed the third with an unobstructed swing.

The rookie wanted to collapse back in the sand, but if there was one thing his training did prepare him for, it was completing the damn mission no matter what.

Lurching up, Rovo saw his savior dispatching the last soldier. Or rather, saw the results. Javelin's suit worked just fine, keeping the man almost invisible.

"Thanks for the save," Rovo said, climbing back into

the drop shuttle's cockpit and confirming the communications array still worked. "I would've had'em though. Another minute."

"Would you now?" Javelin replied from somewhere—it was difficult, Rovo found, to have a conversation with someone when you didn't know where they were. "Way I see it, I saved your bacon, rookie."

Now the Twilight Rangers were calling Rovo rookie too?

"You see whatever you wanna see," Rovo replied, tapping into the broadcast again. "Keep quiet a minute. I have to sell an invasion to a bunch of people that want me dead."

Once he started talking, though, Rovo found the words streaming out as they usually did. He opened with an emergency declaration, telling all those ships up there that the incoming shuttles had nothing except death on them. Backing up the argument, Rovo asked those DefenseCorp ships to contact the shuttles themselves, see what they said.

"You'll find they won't answer, even as they send you the right docking codes," Rovo said, pulling towards a conclusion. "Don't let them land on your ship. If you do, you'll lose it. And, if you have a fighter or two, send'em out to help us torch these bastards."

Javelin had popped his helmet and stood watching Rovo from beyond the shuttle while the rookie finished off his address.

"A true speech for the ages, man," Javelin said. "Might've shed a tear."

Rovo would've rolled his eyes, would've come back with something sassy, but the drop shuttle sparked up a new noise that sounded like its batteries were overloading.

So the two fighters ran into the sand instead.

The Cells

If Aurora bought her survival by bringing the DefenseCorp guards into the science lab behind her, she sold it again when the power died. The cells, blocked by laser-reinforced gates, went dark with the hallway, banishing everyone to blackness. Curses rang out from some voices while others tried to wrangle a disparate group into some orderly semblance.

Aurora pulled herself up, her visor displaying a lovely litany of issues her power armor had picked up during the sprint and subsequent ramming. The suit's bones had fractures, Aurora's left leg had a busted knee joint, and if she wasn't careful, the armor's ability to help her move its heavy limbs would fall apart.

That last would leave the Sever captain little more than a sitting, vulnerable statue.

The visor did, though, accommodate for the lighting lack. Flipping to an infrared spectrum, Aurora could see the confused jumble that'd chased her as they reoriented themselves. Some pointed weapons—blueish blurs due to their cold temps—towards Aurora, while others aimed them at the cells.

The atmosphere had a wire's tension, waiting to be snapped.

"Please don't shoot," Aurora tried, the suit amplifying her voice loud enough to overwhelm all the others. "The things in here might be dangerous, and we're all on the same side."

"Same side?" Replied the man who'd led the charge. "You're a killer, and a traitor."

"I'm trying to save you," Aurora replied, taking a step back all the same. The more distance she put in now, the easier her eventual spin-and-run would be. "Vana's trying to turn you into these things."

Murmurs among the crowd. More weapons pointing her way, but nobody had fired. Yet.

"Yeah?" The same man, apparently the moment's appointed leader, said. "And just what the hell *are* these things?"

"Experiments," Aurora said. "I don't have time to explain now, but when you get back to your ships, look up Dynas. Helix. You might not find anything, but keep digging. It'll all be there, including why your bosses died today."

"That's not gonna work—"

The reply cut off as a glass cell on the left banged. Aurora saw the oblong red-and-orange shape move like a stalking cat in its cage. It'd tested the gate and found the electric barrier missing. No shocks. And it screamed.

Aurora shivered as the vibrating hiss-shout rang through the hall, a noise like an eviscerated throat pushing all the air it could muster. Like some horrible pack, the creatures in other cells matched the cry, ringing out in the same tormented tones.

Perhaps this was another experiment, one turning the already-twisted soldiers into hunting groups rather than bloodthirsty individuals.

Either way, it was time for Aurora to go.

"If I were you," Aurora said, continuing to back-pedal. "I'd get to your ships and leave. Nothing good is going to happen here."

She whirled around as the voices called for Aurora to stop, to deliver more information and explanation. Aurora ignored them, even as she heard the cell doors continue to bang, heard the first glass start to crack. She had to find Vana, and then get the hell away from this nightmare planet.

The hallway walls presented themselves in soft blues, their captured heat giving Aurora enough to tell where to walk. The cold view didn't tell Aurora where Vana had gone, though, leaving a frustrating maze to interpret.

This maze, though, wasn't just walls.

As Aurora crunched away from the fighting behind her, the cells beyond banged and cracked as their occupants sought the same freedom earned by their brethren. Drawing her rifle and speeding up her pace, Aurora tried not to let the strange cries, most close enough to a human scream, distract her.

Hard, though, to ignore it when a cell breaks apart before you, its glass scattering across the hallway. Aurora had her rifle up and ready when the thing stumbled free. With bulging, irregular muscles declaring genetic play gone wrong, the person, wearing nothing more than a thin, torn robe, looked Aurora's way with the same wild-eyed chaos the Sever commander had seen from the *Prisa* turret when Sever had landed here.

"Sorry," Aurora said, and meant it.

Muscles or no, the rifle did its work and sent the victim

smoking to the ground. Aurora stepped over the body, continuing deeper. Three more cells broke as she walked, each one disgorging another experiment to be eliminated. As disturbing as the creatures were, they at least had little regard for tactics, choosing blind charges over anything truly dangerous.

So long as Aurora's rifle had energy, she could keep searching.

Gregor had used footprints in the carpet to track Vana from their first encounter to the bay, but the hard floors here didn't offer such easy answers. Instead, Aurora tried to eliminate paths through intuition and possibility. With the power still out, doorways with scanners weren't going to open. Aurora could bash through them with time, but rather than kick in every option, she tried to guess where Vana might be heading.

The bay would've been an obvious choice. With most of her rivals for DefenseCorp control dispatched at Aurora and Gregor's hands, Vana could've retreated to a ship and taken it up to the fleet. Declare her control there, and perhaps find herself at the head of a vast corporation ready to seize the galaxy.

Instead, Vana had kept on running. At least, Aurora had to assume that. She supposed the agent could've snuck into one of those ships and sat there, but the aggressive security suggested otherwise. Which left a question: why flee back here, to these experiments?

Perhaps to drag Aurora through more monsters that might take her out.

Perhaps to lose Aurora in the cell maze.

But there were signs, difficult to read in infrared spectrum but there nonetheless, on the walls pointing out directions. This turn would take Aurora to a containment lab, whatever that was, while another would bring her to the centralized supply. Neither seemed likely destinations for an agent pursued, an agent pulling off a brutal takeover.

Administration, though? That made for a more plausible option. Once Aurora caught the placard posting the proper direction, she broke into a jog. Her power armor protested, weakened joints and broken motors causing Aurora's run to list right-ward, necessitating an occasional lurch back to the left.

Annoying? Very.

On the long list of battlefield problems Aurora had dealt with? Near the bottom.

The doorway into Administration had the same look as all the others: dead scanner, heavy slat discouraging slam-bang rushes. It also had one crucial difference: a brighter blue shade than the other doors Aurora had been passing by. That meant one thing: heat, possibly from a few living bodies on the other side.

Aurora frowned at the door for a long breath, but no miracle presented itself. A quiet entry just wasn't going to happen. Getting closer, Aurora planted her left foot and swung her right. Her booted foot banged into the door once, twice, three times. Every strike bounced up the power in the kinetic booster a little more, and the visor chimed when Aurora hit maximum.

For the big kick, Aurora aimed low. Punched in all the power she could muster, and the strike echoed a cracking peal through the hall. Her low kick drove the door off its sides and sent it flying end-over-end up into the room instead of down to the floor. Flashes greeted the door, lasers striking its metal instead of continuing past and hitting Aurora.

Bringing her rifle up to her shoulder, Aurora followed the door in as it clattered to the ground. Two agents stood opposite, crouching behind a workstation-coated desk. The whole room matched their chosen spot: desks and wide screens now dark. No lights, and the agents proved their disadvantage by peppering their shots towards where Aurora had been, not where her strides carried her.

They couldn't see Aurora clearly. Couldn't get a clean shot as Aurora barreled through the room. Using the desks and their contents as cover, Aurora bent down and used her shoulder to knock the furniture over, sending components flying and masking her steps with clattering junk. She could see the agents, their orange forms giving themselves away, as they started to make their own moves towards a different exit, this one labeled for emergencies.

"Stop!" Aurora shouted as the two agent realized their likely loss and broke. "You won't make it!"

There were moves Aurora made not expecting them to succeed, motions she gave towards a moral universe or a clean conscience, as if to be able to say, when some fateful person asked, that she'd tried to find a peaceful out.

Those moves never actually worked. They provided the cover for the shots that came next.

Except, this time, the agents did stop. Their hands went up, and the sharp knocks as their pistols hit the floor stunned Aurora enough that she said nothing to her new prisoners.

"Don't kill us," said the agent on the right, standing in the one open area in the room's center. "We surrender."

"Whether I accept that or not depends on what you can tell me," Aurora said, finding her voice. A few crunching steps brought her to the still pair. "Where's Vana?"

"She went on," said the other, a woman and an older one at that, a voice husky with time and stress. "We were supposed to delay anyone coming after. Unless we were lucky enough to kill you."

"Delay why?"

"Don't know," the man said, "but she's heading towards her ship. We were going to meet her there."

So Vana was trying to escape, just in her own way. Maybe she didn't trust all those people who'd worked for the group Aurora and Gregor had executed. Probably a smart play.

"Then I don't have much time," Aurora said, taking a moment to step on and smash both of the agent's pistols. They crackled and puffed beneath her boots. "How about you two head back the other way. There's some Defense-Corp people back there that might give you a ride if you ask nice."

"Through the cells?" the woman laughed. "We'd never make it."

"Your choice," Aurora said, not stopping as she went towards the exit. "If I catch you following me, I'll shoot."

The Sever captain didn't look back. The visor would tell Aurora if they came after her.

"Wait!" The man called as Aurora hit the exit door. "You're with Sever, right? The group Vana said was attacking us?"

"What does it matter?"

"Because there's something you should have." Aurora turned as the agent fished something small from his pocket. "I can't really see where to throw it?"

"At the emergency sign."

When the object left the agent's hand, it held enough heat to look like a soft green, then blue blip. Leaving her rifle up and ready in her left hand, Aurora snatched the object from the air. Took a good look at it. A drive, like the one Vana gave Sai back on the *Nautilus*.

"What's on it?" Aurora asked.

"Not sure," the man replied. "Vana said that if we didn't kill you, we ought to give you this instead."

"So nice of her." Aurora slipped the drive into a pocket slot on her right leg. "Get going."

The two agents didn't offer up anything else, though Aurora didn't wait around to see what choice they'd make. Whether they lived or died wasn't Aurora's concern.

The emergency exit led to an isolated stairwell heading up and down. Orange diodes lined the steps. Aurora had to take a guess, deciding a sudden escape hatch would be more likely down below than up top. Any orbital attacks would start above, leaving a down-under getaway more plausible.

With her veering, battered armor, Aurora jumped from one landing to the next, every bang getting her closer and closer. Finally, Vana had run out of places to hide.

The Underground

Hitting the lift button should've shut the doors, should've blocked the fires, the explosion. Hitting the lift button did nothing, because in the same instant Sai punched with his katana, the base stopped pulling power. The mines exploded, destroyed the battery housing, and before Sai really understood the depths of his danger, all the lights went out, leaving the only illumination coming from the expanding orange-red glow.

Heat and its attendant flames washed over Sai and Perro, the latter screaming in what he must've thought would be his last words. Sai's power armor screamed too, telling him what the leaks in his damaged suit already said by touch: another few seconds and he'd be as fried as the agents outside.

Reversing the katana, following desperate instinct to get away from the heat, Sai cut down into the elevator's floor. The katana's strike added sparks to the fire, one that found Perro's suit a lovely treat. The man looked like a candle, waving his arms as the flames enveloped him.

A second cut, then a third. Sai's eyes watered, his legs

burned. He smelled his own hair starting to smoke.

A fourth cut and the floor fell away. A half-meter square made larger when Sai kicked off another piece.

"Go!" the swordsman yelled, though his words vanished in the fire's roar, a constant engine noise as it ate the oxygen.

Whether Perro heard Sai's shout or not, the burning man and his svelte suit stepped and fell through the hole as Sai kicked again, trying to get the space large enough for his armor to fit. Not that it would matter if the plummet went many meters down, but a fall promised a better death than fire. Another kick, another small piece.

His visor screeched louder. The armor itself grew hot now, its own cooling unable to compete with the continued hot blast from the blown-open furnace.

The answer came when the visor posed a question, asking if Sai wanted to evacuate his compromised armor. Taking one final step across his makeshift hole, Sai dropped his katana, letting it fall away into the dark below. The blade might pierce Perro, but if Sai had to choose between the mercenary's life and his family's sword, well, he already had.

Standing over the hole, Sai told the armor to kick him out. Gears ground against molten fixtures, but the power armor managed one last command. For an instant, Sai felt suffocating heat. His eyes, still closed, burned. His cropped hair completed its simmering into straight fire.

His stomach dropped as Sai fell through the hole, the sudden speed and cooler air shunting out the fire in the short instant between dropping through and a bouncing, bone rattling collision with what felt like a firm pillow. Sai rolled off, coming to rest on his back, looking up at the orange glow above.

"Might want to move in case that lift falls down," Perro

said, his voice more a rasp than human words. "Thanks for nearly killin' me with that damn sword."

Sai wanted to get up. Wanted to see how Perro still lived himself. Right then, though, his body seemed content to bask in its own ruin. Sai had been burned before, on various missions and by various lasers, but no inferno quite matched that one. The skin suit he'd been wearing beneath the power armor coated his body from head to toe, going right up to his neck, and it appeared to have done its job: Sai hurt, but he hadn't lost a limb.

His face, though, tingled with a different pain. A reach up confirmed Sai's eyebrows had vanished, as had his hair. A shocked, numbed feel tingled with his touch, one Sai figured would turn to agony in not too long if he didn't deal with it.

"C'mon," Perro said, and Sai saw the man's hand reach over. "You look like hell. Let's see if anythin' in my suit survived."

"You did," Sai replied, taking the hand and getting to his unsteady feet.

Light didn't shine at the shaft's bottom, but the glow above gave enough illumination to show Sai the padding made for a runaway elevator. Fortunate that DefenseCorp kept its safety regulation game up to par. The katana stuck up from the cushioning like a flag, and Sai, every motion stretching his torched skin, drew out the blade.

Perro, in his moments alone, had scrambled to an alcove off to the side. Sai expected a maintenance closet or some small place for a workstation monitoring the lift's status. Instead, Perro's platform looked like it opened onto another floor, one not listed on the lift's panel. A door, complete with a powerless scanner, sat unmarked and waiting.

"Strange to find a door down here, right?" Perro asked

as Sai sat on the landing next to him. The mercenary started rifling through the charred remnants of his old suit. "Then again, knowing this place, maybe it's not so strange."

"I doubt we'll like what's on the other side," Sai said.

His skinsuit had patches where the cloth had burned away, and Perro's didn't look any better. Neither had any weapons beside the swords, Sai's katana and Perro's red, buzzing blade, anymore. That their pistols hadn't blown up on them, instead melting away, was a stroke of luck and solid design by whomever made the things.

"Here," Perro said, handing over a crinkled tube with its cap missing. "Think it burst during the blast. We can split it."

The salve didn't cover half of Sai's burns, but he spread it as thin as he could manage. If nothing else, the cool lotion would keep Sai from passing out from the coming pain. Perro went for his application, and together the two sat on the landing, watching the orange glow above.

"We should've died in there," Perro said finally. "Can't believe you with that sword. I just—"

"I saw," Sai interrupted. "I thought you knew how to keep your head in a crisis?"

"Oh, 'cause we've all got experience with getting blown up, right?"

"It's not the specifics that matter," Sai replied.

"If you think I'm gonna get all up in arms about what you're insinuating, I'm not," Perro huffed. "I can take a word without losin' my cool."

"Clearly." Sai stood, let his muscles tell him how much they hated the idea. "If the mines worked, then there's no power in this base. We need to find another way back up top."

"Still want to fight, don't you?"

"Until I find out we've completed the mission, yes."

Perro laughed, shook his head, "That's what I don't get about you types. The mission doesn't matter if you die doin' it, man. What're you getting paid for this? Who's hiring you?"

"Nothing and nobody." Sai turned to regard the door. Took his katana by the hilt and lifted it. "This one's not about the cash."

"Vengeance, then?"

Could be. Sai would've bought that argument if Aurora pitched it that way. He certainly owed Vana some payback for the night on Gillane Four Sai spent getting punched up at an ocean spike's bottom

"The future," Sai replied. "Not mine, but my family's."

Now Perro cackled, a disbelieving laugh that had Sai tighten his grip on the katana hilt. That had him twisting his feet ever so slightly, ready to deliver an end to the mercenary.

"A family man way out here? Where are they?" Perro threw on a look of horror. "Don't tell me you left'em up there?"

"Stop," Sai replied. "Please, for your own damn sake, stop or I'll end you here and now."

"End me?" Perro asked, all the laughter, all the play gone. "Why don't ya go ahead and do that, then? I'm all torched, stuck at the bottom of a lift with a bomb goin' off up top. My team's disappeared, and the only other people on this planet want to kill me, so yeah. Do it. I'm not gonna stand in your way."

Stay in the fight long enough and you'll see someone on the edge, a shove away from cracking. To save someone like that, you had to show them a different path.

Sai struck with the katana, a long slash into the door.

The cut blew through the door's dirty skin, cutting right through to the other side. A thin barrier, then. Ripe for a couple wounded fighters to get through.

"C'mon," Sai said. "You can pity yourself all you want when we get out of here."

"Now there's motivation," Perro replied, but the man stood.

Held his red blade like he meant to use it.

Two more cuts cleared the door, opening a dark nothing beyond it. Sai could've used the visor and its different spectrums, but he'd have to rely on what nature gave him this time. And what nature gave him was a gray-black tunnel disappearing away. Unlike the polished hallways above, this one looked like the base's reject, its mottled walls and floor suggesting a rapid expansion without care taken for appearances.

"Feel like we've found another world down here," Perro said.

"Maybe we have," Sai replied. "Be careful. There might not be agents down here, but this place exists for a reason."

"You thinking we go ahead with just the wristlets for light?"

"It's what we've got," Sai said. "Guess we'll have to use 'em."

Leading off, Sai took his first steps into the tunnel. The cold ground matched the cooling air as every step brought Sai further away from the open furnace. A sweet scent came along too, almost sterile and sticky. Like cleaning chemicals.

Behind Sai, Perro stepped off too, following with a respectable distance. Good. Meant the mercenary hadn't totally forgotten himself and the necessary space needed to swing that blade in tight quarters. Sai had his own katana held up before him, ready to parry left or right, ready to attack with short cuts forward. A raised overhead swing would get the sword stuck in the ceiling, and any side-to-side sweeps would hit the walls.

The orange glow lighting their way dissipated a few steps in, leaving Sai embracing his own words out of necessity. With his burns making their presence known, Sai held up his left arm and tapped up a flashlight program. The wristlet's battery wouldn't last too long blasting white light, but a dead battery wouldn't matter if, well, Sai died walking into something he couldn't see.

Together the pair went ahead, skin-suited feet padding along the hard floor. Sai expected intersections, a standard grid, but instead the hall kept going, a single corridor leading on. The walls sported no decoration, only occasional crude signs asking anyone coming to stay alert for escapees.

"Well that's fun," Perro said when they came across the first notice. "Wonder who they kept down here?"

"Might have some idea," Sai muttered. "Let's keep going."

The end came sudden, without any door or other marking. The tunnel widened out into a cavernous chamber, the ceiling rising up and away from Sai's wristlet light. Not that he noticed, not that he cared. Sai had his eyes focused on something else.

Across the room's center, glass podiums, some smashed and others overturned, existed in rows. Tubes lay scattered at their feet, many tracing back into a long bundle disappearing into the dark at the room's opposite side.

"This is real weird. We shouldn't be here," Perro said.

"No, this is exactly where we need to be," Sai said. "If Vana is the head of this madness, then we've found the heart."

Friends In Need

THEY CLIMBED death's ladder into space. Every meter blazed with a laser's spitting fire until Aurum Three's surface disappeared beneath clouds and swirling sand, until the only things Gregor saw outside his turret's windshield were shuttles. Always more drop shuttles, crowded with suited soldiers rising towards Gregor's former friends.

The *Prisa* caught Rovo's message when it came, a short warning that Eponi wasted no time re-broadcasting as far as Sever's ship could send. The rookie's words said the coming shuttles offered only destruction, and Gregor caught hope that the fleet might listen. That fighters might join Sever's battle against the automated ships and turn a tough fight into a rout for the good guys.

Gregor hoped, but he didn't believe.

"Those bastards are calling us liars," Eponi's words came over the intercom as she twisted the *Prisa* into a gut-wrenching swoop, sending the ship upward and away from another shuttle cluster and their constant, pestering lasers. "We're either traitors or idiots or both, you listen to them."

By Gregor's count, they'd downed three shuttles so far.

Three flaming wrecks crashing down to the surface out of at least twenty, if not more. So many shuttles being here told Gregor the disparate fleet wasn't just a show of force for Vana and the other DefenseCorp brass coming by, but a supply mission. This wasn't just a demonstration, but a delivery. The fleet's own shuttles would be bringing death right to their doors.

"I'm beginning to think they don't want our help," Tarla said. "Votes to abandon them to their own stupidity?"

A younger Gregor might have taken Tarla up on that. He'd watched enough power-hungry, oblivious people and organizations strike too hard for victory and lose everything in the process. Those that survived tended to learn from a crisis, and the ships that survived this assault might too.

Outside, the *Prisa* broke the atmosphere, bringing dark space into full flush and, with it, the fleet's sparkling outlines. Running lights flared, with smaller craft looking like shooting stars dancing between huge cruisers and frigates. So much cash, so many lives invested in what lay outside Gregor's turrets, and most of those lives had no idea what flew their way.

"This was not their choice," Gregor said as Eponi flew the *Prisa* out of turret range, into a neutral zone between attack and retreat to let the ship's shields recharge. "They are following orders without knowing the consequences."

"Galaxy's a tough place," Tarla quipped back. "It's not our job to protect them from their mistakes, especially if it's gonna cost me cash."

"I thought we didn't want these monsters spreading?" Eponi asked.

"So we hang at the edges. Any shuttles try going long, we take 'em out." Tarla always seemed to have an answer for everything. "Don't all these people want you dead anyway? Let your enemies fight. It's a great tactic."

"And fun to watch," Briana added.

"We will not," Gregor said. "The people on those ships are innocent."

Tarla laughed, "Innocent? Sounds like that might be you, big boy. Nobody working for DefenseCorp believes they're the good guy, unless they're too dumb to see what's going on. Eponi, you heard me. Get moving, let them play with their toys."

Gregor sat back in his chair. The stiff turret setup didn't give him much room: the cramped fit made sure the turret itself moved taut with his every twitch. A design focused on achieving an end. Gregor could argue he was much the same. A fighter meant for nothing else.

And he wouldn't be sitting this one out.

On the scanner, glowing on the console screen near his fingertips, dots swarmed as the shuttles approached larger ship squares. The fleet's promised starfighters showed up too, dashes forming a lazy wall between the *Prisa* and the upcoming shuttles. Before too long, the pilots would have to decide to engage, and once those shots fired, changing minds would get even harder.

At the fleet's fringe, close to the atmosphere's edge and the fighter screen, a shuttle neared a waiting light frigate, the *Volucris*. The small frigate, designed to handle starfighters and fleeing transports, wouldn't have much crew. They'd be destroyed by the suited soldiers. Torn apart.

An example.

"—that's why I'm saying we go back down," Tarla was speaking. "We pick everyone up now, while Vana's little murder friends are still making their way through the fleet. Then we just play clean-up."

"Head for the *Volucris*," Gregor said. "Drop me, if you want. I am not abandoning them to die."

"That's on the other side of the fighter screen," Eponi warned.

"Are you scared?"

"She's smart," Tarla replied. "But if Gregor wants to get himself killed, Eponi, then I don't see why we shouldn't let him. One less share to pay out."

Whether she did it for Tarla or Gregor, Eponi started the *Prisa* into a shallow reversal, skimming the atmosphere's edge back towards the shuttle line and the *Volucris*. DefenseCorp's starfighters began their own move, shifting to cut off the *Prisa*.

"Oh, look," Tarla said. "Seems like your friends are making good on their threat. Should we destroy them on the way, Gregor?"

"Tarla," Eponi cut in before Gregor could talk. "Please, just shut up for a minute so I can fly? We're getting to the damn frigate, and we're gonna save all these morons from themselves."

Gregor rode those words up from his turret back to the *Prisa*'s central chamber, embracing zero gravity and its ability to make movement in a twisting, dodging ship that much easier. A quick command opened up his power armor, its whirring arms and legs expanding to let him in. The visor clamped over his face, and again Gregor saw his vitals, his suit's stats splayed across his eyes.

Briana joined those numbers and their green, healthy glow. The Twilight Ranger kicked herself into the center with Gregor. Her big cannon didn't work with its broken batteries, but she'd scrounged up a spare rifle to pair with pistols.

"Think you could have some fun and not invite me?" Briana said when Gregor looked her way.

"Apparently not."

Briana looked like she had something else to say, but Eponi overruled her words with a sniped call to get down to the *Prisa*'s hatch. Ducking and dodging fighters meant this wouldn't be a calm, gentle docking but a sling shot launch.

Briana didn't have her own power armor, so she had to pull on a flexible evac suit. Bright yellow to assist any rescue attempts, the evac suit had the flexibility to move but thin paper's protection. Rather than holsters, Briana had to slide her pistols through loops meant for rescue grapples. She slung the rifle around her shoulders, where it floated as though possessed.

"Don't you dare laugh," Briana said when she finished the floppy, stumbling dance to get the suit on. "I've killed for less."

"I do not doubt it." Gregor laughed anyway, short but loud enough for her to hear.

Knowing he was about to get into a good fight did wonders for the man's mood.

The two set up at the *Prisa*'s bottom hatch. A whirring click sealed off the rest of the ship as Eponi approached the launch point. Briana and Gregor, standing upside down to use their legs for added push, waited.

"Almost there," Tarla said, taking over so Eponi could focus on keeping the *Prisa*, already buzzing with hits to its shields, alive. "Hope you two know what you're doing. That shuttle's already docked. You'll be late to the party."

"Better late than early," Briana said, her voice tinny in the evac suit's cheap comm gear.

"More targets that way," Gregor added.

"You're both crazy, and I love it," Tarla said. "Get ready for vacuum. Hold for one then go."

The hatch slid open, air sucking at Briana and Gregor.

Tarla shouted go and the two moved their arms off the hatch's sides, Gregor going just before Briana. Without resistance, and with Eponi pulling the *Prisa* hard against their momentum, Gregor shot through the hatch into black space.

Like a missile cutting through a void, Gregor crossed the interstellar chasm between the *Prisa* and the frigate, a gap awash with laser glows from fighters, the frigate, and the *Prisa*. Yellow, orange, and blue shots flashed across Gregor's visor, all giving away to a broader white aura as the Sever squaddie neared his destination.

Passing through the magnetic field coating the *Volucris's* docking bay felt like getting splashed with cold water. The frigate had enough mass for some gravity, and the sudden return to oxygen-suffused air slammed Gregor's momentum, crashing him into a slow roll along the bay's floor. Wide enough for the drop shuttle and several departed fighters, the bay offered Gregor ample room to tumble along without impact.

Though the world outside his visor turned like a bad dream, Gregor timed a double-palm press to re-orient himself and reverse his body, putting his feet in prime position to catch the frigate's interior wall. Slamming into the metal, Gregor heard the lovely chime from his kinetic boosters. He spent the energy immediately, jumping back towards a certain yellow streak following ever-so-slightly right of his position.

Growing up on an outer space mining colony meant such casual past-times as playing catch never happened for Gregor. He'd never passed an afternoon riding the high that came with cradling a ball in a glove or in his arms.

Any missed moments vanished when Gregor caught Briana's speeding shape. His boosted momentum didn't quite cancel Briana's own, and Gregor's power armor wasn't exactly a pillow, but the two crumpled into a slow, bouncing landing into the frigate's bay nonetheless.

"Hey, we're alive," Briana said, untangling her limbs from Gregor's. "Nice catch."

"You are welcome," Gregor replied, then he shoved Briana aside, drawing his pistol to meet two frigate dock hands and their own raised weapons. "And you two need to run."

Wearing DefenseCorp crimson and wielding their own rifles, the two troopers greeting the drop shuttle paired haughty denial with more than a little fear as they contemplated Gregor's pistol. They both had to know the power armor more than trumped their weapons, even if the two might manage a shot before Gregor made it to his feet.

"You're way outnumbered," said the one on the left, going with bravado over bravery. "In a second that shuttle's going to open its doors and you'll be swarmed. Hang it up now and we'll tell'em to go easy on ya."

"They will—" Gregor stopped when Briana held up a single finger.

"You've got one second," Briana said, "before he shoots you. Then I'll shoot you. And then we'll kick your bodies outside, so everyone can see this dumb rock's two newest moons."

The left one smirked at the threat, opened his mouth again, but didn't get anywhere before Briana, sloppy suit notwithstanding, swung up and loosed a rifle shot. The laser sliced through lefty's rifle, leaving its barrel smoking and a black mark on the bay's ceiling.

"Run, little ones," Gregor repeated.

This time, the two soldiers did as they were told. They sprinted from the bay, with Briana calling after them, telling the cowards to shut the door on the way out. The drop shuttle's side slats had started to open, a whining grind, and Gregor wanted to keep his prey where he could find them.

Reaching over his shoulder, Gregor pulled his hammer free. Felt the haft in his hands. He'd swung the weapon many times today already, against weak enemies. The hammer deserved a contest, and—

"Hey," Briana said. "Pay attention, killer. You show me where they're hiding and I shoot. Got it?"

Gregor tapped the hammer's head on the docking bay floor, as the first clacking noises filled the bay. Boots hitting the floor, invisible suits turning their way.

"Understood," Gregor said, and the hammer man went to work.

NINETEEN

Fancy Flying

EPONI KNEW Gregor and Briana made the jump when Tarla swore, impressed. The pilot would've watched as best she could except the *Prisa*, like a kart racer walking into a crowd, had a following hounding her every move. Starfighters jockeyed for attack runs, their swarm the only thing keeping the corvettes from launching missiles on the risk those damn projectiles might hit their own side. The fighters could've cleared away, but they had their own reasons for sticking to lasers over the harder weapons:

Profits. Missiles cost way more cash than a few energy beams, and DefenseCorp knew the balance.

"Can't believe they pulled that off," Tarla said. "Figured they would miss the mark and burn up in the atmosphere."

Eponi flipped the *Prisa*, snapping downward to throw the frigate's lasers into the pursuing fighters' flight path. The space over Aurum Three had filled up with shuttles heading towards their chosen targets. And DefenseCorp greeted the killers with open arms.

"You let'em go anyway?" Eponi asked, wincing as the shields soaked another direct hit.

The *Prisa* wouldn't absorb many more. Then Tarla might be trying her own space shot.

Eponi? She'd go down with her ship.

Her beautiful ship.

"You think I can stop Briana when she gets an idea?" Tarla laughed. A marvel that she kept her voice so carefree, as if they weren't surrounded by all this danger. Eponi ought to learn the skill, seeing how often Sever put her a laser's flash away from death. "Best I can do is try to get her thinking what I want is what she wants."

"Bet that's not so hard for you."

Eponi had to make a choice. She couldn't keep dancing in this narrow spot in space for long. The starfighters were forming a web with the corvettes, pinning her inside where the frigate or some other turret-blasting punk would torch her to nothing. She could arc back towards the atmosphere, reverse the shuttle ladder and see about making it to the surface. Or the *Prisa* could take Tarla's original suggestion and head to deep space to wait out the fighting.

Both of those would leave Gregor and Briana for dead.

"You think I manipulate the Rangers that much?" Tarla said. "Like I'm some mastermind pulling all the strings for my crew."

"About sums it up, yeah."

Well, until Eponi had a direction, she wasn't going quietly. Gregor might not want DefenseCorp fighters blown outta the sky, but Eponi could still give'em a haircut. Twisting the *Prisa* away from the planet and heading towards a corvette with its starfighter duo, Eponi watched as six other fighters formed up on her rockets, lining up their lasers.

"I don't run a cult, Eponi," Tarla said. "We make cash, and we have fun doing it. Even Sanje, who'd spent his whole life flying fertilizer, came onboard. That's about as cushy a gig as you can get in this broken galaxy."

Eponi did not know how cushy fertilizer flying could be, maybe because the idea of it made her vomit ever so slightly. Or maybe that was the energy readings as the *Prisa*'s shields took another hit and went critical.

"That's what brought them here, huh? You told them they'd make cash fighting us?" Eponi said as she depressed the trigger, spitting fire from the *Prisa*'s cannon-and-turret combo. Without gunners in the seats, the *Prisa*'s side guns followed her orders and lanced their light towards the corvette. "What a deal."

"It was a damn deal. Vana offered us more cash than anyone else. A lot more," Tarla hesitated as lasers flew out front. "Are you going to get us killed, Eponi?"

"Trying not to."

Eponi's fire made the corvette blink. The ship panicked, launched a missile barrage towards the *Prisa*, but the hurried volley was dumb-fired, a standard tactic to make a charging ship change its course. Nobody lived through a dozen missiles hitting you head on, though the corvette probably expected to lose a few when Eponi made desperate attempts to shoot'em from the sky.

Except Eponi pulled her hand off the trigger as soon as the white puffs appeared, as soon as the console at her hands yowled that their death was coming, and fast.

Pushing forward on the stick, Eponi dialed away her laser energy to her engines, giving the *Prisa* a boost that sent it into a shallower dive. Those missiles rocketed right over, whistling ion trails like shooting stars heading for the fighter pack tight on the *Prisa*'s aft. With the *Prisa* blocking the view, and the missiles not targeted their way, the fighters had a snap second to realize how screwed they were.

Tarla whistled as the explosions bent the vacuum behind them, fighters whirling away or crashing into each other in wild attempts to survive. The corvette's escort pair, expecting a head-on assault, overshot Eponi's maneuver and flew right into the mix, their dots fizzling off Eponi's scanner as debris knocked them from the fight.

The *Prisa*, meanwhile, flew towards a blank spot in space. Eponi might not be near Briana and Gregor when they needed a ride, but she was alive, and for now that'd have to do.

"That, I think, was the finest move I've ever seen," Tarla said. "You took'em all out."

The praise didn't get anywhere. Died on impact with Eponi's ears, so fast the pilot barely registered the words. She had her eyes glued to the scanners, hoping for some dots to come back, hoping for—

"Turn on the comms, standard rescue frequency," Eponi said.

"What?"

"You heard me. Do it, Tarla."

"They have so many ships," Tarla said. "Don't be the hero that dies doing something stupid."

Eponi swiped the console off the scanner—dangerous for a pilot to go blind, but screw it—and tapped open the channel. Words poured in, garbled, overlapping requests for pick-up, for medical help. Some cruiser announced it was getting a rescue shuttle going, but it would be minutes.

Too many minutes.

With Tarla muttering curses beside her, Eponi turned the *Prisa* around. Took in the full results of her efforts. Like starlight through a blizzard, the debris cloud showed grit and gristle. Starfighter parts spun, bouncing off one another and breaking apart into smaller swarms. Ejection capsules drifted through, and Eponi saw at least three free-floating bodies in their suits.

Despite looking like they spun in place, everything in the mix sped along at high speeds unencumbered by gravity, by friction. Every impact threw more sharp spears into play, jagged edges that could kill a pilot.

"Get a suit on and get down there," Eponi said. "You have thirty seconds."

"This is why you're here, isn't it?" Tarla said as she picked herself out of the seat. "Your damn squad never committed to this life. Never."

"Tick tock," Eponi replied, aiming in on the closest body while she opened the comm channel. "Hailing all you jerks, this is the *Prisa*. Despite shooting at me and blowing yourselves up, we're coming to get you. Hang tight and we'll scoop you up one by one."

Eponi's words caught silence, then came protest, a storm calling out Eponi's actions from all corners. The pilots themselves offered choice words describing Eponi's flying, the *Prisa*'s looks, and what Eponi could do with her rescue. The larger ships, the ones taking too long to send anyone out, ordered Eponi to stay away or they'd send in more fighters.

"Thanks for the kind words," Eponi said after the chatter died down, the insults petering out as the spinning pilots started realizing how doomed they were. "I'll keep them in mind as we reel you in." Muting the signal, Eponi flipped to the in-ship intercom. "You ready, sweetie?"

"You calling me sweetie?"

"Just trying to help you think nice thoughts as you catch those pilots for me." Eponi frowned as they came up on the first one. She was doing the rescuing, and the DefenseCorp pilots were being such ass hats. "On second thought, ignore that. Treat'em like the ungrateful idiots they are."

"Much better."

Turning back to the rescue band, Eponi expected more flak. Instead, she caught worry. The pilots weren't chattering about the *Prisa* anymore, but were trying to raise their home ships. Trying, and getting silence instead of rescue shuttle timetables.

Eponi swiped back to the scanner, looked at the shuttle stream. More had docked at all the closest frigates, a couple light cruisers. DefenseCorp kept the bigger ships farther out, but the drop shuttles progressed towards them too, a steady line.

The invasion continued as Eponi and Tarla picked up one pilot after another, each one getting over their name-calling in a hurry once they realized no rescue would be coming from their homes. Especially when new messages came ringing across the rescue band, from the very same frigates and cruisers that'd been so adamant shooting down the *Prisa*.

Eponi listened, flew from body to body as the calls cascaded. A drop shuttle had docked, and now a frigate's garrison had stopped responding. Sealed bridge doors were being breached. Offered surrenders went ignored, and some transmissions ended only with panicked shouts. Screams.

Numb, Eponi counted the shuttles on the scanner. Only six had docked with their targets so far, and already chaos had broken out. Other ships interjected, asking questions and getting, with all the crosstalk, all the scattered information, only one clear answer:

Nobody could see what was attacking them. People were dying, and nobody knew why.

The shuttles crept closer, and Eponi hugged herself.

Closed her eyes and tried to be somewhere else, somewhere Sever hadn't failed. Where all she had to do was get a ship to ground, collect her cash, and drink the day away in some bar. No lasers, no explosions, no death.

"Hey," Tarla tapped her shoulder and Eponi's eyes opened. "They're all on board. A couple minor injuries."

"How many didn't make it?" Eponi asked.

Tarla grimaced, started to say something when Eponi's console chirped. An incoming hail. Eponi shook away her previous question. Self defense. She didn't want to, didn't need to know what it cost. Instead, Eponi tapped to a different story.

"*Prisa*, didn't expect to see you up in the air," Deepak's voice, his fuzzy picture came onto the console. "We're in system now and closing fast. Mind telling me what's going on?"

Sometimes opportunity didn't come at the end of a race, or with a laser's flash. Sometimes, you just had to say the words.

"Admiral, you have to take command," Eponi said. "There's nobody left to run the fleet, and Vana's soldiers are docking now. They won't listen to me. You have to tell them to destroy the drop shuttles or—"

Deepak cut the comm before Eponi finished. She dialed back to the rescue band, waiting, and then heard Deepak's voice cut above the panic.

"This is your new commanding officer," Deepak said, throwing in his name, rank, and the *Nautilus* for good measure. "The incoming drop shuttles are hostiles. Destroy them with anything you have. If they have already docked, seal off your bays and your bridges. Send your coordinates to our cruisers and we will dispatch strike squads to rescue you."

Eponi sat back, listened as Deepak continued outlining the new objective.

"Hey," Tarla said again, and Eponi looked her way. "You off the clock or something? There's a whole bunch of shuttles that need blowing up, and you have pilots in your turrets that want some revenge. Whaddya say we have some fun?"

TWENTY

Moonlit Chat

THE BASE FALLING dark didn't stop the shuttles. The open-air loading zone kept bustling with agents using wristlets to guide the drugged phalanxes into their death boxes. Rovo and Javelin, hustling in their suits, took the long jaunt around, coming in behind a building that looked shredded, as if a bomb deep inside had blown it apart. Javelin had wanted to use the same escape hatch he'd taken to get out here, but Rovo shot that suggestion down.

He'd been cornered in those tunnels enough, thanks.

"Almost done," Javelin said, chuckling at the end. "Guess we're getting both contracts then."

"Both contracts?"

"Vana paid us to keep this goin', and now Tarla's getting us paid to get you out." Javelin's grin shown in the combo star-and-engine light coming from above. "She knows how the game is played."

"Lucky you."

The two nestled in tight to the torched building's rubble remnants, watching as the last shuttle's slats slammed shut. Its jets flared a second later, the shuttle on the same set route as its fellows heading into the fleet above. While Sever's mission parameters had been blown all to hell—the goal had been to stop Vana, though who knew if the agent still lived—Rovo itched to dash out there, shooting away at the shuttle to stop it.

And he might've, except Rovo's arm stung from the stab he'd received courtesy of Vana's invisible monsters. His chest panged where cracked ribs demanded Rovo lie down, and a twisted ankle, delivered courtesy of a dune and a bad step, hit him with a final, insulting ache. Altogether, Rovo's body roster said a run-and-gun assault on an enemy squad would turn out crappy.

"There they go," Javelin muttered. "Was wonderin' how long they'd stay and play."

The agents that'd been directing Vana's soldiers swarmed like bees given a critical directive. Ditching the carts and even a few spare suits hanging on them, the agents broke for five ships on the landing pad's edge. Rovo knew them by their shapes: svelte, sharp rectangles with mirrored plating, the craft dominated DefenseCorp's stealthier side, designed to throw off scanners while maximizing speed both in atmosphere and without.

Boarding ramps dropped as the agents approached, some picking up belonging bags already laid on the ground in lines. The agents flashed their wristlets at the bags as they neared, lighting up name and number designations. Rovo couldn't read the words from the distance, but the agents took only seconds to pick the right ones.

"Looks like Vana isn't going to stick around," Rovo said. "I don't get it. She had everything she needed here to keep making the suits?"

"Not anymore," Javelin nodded towards the blown building. "Maybe they're giving up?"

"Too fast. They wouldn't have had time to get all their things together," Rovo said. "This was planned."

"You think they blew up the building then?"

"Who knows what Vana's willing to do. She's the one that turned a bunch of civilians into infected killers, remember? Hell, she hired you."

"Hey now."

As much as Rovo enjoyed giving Javelin crap, they couldn't sit in the wreck's shadow forever. Eponi and the *Prisa* had disappeared up above, out of the range of Rovo's suit-based comm array. The rookie could walk away from the action, find a nice dune to wait out the night in hopes Sever survived.

But that would be the coward's choice.

Rovo checked the squad band again, sending out another query, and caught back silence. Javelin did the same. Even without the jamming, if any Sever or Twilight Rangers remained on the planet, they were deep enough in the base to block signals. If information was going to be obtained, Rovo would have to get it the old fashioned way.

"Why don't you put that cable to good use?" Rovo said, pointing ahead to the steady agent stream as more came from all directions towards the landing pad. "Think we can snag one for a conversation?"

"You're wanting to start a new fight?"

"You have a problem with that?"

"I might," Javelin said, watching as Rovo moved a hand to the scythe on the rookie's waist. "I see that hand. Better not move it anymore."

"Not for you," Rovo waved again towards the agents. As he did, the first stealth ship sparked to life, its ramp rising along with the craft. "For them."

Rather than follow the shuttles towards the fleet, the stealth ship rose over the base and then jetted off across

Aurum Three's surface, staying low until it vanished over the horizon. Definitely running, definitely not looking to get caught.

"All right," Javelin said. "You get us in trouble, I'm saying you took me hostage."

"Means you lost to a rookie, you know that?"

"You think I got pride?"

His point made, Javelin shoved off from their position, shutting his suit's visor and disappearing into a blur. The advantages drew a soft sigh from the rookie. How many missions would go so much easier if the targets couldn't see you coming? If, with the juice Vana made from Kaia's blood, you could run in through anywhere, be strong enough to take just about anything?

Based on the agent walking along, watching her wristlet as she went towards what was probably a safe escape, the result was pretty damn scary. One second she stepped along smoothed sand towards a ship, and the next Javelin had her mouth covered, a knife pressed into her stomach as he dragged her back towards the shadows.

If the other agents saw, they didn't break from their plans. Rovo, rifle ready in case Javelin's move brought trouble, didn't need to pull the trigger. Aurora's voice floated by, talking about the mission over the moment. Vana's agents needed to get away before they all died, before they were captured. One missing member wasn't worth the risk.

"Make it quick," Rovo said when he approached the agent, "and we'll let you go in time to catch your ship."

Javelin had her pulled into the ruined entry, a place that looked like a tunnel leading into the blown building. Its door hung off the side, leaning out and blocking the view from the stealth ships. Shadows cut the silver light around them, the noise a whirling wind and running foot-steps combo.

All in all, a good interrogation setup.

Removing his hand, keeping his knife, Javelin stayed behind the agent, who propped up a look that said she was very, very done with all this.

"Make what quick?" The agent said. "Are you and your friend others that skipped a dose? How many old power armor suits do we have on this damn base?"

"What?" Rovo said. "More?"

"Another one like you," the agent replied. "I can tell you more if you let me go."

"I'm not here to kill you," Rovo said. "Tell me. Who was the other one?"

"Then have your buddy his knife away and I'll talk."

Rovo nodded over the agent's shoulder. Javelin brought the knife's edge off the woman's uniform, sparing her a centimeter to breathe, but only that.

"He looked like you. Power armor. Different color. Also had a sword instead of," the agent faltered, looking at the scythe, "whatever the hell that is."

"Where'd he go?"

"He had another with him, that's who told me about the skipped dose. They were going to medical."

"And that is?"

The agent squinted at Rovo, mouth open in a confused gape, "How do you not know? You've been here for months."

For months? What did this agent think was going on? Rovo dismissed that line as soon as the question flared. No time to correct the agent's theories. It sounded like she'd seen Sai, and if Sai had come by here, he probably wasn't on the *Prisa*. And, if the swordsman wasn't responding to open queries on the squad band, then Sai might be in trouble.

Rovo would not, no matter what Tarla said, be useless.

"Memory loss. It's a side effect," Rovo flubbed together. "Now, where?"

"You could've taken a lift before the explosion," the agent said. "Now, you might be able to get in on the other side?" The agent pointed straight across the landing pad, along the wide open gate towards where all those ranks had been fitted with suits. "Without power, who knows though."

"Last question." Rovo had his path, now he needed understanding. "Where are you all going? What's happening here?"

"That's more than one question," the agent snapped back, but the irritation faded as she answered. "Honestly, we don't know. Vana told us to see the shuttles off, then make it to our ships and run. We're scattering around the galaxy. I don't know what comes next."

Rovo waited, but the agent didn't offer anything else. Maybe she told the truth. Could be Vana was liquidating her force, or sending them out to wait for her next big move. It sucked when a question answered only brought more questions, but Rovo's boots itched to get after Sai.

"Okay, get going." Rovo jerked a hand at Javelin, who let the agent loose. The woman didn't bother sparing a second look at Rovo, but kicked off into a dead sprint.

"She's gonna tell her friends about us," Javelin said. "Should've let me finish her."

"Her friends don't give a damn about you and me," Rovo replied, and to back up his own words, he broke into a run across the landing pad.

There weren't so many agents still boarding the ships. Only two even remained, and of those agents grabbing their bags, Rovo caught a couple glance his way before returning to their flight. They had their mission, Rovo had his, and neither cared one bit about the other anymore.

The agent's directions proved accurate, leading them to a sloping structure easy to miss among the dunes. Like a wedge placed on its side, the building jutted a single story up from the ground and seemed, compared to the other places Rovo had been here, older than everything else. The door, a single, thick and somewhat rusted thing, had a tacked on scanner with visible metal straps tying it to the door. A sign, also tacked on, sat above the door and declared the building restricted in bold red letters.

"Building's restricted and it doesn't have a name?" Javelin said as they approached. "Something bad's going on in here."

"Guessing this wasn't included in your tour?"

"Tour? Vana showed us the kitchen, the bathroom, and gave us our suits. That's all."

"And yet, you still went to work for her."

"Cash is cash, my friend."

Rovo aimed his rifle, dialed up the heat to its max, and plugged two shots into the locking straps. The laser melted through, leaving molten orange in its wake. The rifle couldn't sustain too many shots at the high temps, but the two were enough: one hard kick and the door broke in.

Cold metal stairs sat inside, heading down. No lights, naturally. Dust caught the silver glow, escaping into the outside. In the relative quiet—the agents and their ships had all left, leaving sounds to the dwindling shuttle noise—Rovo picked up something new, something that had him starting forward even as Javelin stepped back.

The rookie had been around Sai long enough to know a katana's ringing clash when he heard it.

Flaring his wristlet to give him some light, Rovo took off down the steps, every clank driving Tarla's *useless* further from his mind.

Reasons

THE EMERGENCY EXIT didn't make sense unless you knew the base's purpose. Aurora bounded down the stairwell, accepting its placement next to the administration room as a concession to the disasters possible when playing with people. If Aurora had guessed right and the base really was the original home of the Raider program, then putting a quick exit without any hungry cells in between made sense.

It also made the makers cowards, unwilling to face the consequences they brought upon themselves with their reckless experiments.

Passing by a few landings brought Aurora to the stairwell's bottom and an open door, scanner glowing green. Overhead, again, the word 'Emergency' flared its red and white announcement. Below and beyond, no hallway presented itself. Instead, a broad chamber swooped down and away from the entry, scooping out enough space for a ship.

One Aurora recognized.

Any overhead lights remained dead, but, befitting its purpose, the chamber had diodes all along the floor tracing a path to the parked ship. Renard's old vessel—Vana's now—sat on its struts, boarding ramp down, ready and waiting to embark.

Every instinct told Aurora going into that chamber, approaching that ship would be a terrible idea. The doorway's sides kept Aurora or her visor from seeing anything waiting for a step inside, while potential threats could come down the ramp or come around the ship, leaving Aurora caught without any cover.

Every instinct said a retreat back up, a potential alliance with the DefenseCorp soldiers or a reunion with Sever would present a better alternative. DefenseCorp's own logic dictated as much, preferring careful assaults—and the extra billings—with large numbers over individual heroism.

But Aurora wasn't here for DefenseCorp, and she sure as hell wasn't here for the cash.

Raising her rifle, willing her power armor to keep going for a little bit longer, Aurora took the first step beyond the threshold. Snapping left and right, the Sever captain confirmed only dwindling darkness sat to either side. While the diodes didn't get their light to the corners, Aurora hot-swapped to the infrared spectrum to confirm, with deep blue shading, that nothing waited.

The absence continued as Aurora descended towards the ship. Every step, Aurora thought an attack would come. Every step, nothing happened.

The ship stirred, pulling Aurora's attention. An engine's awakening whine echoed around the chamber. Aurora didn't see, couldn't tell where the ship's exit would be, or how one might operate if the base had no power. Maybe Vana had some plan to blow her way out.

Or this was all another ploy.

"So you followed me all this way," Vana's voice sounded close. Right in Aurora's ear.

Aurora spun towards the noise. Looked and saw nothing in the shadows. She listened, trying to hear the padded falls of feet hitting the ground. Aurora again flipped to infrared and saw nothing. Her visor gave no indication of a threat.

"You won't find me," Vana continued, though now her voice seemed to bounce around the room. "We've made some improvements, you know. Renard really was a genius."

"He was a monster."

With nowhere else to go, Aurora decided to keep on heading towards the ship. If she couldn't see Vana, then Aurora had to restrict her options. Inside the craft, the agent wouldn't have room to hide. Wouldn't be able to vanish and re-appear.

"They all are," Vana said, injecting passion before splashing it cold. "Or, I should say, were. Thank you for that. You have done the galaxy a great service."

"Glad I could help."

Reaching the center platform, Aurora saw exactly how the ship might escape. The diodes washed out the light, but above a clear tunnel led up and out to Aurum Three's night sky. Grit interrupted the view, flowing sand proving the tunnel wasn't wide open, but sealed over with glass. Easier, though, to break that than burrow free through sand and rock.

"You have," Vana said, earnest and apparently in no rush to stop Aurora's advance. "Everything that I've wanted, you've given me."

"Doubt that." Aurora set one foot on the ramp, waited. "Where are you?"

"Here," Vana replied, again sounding so close. "Don't worry, you'll see me soon."

"Stop playing games."

A laugh, "Games? I'm sorry if I am not as direct as you, Aurora. My objectives aren't simply solved with a rifle. You have the drive, yes?"

"Your friends gave it to me," Aurora said, taking another step up the ramp.

She'd yet to see any sign of Vana in the chamber. The room's sloping walls made it possible for an echo, or maybe a direct broadcast to get Vana's voice sounding the way it had, but the agent's continued vanishing act had started to wear thin.

Time to force Vana's hand.

Aurora turned and ran up the ramp, pushing power into her damaged boosters to kick that extra step. If Vana waited inside, planning an ambush, the sudden burst ought to ruin the surprise. Three long strides took Aurora into the ship's center room, a familiar couch along one wall—seen when Rovo was a hostage, described during Sai, Eponi, and Gregor's sabotage mission—and nothing else. The card played, Aurora went right, heading for the cockpit.

Vana had to protect the ship. Its stealth abilities were the safest way for her to get off world.

But the cockpit proved as empty as everywhere else. Amid the consoles, though, a light blinked. An incoming hail. Already feeling sick, feeling like something had gone very wrong, Aurora went forward and tapped to answer it.

Vana's face faded in, the view behind her shifting. The agent moved, her wristlet's camera capturing the motion as she went. Aurora caught the dark, caught the diodes, and then saw the very same stair she'd just walked down. Aurora started to turn, when a different noise erupted.

The boarding ramp, sweeping up to a close, and the ship's door slamming shut to meet it.

"Sorry, Aurora," Vana said. "I know how much you wanted a fight. That, though, simply isn't me."

Aurora should've been angry, should've been bashing her way out. Instead, she popped her visor, looked out the ship's cockpit to see Vana standing outside. Or, rather, Vana's face seeming to float above a blur. The agent had found her suit, but why was she choosing to strand herself here?

"I don't understand?" Aurora asked, curiosity quelling her frustration.

"I'm trying to ensure the galaxy *does* understand," Vana replied. "You and that drive are one piece. My agents are another. The destruction above us a third, and many more besides. You've done everything I could have asked for, you and your Sever squad. So I'll thank you now, and wish you a safe journey."

"You'll wish me nothing," Aurora said, swiping at the console, trying to find a way to stop the ship.

Its engines continued spooling up, the maneuvering jets rattling to life and picking the craft up off the ground.

"That's not something you get to decide," Vana said. "You're a soldier. Follow orders, as you do so well." Vana put up a small smile. "You'll never hear from me again, just as I look forward to never seeing you. Goodbye, Aurora."

The transmission cut, and with it Renard's ship, in its autopilot grip, settled on a pre-programmed course. With the jets firing, the ship began to rotate up. An automated voice called for everyone to find launch positions. Aurora's power armor locked its boots to the floor when Aurora asked, keeping her from sliding.

All the motion kept Aurora from digging into Vana's

words. Spend too much time running dangerous missions and you'd run into plenty of people wanting to get all cryptic with their final proclamations. Better to take care of the problem and sort out the trash later.

Aiming her rifle, Aurora shot into the cockpit's glass, burning but not breaking it. Too thick, perhaps, for a shot to pierce, but the rifle's work wasn't meant to blow a hole. That came now, as the ship neared its vertical launch. Kicking with her boots, firing boosters charged by the hops down the stairs, Aurora sprayed more fire as she rammed the windshield.

The ship didn't give Aurora up easy, the glass splintering before breaking, dragging and cutting into her armor. Still, her momentum brought Aurora through, albeit with less a glamorous leap to freedom and more a slow, tumbling roll off the ship's nose and down to the ground. Aurora landed hard on her back, the air whooshing from her lungs while her eyes caught the visor's frantic blinking alert.

A spacecraft was about to blast off, and Aurora lay right beneath its rockets.

With a silent curse and a lurch, Aurora tried to roll away. Tried, and found her power armor sparking out, unwilling to shift. Above, the rockets grew brighter. The heat increased. Moving felt like shifting a million kilos.

Escape one problem for another, and this one didn't have an obvious solution.

Until, scraping along, something dragged Aurora away. Like getting hitched to some fast craft, Aurora slid on her back along the central platform, off onto the smooth, sloping side. The starship ignited, flaring up as Renard's old vessel launched. The warmth squeezed through Aurora's suit, heating up her legs, her chest, her head.

Then the rockets left and, aside from the shattering

glass above, which proceeded to rain down into the chamber in large chunks, the room sat still and cool.

"Eject," Vana said, stuffing a knife up beneath Aurora's visor into her neck. "Eject or I kill you now."

Aurora's visor finally read the threat, highlighting Vana's form. So helpful.

"Why'd you save me?" Aurora delayed, debating whether she could get away, maybe draw a pistol. With her armor busted, though, neither option seemed good. But there was a third. "No way I survive the rockets."

"The drive, you idiot," Vana hissed, and now the agent's suited head moved into Aurora's vision. "If that doesn't get out, this might all be for nothing."

"What 'all'?"

The knife wiggled, found the slightest slack, "Haven't you figured it out yet?"

"Like you said, I'm just a soldier."

"And I am out of time," Vana said. "Eject, please. I wouldn't want to hurt the drive when I take your life."

"Now that is some motivation," Aurora replied, sliding her left hand near the slot on the armor where she'd put the device. "What's on the drive, Vana?"

"Everything about this base and what Renard tried to do with it, what I actually did. A story that needs to be shared." Vana said, then tightened her grip on the knife. "I know how power armor works, Aurora. I'm giving you five seconds."

Balling her left hand into a fist, Aurora raised it, "You want the drive? Here's the drive."

Vana's reaching fingers seemed a blur, but Aurora felt them nonetheless as they touched, tugged at her closed hand. Like a spider striking, Aurora opened her fist and grabbed Vana's hand. At the same time, Aurora reached up, put her right palm on Vana's arm.

And activated the Shock-Jock.

Made to jolt a soldier back to life, the power armor's emergency function shot enough current through Aurora's hand to blast Vana away, knocking the knife loose as the agent fell back. Aurora followed up the shock with a second command, popping the power armor loose. Blowing its own joints, the suit disintegrated around Aurora as she rose up, grabbing for the pistol still locked to the suit's waist.

"A dirty trick, even for you," Vana said as Aurora found the pistol.

The Sever captain snapped her weapon, aiming it where she'd heard the voice. Vana stood, her invisible suit covered with black lines where the Shock-Jock had burned through its reflective circuits. The agent's helmet smoked, and Vana tore it off, casting it away.

"I thought you knew," Aurora said, "anything goes in a fight."

"Is that really it then, your wish?" Vana asked, no smile in those words this time. "You've come all this way, done all this damage, for a fight?"

Aurora leveled the pistol at the agent's exposed head, "You bet your ass I did."

TWENTY-TWO

The Dance

OF THE MANY truths Sai had adopted over his time in DefenseCorp, understanding he would never get to act on his mistakes had been a staple. A mission gone wrong, a shot missing its target, or a plan plotted poorly, all would occur and simmer in history, crystallized in their error forever.

That truth shattered in the dark among the podiums. It shattered when skittering, squelching sounds came from the room's corners. It shattered when the first thing lurched towards Sai and Perro, a bubbling, brackish mass with a single goal: to consume.

Sai had seen these things before, way back on Dynas. Back then, they'd been set upon the swordsman as some sort of test, though Sai never learned whether the goal was to prove the monsters would attack regardless of their chances, or that Sai himself was worth keeping as a test subject.

Impossible to forget, though, what came after. The injections, the burning fevers, the feeling that his insides were about to devour themselves in a frantic rush . . . Sai wouldn't tell a damn soul how many nights he woke up sweating, feeling that same way. Hard to tell if expunging the scourge from the galaxy would make those nightmares vanish, but it seemed worth a shot.

So Sai swept his katana to meet the thing, slicing its frothing mass in two. The goop split around Sai like he was some sort of high tech prophet, giving way to three more creatures scrambling in behind.

"Come on!" Sai said, stepping to meet the rush, his blade stained black.

As a battle cry, the words could use some work, but Sai fell into the motions. A left-to-right cross-cut took the center beast and let Sai step to his left, buying a half-meter distance as he spun the cross-cut around. The wave nicked the creature from the right, slowing it enough for Sai to complete the spin, slicing down the left and coming back across to finish the trio's destruction.

The moves felt like a movie, only doable because these things were barely alive, barely held together. Against armed or armored enemies, the katana would get itself stuck on their bones, their barriers. Here, Sai could flow.

Without the power armor, the swordsman reached a fever speed, catching every oncoming creature in his path. Falling back on all those evenings with his mother and father, Sai returned to the dance he knew in his bones. The creatures, those faded, forgotten things, dove in without regard for their lives. They rushed at Sai from the side, from the back, and dropped from above.

All found their relief on his blade, and Sai in their end.

At least until his foot, bare, slid on the slick floor. Trying to keep his balance, the spell broken, Sai realized he stood in a churning pool. A living person might be slain by a stab or a cross-cut, but a virus like this did not respect such precision. Stumbling, falling, Sai landed on his back in the disease.

And heard Perro shouting, screaming. Not the confident sounds of someone who might come to his rescue. Sai, keeping his grip on the katana, rolled on his shoulder, tried to push himself up. What had been slick, though, now congealed around a new opportunity. The virus sucked at Sai's feet, his legs, his hands. A tingling feel quickly turned to an icy burn, a numbing pull.

The monster Sai had beaten once came for him a second time.

He would not let it win.

Pulling up the katana in his right hand, Sai stabbed it into the floor. The sword's diamond edge bit into the ground, giving Sai leverage. He pushed, fought against the cold tearing at his limbs, and reached his feet. Using the katana again, Sai tried a jump, pushing himself up as he went. The floor betrayed his footing again, and Sai's supposed leap free from the puddle became a falling, flailing stumble.

The man made it. The sword did not.

Hitting blessedly clean ground, Sai rolled through and up to his feet. Looking back, his wristlet's silver cast illuminated the churning viral pit as its tendrils devoured the katana. Whether or not the virus could actually hurt the sword didn't matter: without a weapon, Sai wouldn't live long enough to care.

Instead, he turned towards Perro's broken cries. The Twilight Ranger had cleaved himself into a corner, barely visible under an infected avalanche. With his power armor, Sai would've gone in, fought to free Perro. Without it, he'd only be jumping to his own death.

"Don't you want to save him?" The words came watery, decayed, but recognizable.

Sai glanced to his right, saw a woman he never wanted to see again, but one who, nonetheless, brought some hope: if Sai was going to die in this damned dungeon, at least he could take the right person down with him.

Anaskya didn't much resemble the woman who'd ditched Sever on Wexer after both using and being used by the squad to escape a doomed existence on Dynas. She'd been a premier scientist with a taste for the finer things, a quality that didn't seem to be met here, where Anaskya looked like she'd caught the wrong end of her own inoculations a few too many times.

But Sai would never forget that face, no matter how marred with disease, how warped with her own failures.

You don't lose sight of the one that almost took you from your family.

"I'd rather kill you," Sai said, looking for a way to do just that.

Anaskya, though, didn't seem like she belonged to her old body anymore. Like the creatures Sai had been slicing up, Anaskya's arms and legs looked largely dark and writhing, with only a patch starting around her chest and continuing up through her head remaining recognizable. Sai could throw a good punch, could try and snap a neck, but would any of that really stop her?

"You won't have to," Anaskya replied. "I'll be dead soon, as will everybody left here. Then this virus will cover the planet. My life will have its legacy in the creation of another. What more can one ask for?"

"A little sanity, maybe?" Sai turned back to Perro, still struggling. "Can you tell them to leave him alone?"

"Why would they listen to me?" Anaskya laughed, a gutted sound, like a fish gulping for air. "Their only thoughts are hunger."

"Is that what's going to happen to all the suits in the shuttles?"

"Vana started her crusade?" Anaskya said. "Then yes, eventually. Once their suppressing doses wear off."

"But why? What's the point of killing all your soldiers?"

"You'll have to ask Vana that," Anaskya frowned. "She's the one who ordered me to revert the virus. With the girl's blood, they could have been invincible. Instead, she wanted them turned into bombs."

"And you did it without a second thought."

"I did it with many second thoughts, ones I shared with Vana many times after her agents took me," Anaskya said. "She ignored them. She forced me to create this. These."

"Why would you? If you knew you would die anyway?"

"You're a father, aren't you?" Anaskya asked. "These are my children. They might not be as I hoped, but at least I saw them live. Without Vana, I would've had nothing. My work would have gone to waste."

An odd calm settled over the swordsman. Perhaps the same calm that seemed to have hold of Anaskya. They were both doomed, destined to be fodder for those things once they finished Perro. Knowing Anaskya would follow him into the beyond, sharing a last conversation seemed almost normal, seemed the only thing Sai could do.

Running for it played a brief stint in Sai's decision roster. He could make a sprint into the dark, guiding himself through random turns with the wristlet and hoping he'd find an exit before the monsters found him.

And yet.

"Two choices," Sai said. More creatures had entered the room, no doubt the dregs of Anaskya's experimental supply. Perro had gone silent, though the mob still enveloped the man. The rest gave the scientist a wide berth, like a family respecting their parent. "I can give you a quick death now, or you can let these things devour you."

"As they will you after I am gone. Why give me the better end?"

"Because it will be the last satisfying thing I do."

"Do you really hate me that much? Am I so awful?"

"Yes." Sai squared up. Ready to go. "Choose."

Anaskya looked down at herself, then shook her head, "I'm sorry, Sai. If I am going to die, it will be by my own creations."

Perfect. Much more fulfilling to take down an enemy who fought back, rather than one that just gave in.

Sai went for a punch. A straight-up jab from nowhere meant to take Anaskya out before she could bother with a defense.

His fist never made the connection. Another creature, one Sai hadn't seen coming up behind him, tackled the swordsman to the ground. Anaskya issued a wet laugh as the creature piled onto Sai, its sloppy, writhing mass bearing him to the floor.

The creature, though, still had a body, and Sai still had his strength. Pushing off with his arms, Sai rolled the creature and himself onto his back, driving his elbow into the thing's face. It felt like smacking a pillow stuffed with steak, but the blow stunned the thing long enough for Sai to get up, to whirl around with his wristlet find no sign of Anaskya.

Sai kept turning, trying to find what path Anaskya might've taken. He moved as he looked, stepping away from grasping arms. He refused to buy into the despair that Anaskya had vanished, that Sai wouldn't get revenge's last satisfaction. That way led to a darkness deeper than any found down here.

The wristlet caught a crimson glimmer, and Sai keyed in on Perro's blade. The buzzing sword must've falling from the man's grip, its edge peaking out from beyond the creature trio swarming the mercenary.

If Sai couldn't catch Anaskya, then he might as well die doing something right.

The swordsman dove in with a right hook, splattering the central creature's gooey fibers and knocking it into the one on the left. The sucking noise as the creature's sticking tendrils peeled off Perro wrinkled Sai's nose as much as the fetid smell swamping the room, but the punch bought enough space for Sai to reach down and snare the sword from its black mire.

The creature to Sai's right realized its feasting had been interrupted, lurching to Sai with a gnashing tendril mass instead of a face. Shifting, amorphous, and diseased the things might be, but they didn't have much for speed.

Sai raised the sword, stabbing forward with it as he did so. Where the katana cut with a refined edge, Perro's blade worked like a hot saw, boiling and slicing in equal measure as its teeth worked back and forth at a speed too fast for eyes to see. The blur burned through the menace, leaving it hissing in two piles on the ground.

Goopy hands gripped Sai's shoulders and tore at his skinsuit, while others snaked around his feet. Reversing his hold on the hilt, Sai stuck the blade backwards along his side, skewering the creature behind him. Its angry howl brought a last smile to Sai's face, one that stayed up even as more infected, dripping hands ripped his feet away.

Falling, Sai landed next to Perro. In his wristlet's light, the mercenary looked rough, with bloody patches covering everywhere and black blotches spreading across the man's skin and clothes. Despite all that, as Sai waved the sword in an arc, slicing through the next advancing creature, he caught Perro's chest rising, falling.

"Oh hell," Sai said, kicking away more hands from sliced up creatures reaching for his feet. "I can't go ahead and die while you're still alive, can I?"

Perro, as expected, didn't respond. The creatures, ever more of them, howled.

"Fine then," Sai said, reaching behind him and pushing himself up. Slicing down with the sword, he cleared away the remnants hounding him below. "C'mon, you bastards. We're not done yet."

If Sai's challenge scared the creatures, they showed no fear in his wristlet's silver light, its every ray catching another monster charging in from the dark.

TWENTY-THREE

Suits

GREGOR'S VISOR confirmed what his ears delivered as boots hit the ground in the docking bay. The drop shuttle's two sides opened up, their wings soaring high and disgorging the dozen inside. Gregor, his hammer in hand, took the lead, charging right towards what he couldn't see in hopes that they would see him.

A swarm would be easy for Briana to cut down.

Harder, too, for Gregor to miss when everyone had themselves all packed together nice and tight. A battle hammer like his wasn't meant for precision.

It did destruction real well, though.

"Blazing right," Briana said, her voice coming in next to Gregor's ear.

The command sent Gregor's first swing left, a wide sweep looking to collect the red threats Gregor's visor laid out for him. He expected the fiends in the *Prisa*'s bloody bay, the mindless ghouls ready to get destroyed.

Instead, his swipe caught nothing. Clicks sounded as boots left the bay floor for the air, and Gregor overbalanced as the hammer hit zero resistance, sending him into a spin even as Briana's bolts splashed blue on his right. She had more luck: Gregor's inadvertent acrobatics brought a target into Briana's path, letting the shooter score two solid hits.

The target didn't falter, kept on running right by Gregor in exactly the way a blind predator wouldn't.

Damn.

"They're not—" Gregor finished with a shout as something hit him hard, knocking him from his feet and sending him rolling across the bay's floor.

Using the hammer to stabilize by hooking its head around some supply crates, Gregor found his feet in time to take another hit. This one, an armored blow to the visor, cracked Gregor's armor against his forehead, swimming his vision and stumbling him over the crates to fall on his back.

Not a great start.

Off to the right, a different noise filled the bay. A grinding sound, metal's shriek as cutting lasers tore into resistance. More signs that these weren't dumb bombs, then, but calculated, trained demons with the means and methods to achieve their goal.

"You helping?" Briana cut through the dizziness. "Because if I don't see that hammer swinging soon, I'm going to be real pissed."

Gregor's visor, as if following Briana's words, pinged another hard alarm. Dead center. Still on his back, Gregor let go the hammer and crossed his fists as a knife, shimmering in the light-bending soldier's suit, swept straight in. Gregor's forearms bounced the blade off, driving it into the floor beside Gregor's head. As soon as the point nicked the ground, his attacker had it withdrawn again, going for another stab.

Raising his knee hard, Gregor felt it hit a blur he

couldn't see, saw the man's second stab overshoot as the thing lost its balance. Gregor reached up, caught the knife arm and pulled down, using the momentum to roll himself onto his attacker as the suited soldier hit the floor.

The knife, free from its sheath, couldn't hide so well as the suit. Gregor used the weapon as a clue, bashing its hilt against the ground—and ignoring punches to his chest and legs—until the man released his grip, sending the knife free to the floor. Delivering a stunning blow to the man's head, following the blurred lines along what otherwise looked like clean blue-black tile, Gregor snagged the knife and used it to put a permanent end to the fight.

"Gregor!" Briana didn't sound so cocky now.

Grabbing his hammer and standing up, Gregor found Briana fighting a retreating battle. One smoking suit lay on the bay floor, but it looked like at least two others had Briana pushing back to the bay's side. Rather than shooting, the Twilight Ranger had her rifle held like a sword, using it to block knife strikes in a frantic defense.

A defense that gave no endgame except death.

With the hammer in one hand, Gregor drew a pistol as he started the run over. He aimed where Briana swung her rifle, where the sparks showered every time a blade caught her barrel. The orange bolts, striking an even keel between strong enough to pierce armor and weak enough to keep the power pack going, dove into the suits and left charred marks on their owners.

If they cared even a little, Gregor couldn't tell.

Briana caught Gregor's approached and changed up her tactics, stopping the retreat to hold the suits there with a furious sweeping series meant to get the invisible monsters to back up a few steps. The first swing with the rifle struck air—a success—but the back swing stopped hard. Briana winced behind her helmet's screen, visible as

Gregor started his own windup, and she dropped the rifle, going instead for a punch at the one that'd grabbed her weapon.

The fist never made it.

A knife slashed in and caught Briana's chest, driving into the armor and pushing her back. Leaving the blade stuck, the attacker must've had some grand second plan. Gregor didn't know because he couldn't see what the man was doing.

But Gregor's visor told him right where the man stood.

Gregor's hammer struck with a force he hadn't deployed in a long time. Anger flooded at Briana's stabbing, at nearly getting gored himself. A rage at how these things broke the rules with their camouflage, at how the new sounds behind them made clear the other attackers had broken beyond the bay and were streaming into the frigate.

In short, Gregor had a lot of reasons to be mad, and he took them out on the idiot who didn't make time to dodge.

The hit broke the suit's reflective coating, sending a bent fracture flying across the bay and out the frigate's open magnetic shield. Flipping his grip, Gregor used the hit's momentum to send the hammer the other way, only to catch Briana's rifle as its new owner used it to block the blow.

Letting the crumpled rifle drop, the suit repeated its strategy, grabbing at Gregor's hammer and holding it fast. The blurred outline matched Gregor, tugging at the weapon, pulling them close together. Giving up grip to throw a punch might mean losing the hammer, and given these things could swing real quick, Gregor didn't want to chance it.

Instead, he pulled. The suit pulled too, their grips

winding around the hammer's haft like two gods stuck in some immortal clash.

Stuck until Gregor noticed a red-black burn coursing through where the suit's head had been. The thing's grip slacked and fell away, revealing Briana with her drawn pistol standing behind.

"Much easier when they stand still," Briana said. "You alive?"

"Are you?"

"Have myself a good cut beneath this armor," Briana replied, wiggling the freed knife now in her left hand. "These things are sharp."

"Yes." Gregor looked back towards the bay doors. "There are more."

"Then what are we waiting for?"

"The odds are not good," Gregor replied. "We could take the shuttle and leave."

Briana laughed, "You, getting scared? Didn't think that was your deal."

"You're wounded."

"And the mission's not over," Briana replied. "Let's go, big boy. I'm gettin' bored standing here."

Having given the concerns their due, Gregor didn't waste any more time simpering over Briana. Together, they went by the drop shuttle and through the sliced bay doors, which now had a still-smoking oval cut through their center from top to bottom. Beyond, the frigate's central concourse broke left and right.

Any easy decision died as the two looked both ways down the long hallway. Standard DefenseCorp posters, both of the educational and propaganda variety, clung to the walls in tatters, some actively burning as laser fire left its evidence. Bodies, too, littered the ground where the frigate's security detail and random passersby had met quick ends.

Those bodies went in both directions too, suggesting the invading force was less intent on taking over the ship than in cleansing the frigate. Again, Gregor's stomach hardened with his heart, his jaw setting at the efficient carnage.

These poor souls didn't know what they were fighting. Didn't have a chance.

"Bridge or engines?" Briana asked, the cocky attitude gone in the face of, well, everything.

"Bridge," Gregor said. "They are after people, not machines."

He also had to bet the monsters wouldn't know how to disable or affect the engines if the creatures made it that far. From what Gregor remembered, the Raider program wasn't known for its soldier's intelligence.

"Think there'll be any survivors?" Briana asked as they went left.

"We will see," Gregor replied. "If not, then we will make sure they are avenged."

As they left the bay behind, the ship's quarters blew by on the right, its door sealed shut. That, at least, gave Gregor a measure of confidence. Someone had been smart enough to close the space, and the monsters hadn't cared to break it down.

Yet.

"You're all in on helping these people, aren't you?" Briana asked.

"I was one, once," Gregor said. "You do not forget being used."

"Says someone who's spent how many years doing just that?"

"Not like this. Not deceived and left to die."

Briana didn't reply back to that, and Gregor was all for the silence. Not that the ship didn't have sounds aplenty. Alarms rang out now, their blistering peals a call for soldiers to find their posts, for everyone else to find a weapon. Nobody, though, burst into the concourse to fight the intruders. Either more intelligent commands prevailed, or anyone with an ounce of courage was already dead.

The bridge proved both those thoughts wrong.

Barred with another, thicker entry, the bridge sat unbreached as Gregor and Briana came up behind. His visor pinging the invisible suits, Gregor counted four attacking the door with the same cutter they'd used to get through the bay. At their approach—the straight concourse offered little opportunity for stealth—two suits turned towards Gregor and Briana.

Unlike the ones leaving the drop shuttle, these two had rifles. The weapons stood in contrast to the invisible armor, glaring in their blacks. Glaring even more in the Defense-Corp shading on the weapons.

The suits hadn't come with these rifles. They'd pillaged the dead.

"Go," Briana said, hefting her own pinched rifle and letting loose.

With hammer high, Gregor charged. He kept to the concourse center, letting Briana fire around him. The two suits focused their shots on Gregor, choosing the rushing madman as the easiest target. Gregor's power armor took the incoming fire with alarm, but the shots hit Gregor's chest, the strongest part, the only plate that might last long enough for him to get into hammer range.

Briana's cover fire made its difference after the first salvo, sending both rifle-packing troops diving away. Their self preservation only sealed their doom, as Gregor broke hard right, tightening the haft and sending kinetic power through the hammer's head. The man tried to block with the rifle, intercepting the hammer high in its arc.

The rifle broke in two, its red gas popping as Gregor's hammer struck home. The kinetic energy bounced Gregor's weapon even as it ruined the man, smiting him to the hallway floor. Gregor twisted with the hammer's rebound, using the momentum to break across the hallway towards the man's partner.

A red flash hit Gregor's eyes and the visor melted, taking the hit and leaving Gregor a syrupy view of the world. A view that still held a clear target: Briana had studded the armor with blast marks, leaving the thing prepping another shot.

Gregor felt the warmth in his stomach as the rifle fired, felt the splatter on his face as his hammer rendered that last shot the thing's finale.

Turning to the pair slicing through the bridge door, Gregor caught two smoking corpses, each riddled with Briana's rifle fire.

"They kept cutting even while you charged," Briana said as she caught up to Gregor. "They might be tough in a fight, but they're still single-minded."

Gregor grunted agreement, setting the hammer aside to tear out the rest of his visor glass. That warm glow in his stomach hadn't gone away. In fact, now that he paid attention to it, the glow felt more like a hot bleed. He looked down, saw where his armor had been, there now sat nothing more than skin, and not much of that either.

"Oh, that's not good," Briana said, moving Gregor's hand away. "Sit, you moron." Briana almost pushed Gregor down as she turned towards the bridge. "Hey, anyone in there? The people that just saved your asses need a medic! Now!"

Gregor blinked. Tried to shake the growing numbness.

A strange feeling, this. Hot, and paralyzing at the same time. Like his very soul was trying to find a way out through the hole. He'd been shot before, plenty of times, but not here, not in the gut.

Maybe that's why he'd kept up his damn courage all this time: Gregor had never been hit in the right place.

Briana went closer to the bridge door, still shouting. Another voice came back, an answer Gregor didn't quite catch. His ears, ringing though they were, had caught a more important noise. A clattering, clanking sound, coming from back down the concourse. Heading this way.

"Briana," Gregor said, almost choking on her name. "There's more."

"What?" Briana asked, flicking a glance back. "Be quiet, man. Save your breath."

There would be time for that later. There always would be.

Gripping his hammer, Gregor pulled himself to his feet, looked towards the approaching noise. Dying defending an innocent bridge?

Yeah, Gregor could do that.

TWENTY-FOUR

The Racer's Gambit

THE SHUTTLE SHONE bright when the *Prisa* lit into it, her turrets joined above and below by flanking fighters as the DefenseCorp fleet came to its senses. Like a body gunning for a disease, the corvettes, fighters, and larger ships sought out the shuttles and burned them apart. Eponi's attack runs came with a larger squad now, splitting the automated turrets between targets.

"And this is why we still have humans at the controls," Tarla said as the *Prisa* took scattered hits, not enough to punch through the shields. "These dumb things couldn't destroy a freighter."

"They nearly killed us," Eponi replied.

Tarla waved away the words as Eponi followed the fighters towards the next shuttle needing destruction, "It was never that close."

Going by the *Prisa*'s own data, Eponi would disagree. Her ship had some hard burns on its hull, and a few parts would need replacing next time they landed. Another fighter salvo might've punched through, sending the *Prisa* and her crew spinning into vacuum.

Then again, close calls were part of the game.

"Sever, you free for assignment?" Deepak's voice patched through their open line. "We've lost contact with one of the cruisers. I need you to buzz their bridge and see if anyone's still in there."

"A cruiser? You mean one of the big boys?" Eponi asked.

"I believe you have experience getting close to a ship's bridge and scaring its officers," Deepak said. "I'm sending you the coordinates."

On the big windshield, a new line appeared, tilting the *Prisa* back towards Aurum Three. Deepak's target happened to be the cruiser closest to the planet itself. Not exactly a surprise—shuttles would've hit that one first.

"He wants us to do what now?" Tarla asked.

"We're supposed to say an up close hello," Eponi replied. "He's hoping their comm systems are down and that's it."

"So fly near to a giant ship bristling with guns that may not be on our side? For no reward?"

"Same deal as before, Tarla."

"When they change the terms, you can do the same," the Twilight Ranger captain sat back in her seat, shaking her head. "You've got a lot to learn if you want to play this game."

Eponi brushed off Tarla's words, focusing instead on the *Prisa*'s approach vector. The cruiser wasn't quite the *Nautilus*'s size, and its rounded bulk lacked the rocky integration with an asteroid, but the ship still had space to spare. It hung over Aurum Three like a rogue moon, its rear jets off, leaving the ship adrift.

So far as Eponi could tell, the shuttles had been going on a one-per-ship targeting strategy, which had made the things easy to destroy as they split from their packs. Even so, plenty found their destinations before DefenseCorp found its sanity, and one must've docked here. The idea of a single drop shuttle taking on a whole cruiser, with hundreds and hundreds of personnel, troops, and weapons on board, seemed insane.

But a concentrated, lethal bunch of invisible marauders might be able to storm a bridge.

Angling the *Prisa* to come up over the cruiser's left side, Eponi siphoned power from her ship's weapons and poured it into shields. While the cruiser's turrets weren't shooting anything yet, their numbers and firepower could roast an unsuspecting ship like the *Prisa* real quick. The pilots in the *Prisa*'s turrets protested, but a quick reminder about who saved them from a real cold vacuum death cut the complaining.

Tarla spent the seconds sending out queries along both Sever and Twilight Ranger frequencies, trying to get someone on the surface to answer. Nobody replied, and, for once, Eponi caught worry on Tarla's face.

"So you do care," Eponi said after Tarla's latest missive went unreturned.

"Hard to make any cash without a team."

Eponi sighed, shook her head. Someday, maybe, Tarla would show a crack in her cocky armor. There had to be something more to the captain than quips and cash.

Outside, the cruiser's bridge made its first appearance. The curved glass span covered the bridge's multi-leveled space, where a bundle of officers ought to be scrambling with the ship's systems. Looking in from space, Eponi had to see past Aurum Three's glaring star, which cast a white-blue flare.

Relying on plain eyesight in a galaxy where ships flew from one planet to another struck Eponi as a little absurd, but she leaned forward anyway, trying to find life.

Creeping closer, cutting the *Prisa*'s engines, they drew near the glass.

Tarla swore as Eponi sucked in her breath. She couldn't, wouldn't be surprised by anything these creatures could do, not after seeing them barrel towards the *Prisa* back in that bloody bay, and yet . . .

Even as the grisly sight filtered in, the cruiser shifted. Its velocity picked up, and Eponi scrambled to kick in the *Prisa*'s own engines, pushing the smaller ship away as the cruiser lifted itself into higher orbit.

"You didn't see a pilot there, did you?" Eponi said as the cruiser passed beneath the *Prisa*.

"I didn't see anyone," Tarla said. "I know I said we'd keep any escapees here, Eponi, but I'm thinking we can't take this cruiser down."

"It's not leaving," Eponi said, looking at her console as it plotted the cruiser's likely direction. "If anything, it's looking to head right through the fleet's center."

"Why?"

Eponi glanced at Tarla, and the two hit the meaning at the same moment.

"Vana really made them into monsters," Tarla muttered while Eponi re-opened the channel back to Deepak. The man picked up quick, his grainy visage popping up on the console.

"Admiral," Eponi said. "That cruiser's bridge is compromised, and I don't think you'll like where it's flying."

The admiral's face showed all the stress and none of the surprise at Eponi's words, "Then I need you to destroy it. We've been able to raise survivors on the ship, and they still control the back-up bridge. If you can cut the front, then we may yet save her."

"You want me to fight a cruiser alone?"

Deepak grimaced, "I don't want you to, but there's no choice. I'll send out the call for help, but while your cruiser is our largest problem, it's not our only one. Other frigates are falling, and there are more shuttles to down."

Eponi found herself repressing another sigh—she'd been doing that too often lately. Kart racers had to believe they were going to win, and that meant keeping downer emotions at bay. Instead, she tuned up the engines, started shunting power from the shields to the turrets.

"When this is all over, maybe you can tell whomever's left to pay attention when Sever gives the advice, okay?" Eponi said.

"You have my word on that, Eponi," Deepak replied. "Handle the cruiser. Good luck."

The face vanished as the *Prisa* began crawling over the cruiser's hull, making progress back towards the bridge. On the first approach, Eponi didn't see any life in the cruiser's weapons. The turrets stayed still, soft and quiet. Just the way she preferred her enemies.

Now, those same spears sticking out into space began to turn. This close, Eponi saw the weapons shift, and worse, shift in unison. No way enterprising soldiers would move those turrets so smoothly.

"You're seeing this, right?" Eponi asked Tarla.

"I'm just trying not to believe it," Tarla replied. "Here I've been hoping these things don't have the smarts to make any big moves."

"They don't need to know much," Eponi said, "teach'em how to set a target, turn on the autopilot. That's enough to ruin this fleet."

"This contract keeps getting worse and worse."

"You want it to get better, tell those pilots to get ready," Eponi said. "I bet this cruiser's not going to like it when we start shooting."

That the cruiser hadn't opened up right away meant the invaders weren't all that smart after all. Set a destination and turn on autopilot, engage automatic defenses? Those were about the simplest options a cruiser like this had, so a big ship meant for a thousand could limp along with just a couple people left.

The *Prisa* and every other ship next to the cruiser would be blipping by as neutrals, maybe even friendlies. As soon as Eponi pumped some lasers into the bridge, though, that'd change. The kart racer could fly fancy, but the *Prisa* wasn't small enough to evade an entire cruiser's fire.

"*Prisa?*" the hail broke into Eponi's cockpit. "This is Blade Wing? Deepak sent us your way, said you might need some help knocking this big boy out of commission?"

Eponi blinked, looked at the scanner. She saw four blips closing on her position. Nowhere near enough to challenge a cruiser.

"Tell me you're a lot bigger than you look, Blade Wing," Eponi said.

"Two fighters, two corvettes," the Blade Wing lead replied, not discouraged in the least by their prospects. "DefenseCorp standard, at your service."

Tarla put her face in her hands while, outside, the cruiser completed its turn. The big ship now had itself away from orbit and facing the fleet, the continuing laser battle sparking between captured ships, shuttles, and the good guys looking, if Eponi squinted real hard, like a finish line.

"Here's the situation," Eponi said. "We've gotta take out this cruiser's bridge, but its shields are up. As soon as it thinks we're the bad guys, it'll send everything it has our way."

"We're not equipped to handle that kind of firepower."

"Oh, you think?"

The wing leader said nothing, and Eponi almost felt bad about the crack. Almost. Instead, as the *Prisa* crested the bridge a second time and looked into its seemingly empty center, Eponi tried to find another option.

"Tell me what you've got," Eponi said to Blade Wing.

"Missiles and lasers, Sever. That's what we're packing."

"Missiles and lasers," Eponi muttered, mulling the options. She needed a gambit here, something that'd give the five scrappy ships a chance against one giant monster. Well, a monster that, right now, didn't know these five ships were the enemy. "Hold on, can you get past me? Form up a few kilos past my engines?"

"Can do."

Matching the cruiser's velocity, Eponi pushed the *Prisa* over the bridge and down in front of the vast glass. Flipping the ship, Eponi put her windshield looking right at the objective.

"You're going to ram it?" Tarla asked. "Because I did not give you the okay to kill me, or destroy my ship."

"I don't work for you," Eponi replied.

Tarla pulled a pistol faster than Eponi thought possible. The Twilight Ranger captain aimed it right at Eponi's head.

"Pull us out of here," Tarla said. "I'm deciding these DefenseCorp ships aren't worth it."

"Don't care what you think," Eponi said, opening the channel back to Blade Wing. "Lock your missiles on me. All of them from everyone. We'll only get one chance at this."

"On you?" Blade Wing's commander asked, in that concerned tone Eponi heard often enough from Aurora.

"It's an order," Eponi said. "When I say, you fire."

Tarla frowned now, still holding her pistol, "Eponi, I don't like this game."

Eponi didn't reply. She had to get the *Prisa* close. Using the ship's maneuvering jets, she shaved bits off the velocity, pulling the *Prisa* closer to the bridge one centimeter at a time. Alarms started dinging as Blade Wing fulfilled its promise, forming up and locking their missiles onto the *Prisa*.

The lock number and the expected missiles kept rising, far past the number that'd reduce Eponi and everyone on the ship to ash.

"Answer me, Eponi," Tarla said. "Or I'll shoot."

"You pull that trigger and we're both dead," Eponi shot back. "This is life with me, Tarla. You take it, you leave it, but for now, please shut up."

And, for once, Tarla did.

Once the locks settled, once the cruiser's bridge came so close Eponi felt she could reach out and touch the glass, she gave the order.

"Fire, you beautiful bastards," Eponi said. "Fire'em all."

Missiles launched by the dozen, streaking towards the *Prisa* as Eponi punched up the engine power.

Time to win the race, or die trying.

TWENTY-FIVE

Into The Dark

WHAT LAY beneath the landing zone became clear well before Rovo hit the bottom. Black spots, puddles still shaking with living material told Rovo all he needed to know. Nightmares brought on by Felix and his diseased creations haunted Rovo's sleep, and here they were again.

"Go back up," Rovo told Javelin, who trailed the rookie by a few steps.

"Go back, why?"

"Because I'm not getting a signal down here and we'll need help," Rovo said. "If I'm guessing right, what's down here is real bad."

"So are we, bro."

"Bro?" Rovo threw a look over his shoulder at the mercenary. "And no, not like this. We need reinforcements. More firepower."

"But you're gonna go right ahead anyway?"

"If Sai's down here, then he's in trouble. You and I are the only ones who know that. We both die, who's coming to get us?"

"If we're dead, man, why would we care?"

Rovo closed his eyes, inhaled and exhaled in the proper order, "Javelin, please go. Now. Before I shoot you to save myself the headache."

Cackling, Javelin finally did as Rovo asked and headed up top. Maybe the mercenary could get in touch with Tarla and Eponi, have them swing the *Prisa* down here if they were all done with the drop shuttles up above.

Or get Gregor and his hammer.

As the rookie stepped off the final metal stair onto a rough floor, though, the sudden solitude lit a different fire in his bones. The last time Rovo had followed Felix into the darker, diseased corners alone, Rovo had been captured and nearly devoured. This time, the rookie had a second chance to prove he could hack it. That he wasn't an easy casualty.

Thinking that and proving it required crossing a growing chasm as Rovo went further into the underground maze. His wristlet caught sparse signage declaring all new subjects head one way while caretakers head another. Forced to choose between the two, Rovo went with the subjects.

Back on Gillane Four, amid the oceans, Vana had taken Kaia's blood in a bid to turn her agents into some invincible fighting force. Rovo had thought, at the time, a stealthy band that could drop in any environment and come away without a scratch would be as bad as things could get. Now? Vana had taken it a step further, choosing to scrap her experienced agents for random, unlucky civilians.

Hundreds had been put on those shuttles, but if the *Prisa* bay assault revealed what happened to the people Sever had left behind on Dynas, then thousands more could be here. Civilians, families even, trapped in these warrens and awaiting the virus that would turn them into mindless monsters.

Rovo hadn't seen those people going along with the agents in the evacuation. Where they might be, what might've happened to them, the rookie tried not to speculate. Especially as the walls around him faded darker and darker with viral patches. The air grew thick and humid, unlike Aurum Three's dry state above. Through the visor, a fetid stench crawled up and into Rovo's suit, prompting coughs until the rookie had the power armor start filtering it away.

New sounds arose as Rovo went deeper, one halting step at a time. A constant, wet drip and slithering, as if swamp-soaked snakes roamed the depths with Rovo. Behind them, growing louder, came the occasional clacks as two hard objects came together. What could've been a machine held Rovo's attention as the bangs hit at random intervals, as if someone swung an object.

Like a sword.

Rovo had heard Sai's katana while he descended the steps, but the blade had fallen silent. Now this, a similar noise? Maybe Sai still fought deep in these catacombs.

Cursing his own wandering thoughts—speculating on the fates of Dynas's citizens while searching for a friend—Rovo broke into a run, taking choices at random and loping through larger rooms filled with overturned desks, destroyed lab equipment and blank, cracked screens on his way towards the noise. Every choice followed the sound and Rovo picked up the pace, using the armor's kinetic boosters for long lunges, as those clangs came slower and slower.

Bouncing off the walls, spraying black around him as he ran, Rovo burst into the largest room so far, one packed with toppled podiums and soaked in churning, dark grime.

With his armor's lights shining from his shoulders, Rovo spun to the right towards the sound.

Sai stood, back against the wall and favoring his left arm. Rovo couldn't seen any more of the man, as dark shapes charged and broke again and again on Sai's sword. A sword which wasn't, somehow, the man's katana.

Not that the weapon mattered now.

Raising the rifle, Rovo squeezed shots off to Sai's left, burning down a pair closing in on the swordsman's blind side. Pivoting, Rovo ran lasers down the line, skipping over any beats that might hit Sai directly.

"Stop!" Sai shouted, the first words he spoke to Rovo. "Perro's on my right."

On his right? Rovo looked and saw nothing but more swarming forms. Shadows, though, did find space through their grasping arms and bending limbs, space Rovo saw Sai keep clear with wide swings.

So Rovo had to be precise. He could do that.

Targeting his shots, Rovo picked off the creatures as they came at Sai and, now, towards him too. Every blue-white blast left an orange flame on the target, a fire that spread as the creatures fell on one another. The sight stunned Rovo until he remembered exactly how Gregor had dispatched the things on Dynas: breaking a pipe and torching the creatures to ash.

There weren't any pipes here that Rovo saw, but the rifle seemed to be up to the task.

"You going to smoke us out?" Sai's shout carried across the room.

The man had a point. Rovo's work had pitch smoke crawling through the room. The rookie's power armor kept it away from his eyes, kept the filtered debris from getting into his lungs. Sai—in a realization that sprang on Rovo like a pouncing tiger—didn't seem to have his suit anymore. If the fire spread, he'd be as likely to die as the creatures.

"Coming!" Rovo called back, launching into a run towards the swordsman.

The mighty sprint started and ended with a single step into the fiery goo coating the floor. Like some comedy show, Rovo's heavy booted feet failed to find traction and slid out from under the rookie, sending Rovo and his power armor for a slide. Flaming showers sprayed up as Rovo's back hit the ground, with more than one creature seeing its opportunity to strike.

Back in the crashed drop shuttle, Rovo had the homicidal trio hitting him one fist and knife after another. Their suits, coupled with whatever drug cocktail Vana had provided, gave those fiends enough strength to crack Rovo's armor, to dive their knives through his protection.

These creatures had none of those advantages. Their gooey hands, their broken teeth tried and failed to penetrate the power armor's defenses. Rovo could've laughed, would've laughed if he didn't feel the same thing that'd taken the rookie way back on Dynas: a slow sucking feel as the virus latched onto his arms, legs, back.

It might take the damn disease a long time, but it would devour Rovo just the same.

The rookie tried to sit up, but the creatures used their weight to push him down. He couldn't raise the rifle either, as other creatures clambered on it, pinning the weapon in the mire.

"Where are you?" Sai called, the words slipping through a soundscape dominated by squelching, hoarse cries.

"Took a bad fall," Rovo replied, running through his options and not finding any he liked.

But finding one he could use.

"Get yourself as far away as you can," Rovo said. "Five seconds!"

He dropped the rifle, an act that sent the weapon nowhere in the muck pool now halfway up his side. Rovo swam his hand through the slime to his belt, where two grenades sat ready and waiting. Getting his fingers around the ridged orb while grimy fists beat at his face, on his chest, took a few fumbling seconds, giving Sai his five and more.

Then Rovo activated the bomb. Counted to three.

Lurching his arm free, Rovo gave the grenade a toss with all he had. He couldn't see it fly with all the creatures covering him now, swirling together in a shapeless mass eating at his armor. He did, though, hear the slightest clank when the bomb struck the ceiling.

Rovo definitely heard the boom when the grenade went off.

Like a rapid dawn, the scrabbling creatures vanished in a fiery wash. Rovo's own armor splashed alerts on his visor claiming the power armor no longer had much integrity. Taking it to space or underwater would be a fast trip to a slow grave. Heat splashed through around the armor's lightest spots at the joints, searing Rovo through his skinsuit.

Damaged armor or no, the rookie surged up, pushing with his arms as viral matter burned around him. Rocks splashed down from the ceiling, where a nice chunk had blown out, its remnants creating a stone rain in the room. First, Rovo checked where Sai had stood and saw nothing. Then, as his visor noted a threat at his feet, he took off.

Two long leaps, sparking as Rovo's armor struggled with the motion, carried Rovo to Sai's former stand. He caught himself on the stone wall, one battered with scratches where Sai's wide swings had nicked the barrier, and Rovo spied Sai's best exit off to the right, a parallel corridor to the one Rovo had taken over here.

Spied it, then lost all sight as the burning debris reached Rovo's vulnerable rifle. The gas in the weapon's power pack ignited in a blistering flash, running through the colors and sending a second hot series flushing through Rovo's joints.

He'd need a long salve bath after this one.

The thought, as Rovo's eyes found their focus again, brought up a smile. Here he was, in a ruined room surrounded by a deadly disease and the mindless monsters it created, thinking about a nice bath.

Aurora always said Sever had to keep its confidence. Why stop now?

"Sai?" Rovo called down the pathway. "You down here?"

"You still alive, rookie?" Sai answered.

"This is nothing!" Rovo said, heading off towards the swordsman. "A little fire never hurt anybody."

Sai, waiting down the corridor with Perro hanging on his shoulder, shook his head as Rovo approached. The rookie's power armor still had one working light, and Sai had a hand up to shield his own eyes as Rovo came close.

"I never want to see another fire as long as I live," Sai said. "How'd you find us?"

"Followed the carnage?"

Outside the burning room, the walls were coated again with black slime. Bits of it sucked at Rovo's boots from the floor, killing any urge to have a nice catchup with Sai. There was a time and place to swap stories, and it would be over a beer on a world very, very far from this one.

"Mind if we keep moving?" Rovo asked when Sai made no motion to head on down the corridor. Instead the swordsman looked past Rovo towards the fire, one already starting to put itself out. "Or is there something I'm missing?"

"My sword," Sai replied. "I'm not leaving here without it."

"And your sword is?"

"Somewhere under all that." Sai nodded back towards the room.

"And if I go get it, we can leave?"

Something in Sai's look, in the way the man had a set stance even with his wounds, even with what looked like half a skinsuit shredded on him, said this wasn't just about the katana. A feeling confirmed when Sai shook his head.

"She's still here," Sai said. "I won't leave till we find her."

"Aurora?" Rovo offered.

"Anaskya," Sai replied. "Our mission here's not over till she's gone. Until the last of this is destroyed. We let her walk after Dynas. Not this time."

Rovo glanced at his armor. Beat-up and burnt, the rookie's only weapons were the two pistols on his belt. Two pistols, and two fists.

It would be enough.

"One katana," Rovo said, "coming up."

TWENTY-SIX

Walk and Talk

Vana ejected her damaged armor, facing Aurora. Both stood in their skinsuits, Aurora holding the pistol towards Vana, not believing what the agent told her. One line after another. As the words came out, Aurora took a step back, then another, buying enough space to keep Vana from any surprise grabs.

The Sever captain had to make the move, because what Vana said made too much and too little sense. The agent spoke about a long forming plan, helped along by Renard's blind ambition and too much greed from those who should've known better. By her telling, Vana had prevented a terror from being unleashed, had been the one sabotaging the future Aurora and Sever were striving to stop.

In short, Vana had been Sever's greatest ally all along.

"Bullshit," Aurora said for the third time as Vana closed up yet another chapter, explaining how she'd kept stringing Sever along to keep Renard under control, knowing she might have to rely on the squad if things went too far, too fast. "You directed everything on Gillane Four.

You brought all this together. Those are your shuttles heading up to DefenseCorp ships."

"Those are DefenseCorp shuttles heading up to DefenseCorp ships," Vana said, sticking to her infuriating calm. "They are bringing the product Renard wanted, the product all those people you slaughtered desired more than anything else. They will see their mistake up close, and learn—"

"They won't learn a damn thing because they're already dead," Aurora countered. "Everyone on those ships is just trying to earn cash, like you and I. They don't know what's coming."

"Trying to earn cash exploiting a terrible galaxy," Vana's voice chilled. "You know what DefenseCorp does to the worlds it 'serves'. You know who loses when your admirals sign their contracts, and who wins."

Aurora wanted to roll her eyes, but stopped herself. Anything Vana said could be a distraction, a play to get her focus away. Even so, Aurora had heard variations on this moral argument time and time again. Yes, there were losers. Yes, DefenseCorp wasn't some savior always helping the less fortunate. Reality wasn't kind.

But getting trite motivation wouldn't help Aurora and Deepak stop what Vana put in those shuttles. She needed real answers, with real solutions.

"Your response to that is to shoot these things out into the galaxy, where they'll kill untold innocents?" Aurora asked. "What happens when they take a ship away from Aurum Three and land on a real world?"

"They'll never make it," Vana replied, curling into a self-satisfied sneer. "Every one of those poor souls will fall apart within a few days. The very virus keeping them alive will destroy them and leave the ships they take as contaminated graveyards. Everlasting examples of what a mistake DefenseCorp made."

"How?" Aurora wasn't a genetics engineer, but Vana wasn't either. Any bomb put into those things couldn't have been Vana's doing. "One of Renard's scientists?"

"Oh no. They had no idea," Vana shook her head. "Like the ones from Dynas, they worked and worked until they received their shot and found their own fate. Too attached to their ends to see the change slipped in by someone even more obsessed than themselves." Vana held up a palm as Aurora started in for another question. "We're wasting time, Aurora. That drive has everything you want to know inside, everything that can show the galaxy what went wrong here, and why DefenseCorp should be torn apart."

Vana backed up a step, glanced towards the chamber's exit, "Now, I have one more mess to clean up before you kill me, if you can hold your murder in check for just a little while longer?"

Things never went well when you let the hostage run the show, but Aurora found herself nodding for Vana to move along anyway. Aurora needed a minute to rerun Vana's words, parse out what they actually meant. At first listen, it sounded like Vana's whole scheme hadn't been about galactic domination at all, but the opposite, via a bloody, terrible demonstration.

As Aurora followed Vana from the chamber, up those same emergency diodes and back into the stairwell, the Sever captain replaced Vana's puzzle pieces where they fit best. The agent could've done everything she said for the reasons she'd given, a systematic undermining of Renard's plan coupled with a cleansing masterstroke to destroy everyone who'd aided Renard's efforts.

And, just possibly, enough records to horrify the galaxy so nobody would attempt it again.

Bold, brash, and more than a little terrible to send so many hundreds, even thousands to death to prove a point.

As they climbed, Vana stayed silent the whole way, as if knowing Aurora had her work to do. The missing key to the whole explanation sat with Vana herself. The motivation. Most Sever missions had a clear-cut villain, whether it was a rabble fighting for rights or another company overstepping their bounds. Those villains had goals: freedom, a valuable asteroid.

Vana wanted to burn down DefenseCorp, but why?

"Doesn't matter," Vana said as they went into the Administration room, still dark. The agent had her wristlet up and shining. The other two agents had disappeared. "I have my reasons and I'll keep them to myself."

"Makes it hard for me to believe you if I don't know why you're doing this?"

"That's your problem."

"I have the pistol."

"Then shoot me if you want," Vana glanced back, looking almost bored. "If you're not going to pull the trigger, then quit it with the threats and let me listen."

Aurora let her finger slide away from the trigger, did as Vana said and let her ears take a walk. Beyond the administration room lay all those cells, labs, and other horrors Aurora had sprinted through while armed and armored. With the power still out, Aurora expected to hear those creatures tearing each other, and possibly the DefenseCorp guards, to pieces.

Instead, silence. A dead, total silence almost unknown to Aurora, who'd spent so much of her life on churning ships, space stations, and other tech meccas. The quiet compressed space, folding in the world around Aurora until it consisted of her pistol, her wristlet and its silver light, and Vana, looking through the room's destroyed exit.

"Nice work," Vana said, breaking the moment and gesturing towards the door. "I always like seeing these get broken. They're all the same, you ever notice? All these bases, all the ships, all the doors look alike."

"Right . . . Are you satisfied? Where is this thing you're looking for?"

"I'm worried we may have done a better job than I wanted," Vana said as they started off. "It's hard to keep brilliant scientists from making progress. These cells were the next stage. Human, animal, alien. All possible additions to the Raider arsenal."

With their steps interrupting the silence, Aurora tailed Vana as they went through the hallways and their broken rooms. The journey went swift, Vana not hesitating as she picked each direction. Their only stop came when they found two bodies stacked amid overturned tables and shattered glass. Aurora recognized them even as Vana sighed.

"They were supposed to wait for me," Vana said, kneeling to check their pulse. "You should have stayed on the ship. Then the three of us were going to finish it together."

"Finish what?"

"You'll see," Vana glared back at Aurora. "Now you have the responsibility."

"I have nothing," Aurora replied. "This is on you."

Vana matched Aurora's steel with her own, "This is on us, Aurora. You had every chance to end this on Dynas. You could've shared what you saw with the galaxy, but you didn't. Your squad ran and hid. You want to earn that superior tone you're so quick to hold, then help me, and make their sacrifice worth it."

They came upon the things that'd killed the two agents

not long after. The monsters bore laser fire hallmarks along with torn clothing stuck in their teeth and claws. Vana muttered something about dogs, and Aurora could see the resemblance. As for the creature's killers?

The DefenseCorp guards had formed themselves into a cohesive force, walking through the labs exterminating anything they found. Vana and Aurora would've been shot themselves, except their arguing about who was more terrible than who drew curiosity instead of weapons-fire. A curiosity that went from intense to extreme when they realized who Vana was.

"Stop," Vana said, heading off a snowballing question series from the trio leading the ten or so fighters running around the area. "You're asking me what happened here? She has a drive with all your answers. Take it and leave."

Rifle lights flipped over to Aurora.

"Know what she's talking about?" asked one gruff man with a face Aurora couldn't see. "And keep that pistol down, please. We're chippy right now. Hasn't been a fun few hours."

That, Aurora could agree with. She fished into one of the skin suit's thin pockets, made for ID cards and other tiny essentials. Snaking out the drive, she offered it up.

"How many did you lose?" Aurora asked.

"Some wounded," the man said. "The people breaking into this place did some damage before they ran. The beasts in here didn't get us, but we found a few who didn't make it."

"Good," Aurora replied. "You should do what she said and leave."

"Don't think you can give us orders," the man replied. "In fact—"

"But I can," Vana cut him off. "You've done well, all of you, and now you need to head home."

"The people that killed our commanders are still out there," the man protested.

"They're not here anymore," Vana replied. "You want to find them, you get back up to your ships and start there. That's an order, captain. One you should follow, for your own people's sakes."

That last line, given everything around them, seemed to make an impact. The leader drew in a big breath, sighed it out, and issued the order to withdraw. As the shuffling steps started back towards the bay, the man offered them an escort.

"That," Vana said, "We could use."

Aurora spent the walk back to the bay wondering how damn lucky she was that the guards didn't recognize her. Without her power armor, Aurora looked little like the battle-ready warrior bashing her way through the base. Even so, Aurora's face and name would've been plastered all over DefenseCorp's desertion logs.

Then again, who would be thinking about deserters in a time and place like this?

Back at the bay, the guards loaded up their ships, an experience sped up as soon as pilots returned to their cockpits, opened up their comms, and heard about the assaults happening up above. All these units here represented the best each DefenseCorp group had to offer, specialized bodyguards now unable to defend their ships.

"Another part of your plan?" Aurora asked Vana as the shuttles departed, all surprised that the two refused passage. "Keep the best defenders away from home?"

"You might not believe me, but no," Vana said. "It's not the amount of death that matters, just the visual. That's all we need to convince the galaxy that Defense-Corp can't be trusted."

"I'm sure that'll make a compelling argument during your hearing."

Vana laughed, "My hearing? There's only two ways I'm leaving this planet, Aurora. Neither will be in stun cuffs."

Before Aurora could reply, Vana walked towards the bay's wide opening, one that looked down over the broad landing pad the shuttles had used. What had been a crowded, flat expanse rippled now, as if a localized quake was occurring beneath the surface. Pits appeared, one after another, sinking down.

"She's moving faster than I thought," Vana said.

"Anaskya?"

Vana nodded, "She wanted to see her creations come to life. I told her they wouldn't survive, but maybe Anaskya found a way."

"Then, agent, you're going to help me stop her," Aurora said, holding that pistol ever tighter.

"Why, Aurora, I thought you'd never ask."

TWENTY-SEVEN

Disease Dreams

Even through the visor, Sai could feel Rovo's frustration. The swordsman ignored it as he, using a scrap torn off from his ruined skinsuit, wiped the katana clean. Rovo could use a cleaning himself: the black grime coated his armor after the search to find the blade.

"He needs help, and he won't get it down here," Sai repeated. "You said Javelin's topside? Then drop Perro off and come back."

"Like you'll wait."

Now Sai fell into his fatherhood well, delivering the best stare he had straight at Rovo. Responsibility stormed from the look, hitting the rookie hard and driving Rovo's own eyes towards Perro, breathing shallow on the ground nearby.

"We can't chance Anaskya getting away," Sai replied. "Without Perro, I'll be able to move fast."

"Without any armor, you'll die fast too."

"A lot of people have tried to kill me, Rovo. Anaskya too. None succeeded."

"Yeah, because I saved your ass."

Sai quirked a grin, "Then hurry up and you might get the chance again."

The rookie slammed a fist against a wall, splattering the black goop everywhere.

"I know you won't wait," Rovo said. "So be careful. Don't be stupid. I'll be back as fast as I can."

Sai nodded and the rookie didn't hesitate another second, scooping up Perro and thumping along into the depths. Without the power armor's light, Sai's wristlet put up a weak white glow. The dark walls seemed to go on forever, as if Sai walked in an endless night. The continual scraping, rasping, squelching noises as Anaskya's creations shifted kept the idea from being peaceful.

At first, Sai followed Rovo's own bangs and clomps, leaving the podium room and its burning disease pools behind. Anaskya had already left before Sai joined Perro, and nothing indicated she'd returned. As to where the scientist might've fled, Sai only had one clue.

Anaskya said she wanted to die by her own creation's hands. While that could mean laying down and finding peace with the first monster to stumble upon her, Anaskya had already given that up when she left the podium room. There had to be another destination in mind for her, and in this labyrinth, aside from the cages and the injection rooms, was the place Anaskya actually did the spinning, turned hypothesis into product. If Sai had to bet on a place Anaskya would go, it'd be where she brought her nightmares to actual life.

The damn maze, though, didn't give Sai much guidance on where such a place would be.

Sketching out a mental map in his mind, the swordsman walked, filling in the spaces as he moved. Sai put the lift shaft he and Perro had fallen down on the lab's far side, with the stairs Rovo descended on the opposite. If the podium room served as the lab's nexus, with easy access to the lift for its subjects to journey up and get suited, then Anaskya's own chambers would be farther back. The lab's very end.

A perfect place to keep a scientist with a fraying grip on reality.

Sai's collected questions continued to grow. He hadn't expected—nobody in Sever had—this mission to be a straightforward assault, but every minute seemed to make things stranger. Not only had Vana assembled a deranged, infected army, but she'd taken the derelict city on Dynas and mined it for human capital. Also, a lab this size required more than one scientist to manage, but Sai hadn't seen a single other lab rat here.

Though adding those numbers to Anaskya's victims wouldn't be a stretch.

But, why would Vana allow her human mine to fall apart? What would the agent gain from showing off all this potential to DefenseCorp, only to have it disintegrate around her?

Maybe Aurora or Gregor found some answers, because Sai sure didn't have anything.

And he'd have to keep going blind for a little longer.

Rovo's clomps disappeared as the viral muck thickened. Sai felt its sucking grip with every step, his bare feet squelching in through the slime. His cuts stung as the disease no doubt ran into Sai's wounds, co-opted his blood for its own purposes. Even if Sai made it up top alive, he'd need some prime medical treatment to keep from turning into the same monsters he'd been carving.

All the more reason to hurry.

With the hallways turning to blackened tunnels, the moldy growth stretching across the corners and building up into writhing piles along the floor, Sai came to what must've been a door. The scanner, identifiable only as a bulge against its black coating, sat as inert as everything else. Where the metal gate ought to stand, a thick muck wall stood instead. Steadying his sword, Sai slashed twice across the top, shearing the slime's support and sending it splashing to the ground.

On the other side sat what Sai had been looking for: while his wristlet wasn't bright, exactly, Sai saw the sole workstation and the hanging monitors leering down from ceiling arms. Anaskya, working in the room's center, would have screens above and around her, along with controls to manipulate robotic assistants.

Those machine partners stood around the space, their limbs coated with the same gunk as everything else. They should've had their own batteries, should've been able to work, but they sat as dead as the rest of the base.

Unlike the rest of the base, though, the room did have another light source. A sunlit yellow glow coming from the right. Sai stepped through the door, expecting an ambush and receiving none. Turning towards the light, Sai saw a familiar back, with shoulder-length hair ratted as slime stretched through its strands.

Anaskya stood over the lab's only clean place, a long table running from corner to corner. Sai's wristlet coupled with the yellow light to show off cellular food stacked in cases, along with vial and syringe racks. Anaskya, though, blocked any view of the light and its object.

"Found you," Sai said. Moving through the muck would make too much noise for a sneak attack anyway. Might as well see if Anaskya had some surprise in store. "Nice place you have here."

"Still you joke. After all you've seen?" Anaskya asked without turning around. "How?"

"Sever's taught me not to lose myself until I give up,"

Sai said, taking a first sloshing step towards the scientist. The muck thickened here, rippled at Sai's touch. It sucked at his skin, like strong tape peeling off with every motion. "And I haven't given up yet."

"That's very nice for you," Anaskya replied, and now her arm moved, picking something up from the case. "In a way, I suppose I haven't either."

"Hard to see how much more damage you could do."

Three long strides would put Sai in striking distance, but he kept his motion short. After falling and watching Rovo do the same, any aggressive run in this crap had the likely end being Sai, on his back, choking as the grime flooded his mouth.

No thank you.

"Vana and I struck a deal. Just like one of your contracts." Anaskya's hand came into view, holding a syringe filled with something red, a cherry color. "She would get her show and all the death that came with it, and I would get my lab and a chance to build my children."

"Good to know I have one more reason to dislike that agent," Sai replied. Two strides now. "What's in that?"

"The little girl's blood held a vector that Vana had me use. A clean option to provide her sacrifices with strength and, at the same time, a swift end," Anaskya sighed as she finished. "She saw the child's treasure as a means to one end, and I saw it as another."

"Is that a nasty surprise you're holding, Anaskya?" Sai asked, trying to keep the scientist talking. One stride. "What's it do?"

"Watch."

Not expecting the one-word answer, Sai missed the chance to charge as Anaskya injected herself, stabbing the syringe into her shoulder. The fluid ran in as Sai stepped into a swing, putting a clean end to the scientist. She slumped over into the muck, her hand still holding the syringe as both vanished beneath the dark.

On the table, beneath a lamp hooked to a battery, sat a pot-sized vat. More cherry liquid sat inside, inert. Sai watched it for a minute, looking for an answer, an explanation, and found none. Anaskya had botched a thousand versions before Sai ran into her on Dynas. Maybe she'd botched this one as well.

Ending a life on a failed experiment. It would be sad if it hadn't been Anaskya's own choice.

Sai eyed the vat. It didn't hold any answers, and the Sever swordsman didn't know what to do with it. Leaving the concoction seemed like a bad idea, because whomever next found it might hit upon the awful formula Anaskya designed. Dumping into the living muck also seemed suspect: Sai had seen the movies, he knew what tended to happen when you mix two terrible things.

But, blending electricity and liquid tended to fry life altogether. Sai had spent a long time figuring out the best ways to short computers and the circuits they ran on, and sacrificing water to the effort tended to work better than many more convoluted methods. Convenient, then, that Anaskya had left her lamp right here with a working battery.

With his left hand, Sai shoved the hot lamp down into the vat. He pushed hard enough to shatter the lamp's bulb inside the cherry liquid, prompting a spark, some smoke, and a rapid darkening inside the vat as the lamp's current did its work. Whatever lived inside should've received a nasty jolt.

"And stay dead," Sai muttered, turning back towards the exit. Once again, his wristlet served as Sai's lonely guide. "See, Rovo? You had nothing to worry about."

Sloshing slow, Sai made his way to the lab's exit. Taking one last look around, he shined the wristlet on Anaskya's half-devoured body, watching for a long breath, waiting for the woman to show some sign her last experiment hadn't failed.

Nothing.

Turning back to the hallway, Sai made it five seconds down before a noise stopped him. Like a machine frothing a drink, the steady churn had Sai closing his eyes for a short, resigned breath. Of course, it would be too good to let the fighter, already bloodied, beaten, and likely infected with something terrible, walk away.

With his katana raised, but keeping his distance—Sai figured the hallway offered some protection compared to a blind rush back—the swordsman listened as the noise grew. Before, Anaskya's creatures had flopped and dropped their way around, sounding like lethal leaky faucets. This came across more like a roiling roar, like a hose on full blast.

The muck rose at Sai's feet, up over his ankles. In the wristlet's light, the slime's color began to change, as if someone had dipped a red pen in the stuff. A crimson cloud bled from Anaskya's lab, frothing and expanding across the black as it came.

Sai saw nothing to cut, saw no creature surging towards him to slice down.

So Sai turned and ran, because he knew, as every story, every film had ever told him: to touch the red meant death.

Hammers and Knives

DEFENSECORP'S POWER armor turned its soldiers into living weapons. For Gregor, *living* became the key part as the power armor registered his falling vitals and moved to act. The suit wrapped around his skin, his bones, and delivered a glorious combination to Gregor's blood as he waited behind the bridge doors. By rights, the laser char through his stomach ought to have brought Gregor low, but the very beam that killed him cauterized the wound, slowing its damage enough for the power armor to carry him to one last fight.

And he wouldn't be going in alone.

With Briana's help, the fighter had made it inside the bridge, where a dozen officers and panicked crew hunkered down hoping for a miracle. Some had pistols, and a couple had picked up the rifles held by the now-dead suits. None looked like they wanted a fight.

Behind the crew, the bridge's wraparound windshield gave a lovely split view showing Aurum Three's golden sands on the right and laser-filled space on the left. Dotted with workstations serving, now, as cover, the bridge otherwise seemed a pristine place. A shame to let the mongrels coming up the corridor ruin it.

"How long?" The captain asked, the man having enough nerve to stand center.

"They are being patient now," Gregor said. "The surprise did its work."

Gregor had thrown an electro-magnetic grenade far down the corridor, the blue-silver orb promising a quick end to any circuits caught in its midst. The charging, invisible quartet must've been smart enough to know the grenade, as they quit their noisy rush as soon as the bomb bounced out.

The halt bought time for Gregor and Briana to get inside, for the bridge crew to loot what they could. Much to the captain's annoyance, Gregor insisted they leave the laser cutter in the corridor.

"I need my ship back," the captain complained. "It's chaos out there, and we're first in line for defense."

"You let the shuttle land," Gregor said.

"How could we know?"

"Can I shoot him?" Briana asked Gregor, loud enough for everyone to hear. "You're dying, I'm hurt, and he's whining about his own mistakes. We deserve better."

Gregor couldn't disagree on that, but he shook his head nonetheless, "Save your power for the suits."

The captain caught the tone, perhaps saw Briana's finger tight to her two pistols, and wisely decided to shut up. Gregor, leaning his head back on the door and enjoying the cool metal against his skin, shut his eyes. The wait wouldn't be long. Until then, he could focus on the pain, and how to fight it.

"Going to make it, buddy?" Briana said, quiet this time.

"I will worry about that when the suits are dead."

"Could be a problem if you die first."

"Then, if you would, shoot them fast?"

Briana chuckled, a laugh that died when a new sound picked up behind them, through the door. The careful tremors as the suits picked up the laser cutter, getting ready to go to work. Gregor caught the captain's eye, nodded. The man returned the gesture, albeit with a deep gulp.

"It's been a damn pleasure," Briana said to Gregor. "We make it through, you should come with us. We could do this all the time."

Gregor gave Briana the slightest smile. He was a Sever, would always be a Sever until either he or Sever Squad stopped existing. No matter how much fun it might be rampaging through the galaxy with Tarla's band, Gregor's loyalties were cast.

His hand tightened around the hammer's haft, the weapon feeling good and sturdy in his grip, even if Gregor himself felt like he needed a thousand year nap. Not now.

Not yet.

The captain raised a single finger with one hand, brought up his pistol with the other. Gregor, relying on his power armor, stood and hefted the hammer. Just off the door's center, he brought the weapon up over his head while Briana stood opposite, replacing her pistols with the diamond knives stolen from the downed suits.

Ready.

The door blurred, the *whirr* sounded and Gregor swung before he saw his target. Two suits held the large cutter, its heavy beam springing to life as the doors swung away. The short, white-blue flame shot a meter between Gregor and Briana, like some divine line separating the pair. With their hands holding the cutter, the suits had no defense except their blurred armor.

Gregor didn't need to see his target to smash it. The

hammer crunched into the suit's shoulder, driving the enemy to the ground with the combined cracking of bones and barrier. As soon as the suit released the cutter's trigger, its beam flashed out, replaced by brighter, colorful sparks as the captain and his officers opened up on the other two suits.

While Gregor raised and slammed the hammer home a second time, his target's busted armor looking like fractured glass on the floor, lasers blitzed around him. The two shooting suits didn't stay put, using their light-bending armor to dip and dodge the incoming fire while returning in kind with stolen rifles. Someone cried out on the bridge, followed by another as the suits ignored Gregor and Briana for easier targets.

Speaking of—Gregor glanced right, saw Briana kneeling over her own victim, working the knives like Gregor used to work a rock puncher. Straight thrusts in and out, grinding the target to dust. She seemed fine, more than fine. Gregor hefted his hammer, tried to find a spot to focus.

Finding these things was a lot harder without a visor to mark them. Thankfully, this close, it was real hard to miss.

The fire stopped coming from the bridge. Gregor didn't know whether the captain's force had all died, or if the suits had them pinned. Either way, without the incoming fire, the suits dropped their rifles and swapped to those diamond knives. Harder to see, deadlier in the mix.

"You take right?" Briana said as they started forward.

"Yes."

Rovo or Eponi might have come up with a clever quip for the occasion, but Gregor never had the mouth for those. Didn't feel much like it either, what with his stomach boiling from that laser blast.

Gregor read the lines as he stepped over his first

victim's wreckage. At a glance, the suits offered almost total invisibility, catching the light behind and mimicking it up front. Gregor hadn't read the technical readouts on how the damn things worked, but Sai had given Sever an overview during the doldrum days on the fringe station. In short, to see the suits you had to find the edges.

There the reflection didn't come through perfect. The seam between the suit and everything else blurred, like the air above hot asphalt. Hard to see from far away, easier up close and with near-death's concentration.

The knife gave the suit away. A lunging strike, going for Gregor's throat in a bid to end the fight in one. A leading shimmer had Gregor twisting forward, taking the stab along the thick plate over his upper chest. The knife bit in, showering sparks and making an ear-piercing shriek, but the point didn't cut through. The charge cost Gregor a chance at a hammer blow, forcing the Sever fighter to lead in with his shoulder.

As Gregor struck, he blew out the remaining energy in his kinetic boosters, launching himself into the suit with enough force to send the man flying. Gregor couldn't see the suit as it flew, but he heard the man land, saw the sparks where the knives struck the floor. Not letting up, Gregor took the momentum into a following leap, rising up with the hammer and smashing it where the blurs showed the man.

The suit didn't wait for the hit. As Gregor's hammer crashed down, the suit curled away, the blurs moving just outside the hammer's hit. The concourse floor dented where Gregor struck, and he flipped his grip with the impact, rotating the hammer and sending it into a sweep fast enough to catch the suit's stab, deflecting it wide and buying distance between the two.

A loud curse called Gregor's attention back towards the

bridge, where Briana sported a shiny crimson line across one arm, her space suit in ribbons as she exchanged knife blows with her target. Her invisible enemy was, now, very much visible with red slashes up and down their armor. Both weren't letting up, choosing instead to take hits than dodge.

Gregor would bet on Briana winning that battle with any sane enemy. Against these things?

His own target took the waver as an opportunity to close. Those knives didn't have the hammer's reach, so Gregor matched the suit's advance with a step back, sending the hammer on another cross swing to keep the suit away. After Gregor's shoulder charge, the suit's pristine reflection sported cracks in spots, looking like broken glass.

Easy to see, still hard to hit.

The suit feinted a lunging stab, pushing Gregor into another counter swat. Using the suit's own agility, the man darted up, taking a leap off the nearby wall to clear Gregor's cross-swing and take a stab at the Sever fighter's face.

A bold, dangerous move.

Once the suit committed to the jump, he lost any ability to adjust his course. Gregor let go the hammer, too slow to bring back, and instead caught the leaping attack. The knife nicked Gregor's cheek, a nothing blow compared to what Gregor had already suffered. To what the enemy experienced when Gregor swung the suit into the wall. The suit tried to pull back the knife, but Gregor slammed the man again and again, the third strike dislodging the suit's grip on the blade.

The fourth hit, amplified by the power armor's strength, sent the suit limp. Gregor added a fifth to be sure, then threw the body away.

Briana's curses continued, and Gregor looked to see

both fighters in worse condition than before. The captain and his bridge crew, behind them, had their pistols out, but didn't seem confident shooting into the close melee.

They wouldn't have to.

Gregor reached down, picked up the dropped knife. Took careful aim, and after Briana withdrew from another cutting stab, Gregor threw the blade. A dart, ready to skewer and end the fight.

Until the knife's hilt bounced off the suit's head, the blade's sharp end falling harmless to the floor. The suit hesitated, and Briana took advantage. This time, her strike hit home, cutting off her enemy's ability to breathe. The suit collapsed, leaving Briana slumped and bleeding.

"Nice throw," Briana said. "Next time, try the other end."

"I'm not good with sharp objects," Gregor said, leaning to pick up the hammer.

Leaning, and falling over. The problem wasn't hard to diagnose from the corridor floor: his power armor's efforts, plus Gregor's adrenaline, had kept him standing. The fight over, those methods dwindled, leaving him hurting, dizzy, and gasping for air.

"Hey," Briana said as the captain's crew flowed out from the bridge to confirm the kills. "Stay with me, big guy. I didn't get stabbed just to let you die on me."

"Not dying on you," Gregor said, looking up at the Twilight Ranger. "I am on the floor."

Rolling her eyes, Briana bent down, put Gregor's arm over her shoulder and brought him up to his feet.

"Captain, tell me you've got a med bay on this scrap pile?" Briana said.

"Back the way you came," the captain, looking too bewildered to take any offense, said. "If it's still standing, there's a bot that can help him."

Briana didn't wait, wheeling Gregor around and starting off that way. Every step seemed to send Gregor's world bouncing up and down. Every sound came hollow, an echo. His legs had disappeared into some numb vacuum. Problems, yes, but ones he could over come. Refill his power armor's drug supplies and Gregor could keep at it.

"We have to help Sever," Gregor said. "The mission is not over."

"For us, buddy, it's definitely over," Briana replied. "We're going to get you a nice bed and some nicer drugs to go with it. And I'm getting some salve so I don't get too many scars."

Gregor wanted to protest, but as with everything else, his mouth didn't want to play along. His eyes fluttered, his tongue tasted something wet, metallic. Gregor heard Briana curse, and then he heard nothing at all.

TWENTY-NINE

Keeping It Close

IF A TRICK WORKS ONCE, try it again. The maxim might not hold up long term—kart racers that relied on one move over and over tended to get themselves crushed—but Eponi figured Vana's infected monsters hadn't been watching her flying all that close.

The missiles locked onto the *Prisa* streaked in hot, while Eponi shoved all the energy she could to the craft's engines. Buzzing the bridge, the *Prisa* jumped forward as the missiles closed, burning towards a cruiser whose sensors, missing locks that never came, stayed unaware. The move had no chance against real observation, people who could see the bait lingering and have turrets chase it away.

Against single-minded enemies that, even if they saw Eponi's move, didn't know what to do about it?

Perfection.

The missiles couldn't adjust their direction on a precise cut. Not in space. They tried to swerve as the *Prisa* bolted forward, climbing towards the bridge's top and over the cruiser. They tried, and their momentum carried the ballistic bombs right into the bridge shields and beyond. Watching through her console, Eponi saw the green flare as the cruiser's energy barrier tried to burn out the missiles, saw it absorb the first two, three, four hits in rapid succession.

The shield's collapse came without warning. The barrier simply ceased to be, vanishing in time for the next five missiles to streak on through to slam into the thick glass protecting the bridge. That glass, like the shield, absorbed the first few impacts, the cracks rippling across armor designed to give the crew behind a chance to evacuate.

No chance came this time, because the missiles kept hitting. Tarla whistled as the bridge collapsed, its glass windshield shattering. Three more missiles arced up through the hole, attempting to find a way to the *Prisa* through the cruiser's inside. Their nova blossoms poured fire, for a hot second, into space.

The blast should've marked the end, should've cut off the *Prisa*'s alarms, but the ship kept complaining about a missile lock. Eponi found the culprits, two rocketing bombs, on the scanner.

"A fighter fired late." Eponi swore, swamped her shields to gas the *Prisa* to its max.

And spared a fringe bit for the twin turrets.

"Get your guns up," Tarla said through the ship's intercom, taking over while Eponi dragged the *Prisa* as near the cruiser as she dared. "Two incoming, and if you let one hit my ship, I'm dumping you out the airlock."

The *Prisa* wasn't small enough to juke and jive between the cruiser's turrets and jutting modules, a dance that could've sent the missiles ramming a random wall—risking innocent lives inside—so Eponi skimmed the surface instead. Bobbing the ship sent the missiles and their predictive tracking into a wave-like stutter, each dip potentially creaming the bombs into the cruiser.

"Some help would be nice," Eponi said, watching the distance die as the missiles failed to fail.

Behind the *Prisa*, lancing into the wash, the ship's two turrets sent their counterfire. Using the scattering shot, the turrets sprayed low-powered light into the gap. The missiles might've dodged Eponi's tricks, but they had no answer for the laser waves. Both bombs popped in quick succession, blue and green clouds erupting and dying quick.

"Thank you," Eponi breathed, starting to sit back in her chair.

"You two just earned your rescue," Tarla said through the intercom. "Nice shooting. Have you ever considered a career change, say, to a small outfit?"

Any answer to Tarla's question vanished as Eponi sat forward, seeing and trying to understand the motion on the cruiser's surface. All those big guns, the ones that'd been passive this whole time, turned, tracking to the *Prisa*.

"Cruiser," Eponi said, flipping to a near-field open band. "Please tell me all those turrets aren't about to blow me to space dust?"

"What?" Tarla asked, as pissed off as Eponi wanted to be. "Why're they shooting us?"

The cruiser didn't reply, a problem that became a crisis as the first laser fired over the *Prisa*'s bow. Eponi equalized the shields with the engines now—they couldn't outrun the cruiser or its turret range—and cut right, angling towards the cruiser's docking bays. They'd have to traverse over the ship's top and down its side, but Eponi's in-the-moment calculation didn't offer another option.

"The scatter shots," Tarla answered her own question, coloring it with a few more choice words as she popped the intercom back open. "One of you morons hit the cruiser. Consider my offer withdrawn, and any damage this ship—"

"Tarla," Eponi said. "Please shut up so I can keep us alive!"

Beams came hot and fast now, forcing Eponi into a jagged dance. With her right hand on the flight stick, sending the *Prisa* up and down, holding close to the cruiser to keep the number of turrets with a firing line to a minimum, Eponi tapped away on the console with her left. Every finger touch pushed power to a maneuvering jet, sending the *Prisa's* body right and left, vertical or horizontal. Like the missiles, AI told the turrets where to fire, so as long as Eponi wasn't predictable they could—

The console blew out. Its screen melted as the *Prisa's* overhead lights died. The ship itself rumbled as another laser struck, an alarm squawking and dying as the ship tried to reroute power to critical systems. Tarla kept cursing, and Eponi, unable to swap power or trigger the jets anymore, did the only thing she could.

"Sorry," Eponi whispered as she nudged the flight stick forward.

The *Prisa* bounced as it skidded along the cruiser's surface. The two hulls ground on each other as Eponi brought her ship up and down in time with the cruiser's irregular skin. Shrieking metal noises made the pilot wince, made Tarla ask her what the hell she was doing.

"Keeping us alive," Eponi said, barely skimming over the lip before diving down the cruiser's far side. Those bays wouldn't be far away now. "We stay close, those turrets can't hit us."

"Won't matter if we crash!"

"We won't."

Her hands sweating, Eponi held the flight stick tight.

She fought back as the *Prisa* juddered with every spark-shooting scrape, the space above flashing whenever a turret thought it had a chance for a final shot. Left to dodge another gun sticking out, right to fall back between two blocky outcroppings. Eponi's eyes stung, but to blink meant death.

Beneath it all, her heart surged. This was the thrill, this was the rush she'd been missing since leaving the karts. Sure, a bubble would be nice. A cheering crowd. But the tight quarters, a game of centimeters at high speed?

High speed!

"Your console still working?" Eponi said. "Say yes."

"It is?" Tarla replied.

"Cut our speed. Twenty percent. Now."

Ahead, soft blue light interrupted space's normal void, coasting above the cruiser's gray metal exterior. A docking bay's telltale sign, and one the *Prisa* would be too fast to catch without some severe shifts.

"Done. Why?"

"Quiet," Eponi said. "Do what I say."

The *Prisa* came over the last mound before the bay, leaving a flat streak before the opening. The *Prisa*'s cut thrust did nothing to slow the ship because space was space and physics was physics. No friction, all freedom.

"Punch the bow jets," Eponi ordered.

Tarla did, proving she knew the cardinal rule of leading a team: let your experts work.

The *Prisa* swung end over end, its cockpit suddenly facing back the way they came, but with the ship's momentum still sending it towards the docking bay. The slow thrust now pushing against the *Prisa*'s old trajectory cut into the speed, slowing but not stopping the ship.

To stop meant to die.

The turrets, using the cleared space around the

docking bay, tried to get beads on the *Prisa*. Their bold orange bolts came in too high as Eponi kept her ship kissing metal, the hull now sitting over Eponi's head, with space and Aurum Three below.

"We can't get away from the hull or we get shot," Eponi said. "When I say, hit the bow jets again. Fifty percent this time."

With a swipe, Tarla made the adjustment. The docking bay's blue light grew brighter. The *Prisa*'s velocity fell.

Eponi had lost her kart racing career making crazy moves like these. All those had been showboating tricks played for crowds and prize money. Not this time.

"Now!" Eponi shouted as the docking bay's opening slid into view.

Tarla punched the console and the *Prisa* swung again, replacing the cruiser's hull with the bright-lit docking bay interior. The *Prisa*'s twenty percent thrust caught up with the ship's velocity as the flip started to push the *Prisa* away from the cruiser and right into the turret's target zone. For a long second, Eponi could see their salvation as it went away from them.

"Port jet, all of it!" Eponi called. "Ten percent main thrust."

The Twilight Ranger captain came through again, punching the left jet to flip the *Prisa* right-side up. With the thrust finishing off their remaining momentum, the *Prisa* slipped inside the docking bay, orange turret fire lighting up their engine wash and nothing more.

"Zero us out, Tarla," Eponi said, the moment's heat breaking into a cold sweat. "Pop those landing struts."

"With absolute pleasure," Tarla said, then laughed, a single relieved chuckle. "One helluva pilot."

Sitting back and staying that way, Eponi stared ahead as the *Prisa* settled into its docking position. The back-up bridge would have their excuses, and the Blade Wing fighter that shot its missiles late would apologize. Tarla would make sure to stick DefenseCorp with the repair bill, plus the fee for keeping its pilots alive.

All that could get worked out, but as Eponi came down from the high, she started scanning the comm bands, trying to find out what'd happened to the rest of her squad.

Levers

Rovo HIT Aurum Three's dark surface, Perro slung over his shoulder, looking for Javelin and finding nobody. The wide landing zone sat empty, though deep pits now spotted its surface. New divots formed, a steady shaking coming from the underground lab Rovo had left behind. Sai's mission down there wasn't playing nice with the foundation.

Maybe Sai decided to bury Anaskya and her virus?

The thought had Rovo turning back towards the door and the descending stair. He could bound down, get to Sai and—

Leave Perro to die?

Rovo had seen the spreading virus. Even if Sai dropped rocks on it, the stuff might continue to grow, might chew through whatever microbes lived in the sand to cover the planet. Rovo needed to find a ride up, convince some hefty orbital lasers to roast Anaskya's leftovers from a safe distance and get the Twilight Ranger some real medical help.

As if answering his thoughts, starship engines and their

crackle-rumble roiled through the whipping air. Rovo watched as one ship after another burst from the base's central structure, streaking up towards the sky. Who flew them? Rovo had no idea, but with Javelin nowhere in sight, Rovo had to try.

"Calling for assistance down at the landing pad," Rovo said, broadcasting on DefenseCorp's standard emergency frequency. "We're stranded in a bad spot and need a pick up."

The transmission beamed out, should've been caught by those fleeing ships. Rovo watched those jets streak on up and away with not a single pause, not a single reply. The power armor's comms unit wouldn't get a signal all the way to space, so Rovo didn't have any hope the *Prisa* would hear him, and he didn't think the DefenseCorp fleet would come to his rescue even if they did get his call.

"Jerks," Rovo muttered, flipping up a particular gesture with his armored hand towards the fleeing vessels.

As new plans formed and failed one after another, a buzzing signal rang in Rovo's ear. An incoming call on DefenseCorp's frequency.

"Hey, man," Javelin's voice came in quiet, fuzzy. "Caught your broadcast. You want a ride, we got it, but we could use some help."

"Where are you?" Rovo whirled around on the sand, seeing no signs.

"East side," Javelin replied. "Follow the signal, you'll find us."

"Us?" Rovo asked, but Javelin cut the call.

Rovo tried to raise the man again, returning the hail on the same frequency. No response. Javelin's signal had been weak, maybe the man had dropped too far out of range. That was the likely answer. Not, you know, any of the other deadly things running around this hellhole.

Summoning up his mediocre directional sense, Rovo put the base's central structure in line. On its west side sat the *Prisa*'s bloody bay, which made the sandy expanse to the East where Javelin said to go. With zero landmarks and little light save what the stars provided, Rovo pushed his power armor into motion, careful to keep Perro settled on his shoulder.

For all the time he'd spent venturing around the galaxy, Rovo had seen very little of it. Most starships, both to protect against cosmic radiation and to keep their hulls thick, presented little opportunity to look outside during journeys. Space stations did likewise, keeping viewing decks limited, making the act to visit one a competition with Rovo's other needs, like getting a drink or watching another bad action movie. In short, the cosmos remained at a distance, a thing captured on screen or in his imagination.

Until now, until his armored boots pounded through the sand amid a dark and dead base. Up above, starlight shone through without interference, silver lances showering the dunes around Rovo. A purple-blue swath cut through the sky above too, diffuse but beautiful nonetheless: the galaxy Rovo had been traversing laid out in its full splendor.

Dashing between dots, tiny flashes in orange and blue made clear all wasn't peaceful up there. Lasers continued delivering destruction, their import and the lives, including Eponi and Gregor's, at risk robbing some magic from the moment.

But only some.

For all Rovo's want of adventure, that bold fire rushing him from his bunk to his power armor on the morning Sever Squad set out for Dynas, these last months had forged that desire into something sharper, more focused. As the sand puffed up with every footstep, Rovo realized he didn't feel the urge to go diving back into Anaskya's disease pit, didn't want to mix it up with one more monster just for the sake of a fight.

Not unless it helped a person Rovo cared about.

"Cliche," Rovo huffed to himself as he crested another dune, looking down on a squat offshoot. "Of course the hero wants to help people."

Like the *Prisa*'s bay but without the rocky home, the structure embraced a rectangle's hard base and a dome's smooth, arcing sides. Built to shrug off a sandstorm, Rovo guessed the building, if this was Javelin's target, would open much like a flower. The sides would swing wide on massive hinges, offering protection to ships coming in and out.

Without any power, though, the bay wouldn't be opening for anyone.

"Guess the hero might have to help them out," Rovo muttered, grinning to himself.

Barreling down the dune, Rovo's size compared to the structure became more and more apparent. The bay towered over the Sever fighter, large enough to hold whole troop carriers or massive freighters. Apparently Defense-Corp expected this place to produce whole divisions, ready to swamp the galaxy with their murderous rage.

A lovely image, that.

Any concerns about an entrance disappeared when Rovo found the main doors already blown open. Someone with a rifle or a heavier weapon had torched the portals, leaving them charred and off to the side. Beyond, the entry hall sat dark, caught by an orange light towards the back, when the hall met the bay proper. The whole scene looked rough enough that Rovo took Perro, set him down outside the doors with his back to the wall.

"Try and stay alive, okay buddy?" Rovo said, snapping off the med kit from the power armor's back and spreading some salve, injecting Perro with an anti-infection cocktail. Whether any of it would make a difference, Rovo couldn't know, but looking at the bloodied, unconscious man, Rovo figured it wouldn't hurt either. "I'll, uh, be right back."

Unhooking his scythe from his belt, Rovo snapped the thing together into its large, sweeping setup. The hall and bay beyond had the space to swing it, and certain sounds hinted Javelin's call for Rovo's assistance wasn't made lightly.

When the *Prisa* docked, with Gregor and Sai embarking on their slaughter quest, Rovo had been in a turret. He'd heard the snarls, the roars, the choked off cries made by the infected as they'd made their hopeless charge. Those same sounds came back down, filtering out through the destroyed doors before getting lost in Aurum Three's nighttime whirlwinds. Mingled in among them came the hissing-whine as power packs burned, the sucking pop as a grenade burst.

The main difference between the bays?

Here, the snarls, scuffles, and cries were much louder. They filled the hall as Rovo stepped inside, the noises bouncing from inside the bay and back out. So many that the sounds blended together into a constant roar.

"Javelin?" Rovo said, beaming out the man's name. "Please tell me you're playing some bad music."

"Worse, mate. We started the wrong party. Get yourself to the middle, and don't be slow about it."

Something flickered across the orange light beyond. A growing shadow, now followed with heavy steps on the floor.

"Stop!" Rovo shouted, a test that the oncoming form failed when it decidedly did not stop, did not slow.

Rovo's old occupation, his original role on Sever, was all about communications. Getting the squad closer to their objectives without conflict, or finding ways to reach enemies and allies. Sometimes, that meant words.

Sometimes, getting the point across meant using a point.

Squaring up, Rovo swung the scythe in time with the charging shadow. Rovo punched up his power armor's lights at the same time, flaring their bright white at the creature. The sudden flash stunned the thing, a shambling half human, half moldering disease, long enough for Rovo's swing to catch and slice the monster like a particularly ugly wheat stalk.

Hero: one. Monsters: zero.

Rovo didn't have much chance to bask in his victory: as soon as his victim's pieces hit the ground, the light beaming from Rovo's armor went all the way along the hall and into the bay beyond. What Rovo had thought were stacked crates, maybe mounds of rusted out metal like the statues in the *Prisa*'s original bay, turned out to be oh so much worse.

Like a concert audience packed into every centimeter, the jammed creatures turned at the new show. Their arms, legs, bodies peeled and parted from each other as the crowd lurched towards Rovo. New growls, hisses, and calls went up as the things started after their prey.

The rookie had wondered where Dynas's other people had gone, what Vana and Anaskya had done with the wrecks not good enough for soldier duty.

Guess Rovo answered one question today.

One question the rookie had no desire to answer, though, was how long he'd last under a thousand-body press. Shifting the scythe to his right hand, Rovo snapped his pistol from his left waist holster, aimed it up above and fired into the entrance hall ceiling. The shots soared and seared into soft panels, breaking them apart. Above them sat the sparse offices for cargo loaders and traffic control, standard for bays like these and, given this base's crappy history, probably never used.

The onrush closed as Rovo looked up, punched in all the energy stored through his kinetic boosters, and prepped the leap of his life. Returning the pistol to his holster, Rovo gave the charging horde a little wave, brought the scythe up over his shoulder, and jumped.

Swinging the scythe, Rovo snaked its point through the hole his pistol opened up. The strike tore off more ceiling, weakening it enough so when Rovo's helmeted head smashed into the panels, his hands sliding up the scythe's haft, Rovo didn't bounce right back down into the waiting clutches of his closest, hungriest friends.

With the scythe digging in, Rovo punched his left hand through the floor and pulled himself up, the weakened tiles falling away beneath him. Scrambling away from the hole, Rovo found himself exactly where he thought: an empty, open office floor with broad windows looking into the bay. There, amid a teeming horde that seemed at times made of individuals and, in the next second, a singular diseased mass, sat a bulbous ship Rovo recognized.

The Twilight Rangers flew in something that could best be described as a gourd with weapons. Orange running lights streamed around the thing, showing a ship besieged. With the bay closed, it's not like the ship could leave, and Javelin wasn't a pilot anyway, so . . .

"Hey," Rovo said, squinting at the ship. "You can't fly. I'm not really a pilot. So what's the plan here?"

"Sanje's inside," Javelin quipped back quick. "He's

ready to go, but we can't leave with the bay shut. Hoping you had an idea for that one."

"Blow the doors open?"

"Tried it," Javelin replied. "Too strong. Or these turrets need more punch. Use that Sever brain of yours, man, and find us a way out."

His Sever brain?

Rovo glanced around the space, looking for a solution. Bare floor mingled with a few half-built desks, as if the people tasked with fulfilling this space had been called away mid-shift. No workstations presented themselves, no large buttons signaling an emergency power source. The docking bay doors did have a manual control, a lever resting dark against the windows. Rovo went to it, tried to pull, but the lever didn't move.

So much for that idea.

Back in the bay, the creatures innovated: climbing over themselves, their limbs here and there fusing together into a kind of mold-covered webbing, the former Dynas citizens crawled onto the Twilight Ranger's ship. Banging their fists on the hull, the clambering things likely didn't pose much danger to the craft.

But they could bury the ship. Rovo remembered the sting as the slime slipped between the slits in his armor, how hard it'd been to lift his arm free from the swamp in the underground lab. It would take a lotta bodies to bind a craft, but there were a lot of bodies down there. They'd get into the ship eventually, or bury Javelin and Sanje so deep the two would never get out.

Rovo looked closer at the lever. It had to connect to gears, some switch that would retract the bay doors. Without power, it might not make that link. Everything came back to the damn electricity.

Unless.

The lever sat against the wall, on a stand where anyone could get a good grip and pull. Rovo split the scythe and crouched, using the freed hook to carve a line into the gray block beneath the lever. One stroke, two and three followed by a punch, and Rovo had himself a look inside. With his suit's lights, the problem presented itself in sheer, stupefying clarity.

This ancillary docking bay hadn't ever been cleared by DefenseCorp. Its control center hadn't been outfitted. Vana could have opened it with an electric push from her wristlet, so why bother with all the little things needed for full time operation?

The manual lever sat ready to go, except nobody had bothered readying it for use. The steel clasp hung on the release, keeping the lever from starting the cascade to open the doors. Any normal base would've had this off, the manual release good to go.

Rovo laughed, drew his pistol and aimed.

Maybe he did have a Sever brain.

Two low power shots sheared off the clasp, and with his reaching hand, Rovo shoved the lock away.

"Get your engines rolling," Rovo said, standing. "That door's going to open up quick."

Javelin started to reply, but Rovo killed the call. Killed it because he saw something reflected in the windows, a shade in the orange light cast from the Twilight Ranger ship. The creatures down below had learned to stack themselves to get on the vessel.

They'd done the same to get in Rovo's office.

Snatching up the scythe from the floor, Rovo swung and caught the first creature across the chest, flinging it to the side. Two more followed, shrieking as they came at him. With his left hand, Rovo popped the scythe's bottom half, forming a circular shield. Thrusting it out like a punch, Rovo bought himself a second's time to holster the scythe and grab at the lever.

This time, it slid with a heavy *thunk*. This time, grinding gears followed the pull. This time, the bay doors began creaking apart.

And this time, Rovo felt grasping hands rip his scythe shield away. Throwing the weapon behind them, Rovo heard the clang as the scythe disappeared through the hole to the floor below.

Not that losing the weapon mattered. He had no room to swing it anyway.

With his back against the windows, Rovo couldn't see anything except more creatures charging at him, climbing over their fellows to get closer, like a building wave.

They pulled at his arms, tugged between his plates, bit at Rovo's visor as the crush pushed him back against the glass. Rovo tried to move, to get his sputtering suit to punch or push, but he'd burned his kinetic energy getting up here. The power armor, beaten up by a long mission, had little left to give.

So, too, did the windows.

As the bodies kept coming, as Rovo tried to find a way out between all the gnashing teeth, the scrapping hands, the glass at his back cracked and shattered. Falling over with the wave, Rovo shouted with all the rest as he plummeted into an angry, desperate, and dying sea.

At least, up above and beyond all the hell around him, Rovo saw the stars.

THIRTY-ONE

Bait and Burn

When Aurora and Vana reached the landing pad, their skinsuits coated with sand, they both noticed the retreating figure. A lumpy shadow sprinting away through the silver light towards a large dune, both the agent and the soldier tried to parse the form.

"It's heading for the other docking bay," Vana said. "The one where your mercenary friends are staying."

"What mercenary friends?"

"Their leader's a fiery one. The Twilight somethings?" Vana mused. "They said they knew you, could counter anything you came up with. I needed a distraction in case you arrived, and they came cheap. I guess you made an enemy?"

Tarla. Of course she'd be here. That might be why Aurora hadn't heard or seen the rest of her team since this mission started. Her hand tight on the pistol grip, Aurora considered, yet again, frying Vana where she stood.

But the agent might still be useful.

"I thought you wanted us to survive?" Aurora asked. "Hiring another group to kill us doesn't seem like it fits."

"Not kill. Delay, distract, mislead. My soldiers had to get away, and so they did." Vana pointed to the distant flashes. "That fleet? They're going to accept their destruction with open arms. Whole cruisers lost to DefenseCorp's own pride. The galaxy won't stand for it."

Aurora wanted to say that wouldn't happen. That Deepak and Sever would stop her. She couldn't get the words out, because, dammit, it looked like Vana had played them all to a win. The fleet up there would get destroyed, and the galaxy would learn what'd happened here.

Vana, though, had one flaw left in her plan. She wanted a clean death or a getaway here at the end. Neither would happen. DefenseCorp paid for its crimes. So would the agent.

"You brought us here," Aurora said, looking at the pitted landing pad. As her eyes covered the surface, grains shook, and a slight tremor nudged her feet. "Why?"

"Anaskya's lab sits beneath us," Vana said. "Only two ways in and out that Anaskya can use, and seeing what your friends already did to our power station, she'll come this way."

"And once we get rid of the scientist?"

"Then it's just you and me, Aurora. Like you wanted."

They approached the small boxlike building, its door blown open. Vana frowned at the opening, hesitating. Aurora gave the agent several seconds to put something together, then waved the pistol at the entry.

"Not what you expected?" Aurora asked.

"I had the lab sealed," Vana replied, running her own plans through her mind and her mouth. "My agents blocked the elevator on the other side. Locked this door. We had the soldiers sorted. Everyone that didn't qualify we left below, and opened the funnel."

"The funnel?"

Vana shook her head, "Renard started it before I became involved. All those poor people from Dynas. We tested the injections, and held them below, waited for them to die or survive strong enough to get a suit. Most lingered."

"Didn't answer my question, Vana."

"You'll figure it out eventually."

The agent made it one step before noises coming up and out the building had her stop. The loud thud as feet pounded the steps, punctuated here and there by a metal squeal as something clashed against the walls.

"Get back," Aurora said, choosing to leave aside the funnel for the moment. Vana didn't have a weapon, and the agent couldn't die here. "Leave me a shot."

Vana complied, moving to Aurora's left. She put up her hands, went into a slight crouch. Ready to spring into some martial routine, as if that would stop one of the creatures. Aurora would've laughed if she hadn't kept her focus on the dark doorway.

A bloodied, torn form burst out, blade sparking off the door frame. Aurora would've pulled the trigger except for the sword, the katana's curving arc catching the starlight. She knew Sai's blade too well, knew in an instant the shredded, grime-coated form before her had to be the swordsman.

Or someone who'd stolen his sword.

"Sai?" Aurora asked, back-stepping to keep things cautious while the man, breathing hard, stared back at them.

"Aurora?" Sai replied, before recognizing Vana. When Sai placed the agent's face, he brought the katana up. "You."

Vana tossed up her trademarked loose grin, "I see you've met our scientist."

Sai didn't joke, didn't reply. He walked towards Vana with a particular determination Aurora knew all too well. In a second, the agent's head would be lying in the sand.

"Sai, stop," Aurora said, but the swordsman ignored her. Vana's smile fell away and the agent started a retreat. "She's not dangerous."

"Like hell she's not," Sai growled, bringing the blade high for a two-handed swing.

Aurora shot. The blue-white bolt seared between the agent and the swordsman, cutting the air with its heat and, at last, making Sai stop. The swordsman glared Aurora's way while Vana's infuriating smile sprang back.

"What are you doing?" Sai said. "She's—"

"She's in our hands," Aurora interrupted. "We need what she knows, and I'm not having her executed here. It's too clean an ending."

"Too clean an ending?" Sai replied, jutting the katana towards the agent. "Every second she's alive, she's working on something worse. She's the mission, Aurora. Right here."

"Sai, look at yourself." Aurora forced calm into every word. "Vana said Anaskya is down there. That we had to stop her before the scientist did something worse than those soldiers. Did you see her?"

Sai shook his head, "See her? Anaskya's done. Her damn virus isn't, though. It's eating through the whole place down there. I think the stairs slowed it down because they're metal, but it's coming, Aurora." Again the katana went up, and again Vana took another step back, though her grin didn't fall this time. "Because Vana here gave Anaskya everything she wanted."

"Not everything," Vana countered. "Just enough for the galaxy to see how—"

"Quiet," Aurora said. "Don't open your mouth unless I ask you to. Sai, put up the sword and talk to us. You're saying there's more of this down there?"

Sai didn't hide the conflict, the katana trembling in his hands, but years following orders created habits that didn't die easy. With a sigh, he let the blade fall to the dirt. Sat down after it, a surprising move until Aurora took a harder look at the swordsman. Beneath the grime, Sai had cuts and bruises running all along his shredded skinsuit. Gashes crossed him up, looking like seeping scars in the starlight.

"It's worse," Sai said. "Anaskya modified it somehow. It's more aggressive now, spreading faster. She called it her child."

As Sai spoke, another tremor ran through the landing pad. Towards the center, pounded sand shifted, sinking into a growing pit. More followed, opening across the landing pad like some spreading . . . disease.

Aurora had to ditch those comparisons for a while.

"She's done it, then," Vana said. "Anaskya kept talking about a better formula, one she'd use if we gave her more time. The girl's blood unlocked it. I told her no and tried to keep her too busy."

"You failed." Sai spat.

"I did," Vana replied with a shrug. "But after it kills us, what then? It's not getting off the planet."

"For now," Aurora said. "Wasn't the blood supposed to let the disease live anywhere? Survive any environment? Could it get into vacuum?"

"Asking the wrong person," Vana said. "That's why I wanted to kill it now."

Sai muttered something about being too late. Aurora, though, looked across the landing pad, beyond those pits to what looked like a large, ruined building on the opposite side.

"Vana, is that the power station?" Aurora asked.

"Was," Sai answered. "I blew it up."

Aurora nodded, "And the power came from where? I don't see solar panels."

"A pipe, drilled deep," Sai said. "A lot of heat from inside the planet. Cooked me."

Missions never went as planned. Something went wrong, something went too right. You had to adjust, read the environment, your own resources, and figure out how to accomplish the objective. Right now, Aurora had seen enough of Anaskya's disease. Right now, she needed a weapon able to destroy it.

"You said the virus chased you?" Aurora asked the swordsman, those pits growing ever wider. A reddish glow tinted the light as it sank down into those holes. "Blindly?"

"It's a virus, not an animal," Sai replied. "Yeah, it chased me blindly."

If Anaskya's molecular monster wanted food, then Aurora figured she could make the thing work for it.

"I'll do it," Vana said. "Lead the virus to the fire?"

"Right idea, wrong person," Aurora replied. "Sai, you watch Vana. If she makes a move, do what you want."

"No reason to risk yourself, Aurora," Vana said. "I'm dead anyway, why—"

"You're not dead, and you won't be." Aurora waved Vana over past Sai, at the landing pad's edge and away from the growing pits. "Sit and wait like a good prisoner."

Vana gave a good glare. Aurora ignored it, watched the agent follow orders, then turned to the problem at hand.

Anaskya's virus, the living creature, whatever it was, seemed to be eroding the landing pad's very foundations. The constant rumbles paired with a burbling hiss now, with puffs rising up from the pits as rock and sand vanished into an indiscriminate maw.

"Careful," Sai said as Aurora walked closer to the pit's edge and looked down.

With the starlight shining in, the pit sloped into a smaller center. There, churning as dirt continued to fall into its pool, was Anaskya's creation. A bright red, sticky, and in constant motion, the virus looked more like a whole bunch of creatures swarming together, limbs all bunched up and coated with the cherry film.

In other words, pretty gross.

Around the pool's edges, as the sand fell away and took the lab's ceiling with it, Aurora could see an open corridor below. The virus didn't seem to be spreading like gas or water: aimless and everywhere. Instead, its momentum pushed it back towards Aurora and Sai, beneath them and towards the stairway Sai had used to get back to the surface.

"There's an opening," Aurora called. "I'm going for it."

"Good luck," Sai replied. "I'll keep her fresh for you."

"Counting on it."

Running around the pit's outside, Aurora went opposite Sai and Vana. She looked back at the power station, glanced down inside the pit, and plotted a path. The hallway below might not get Aurora right to where she needed to go, but with a general direction in mind, the Sever captain had to believe she could get there.

With one last look at Sai, catching the swordsman's salute with his blade, Aurora dropped in.

Sliding on the sand then falling the last few meters, Aurora splashed into the black grime, catching her landing on her hands and knees. Now at the same level, she looked directly at the virus, saw the impression of swirling limbs wasn't incorrect: just as Felix and his monsters became thralls to the disease, this one seemed to do the same.

But for all its bone and brine, the thing hadn't noticed Aurora yet. That had to change.

Raising her pistol, as coated in gunk now as the rest of her, Aurora took a deep breath, then pulled the trigger. The blue-white bolt flared out, struck home, and ignited a fire in the roiling red. The creature didn't make a noise, didn't issue some roar in pain, it just moved.

A surging red wave came towards Aurora, folding over the fire her pistol started and squashing the flames with its own body.

"Guess that worked," Aurora muttered, spinning on her heel and breaking into a sprint.

Raising her wristlet so its light could guide her, Aurora ran, scattering dark slime with every step. Pulling the pistol's trigger without aiming, the Sever captain tried to keep the creature's attention on her. The grinding, squelching noise following her footsteps seemed to prove Aurora had succeeded.

Hurrah.

The hallway didn't help much, ending fast and forcing Aurora to make a right turn. A short jaunt brought her to a huge room, one swimming in virus. The wristlet caught a red blade across the room, lingering near some rocks. A mystery for another time: the pathway she needed to follow sat to her left, and Aurora broke that way as the creature surged in behind her.

Every footfall came with a slide here, forcing Aurora to move with her momentum. She lost the pistol to keep from falling, dropping it as Aurora slid around a corner and used both hands to steady herself against the walls. Pushing off, she kept going, always listening, always hoping.

Until Aurora passed through a small door into a square room with a cushioned floor. Light came from above, an orange glow, along with breath-stealing heat. Looking up, Aurora caught the cut in the lift's floor, figuring Sai must've made the breach.

The plan had worked so far, but nobody mentioned climbing a shaft. Without her power armor, Aurora didn't have a grapple. Didn't have boots that could boost her. Without her pistol, the Sever captain didn't have weapons.

Shaking her head, Aurora backed up to the room's far wall. A clean-cut shaft, the walls didn't offer handholds. No maintenance ladders in this half-assed place.

"Let's hope you're as dumb as you look," Aurora said as the creature sludged its way into the room.

The thick mass groped towards her, rounded tendrils snaking her way as the red flowed in. Aurora took a step forward and jumped. The tendrils moved, following her, reaching for her. Thanking all those agility courses, Aurora planted a foot on one tendril, felt it sink in, felt it touch bone. Landing her right foot on another stump, Aurora pushed off, tore her feet free as the virus surged into the lift shaft.

With her wristlet guiding her steps, Aurora kept moving, using the walls to push off and keep the virus surging after her. The tendrils lunged, creating new footholds. Every step cost Aurora some skin, every step left virus on her legs, her arms, but every move bought her time, brought her farther up as the virus poured into the shaft.

Lunging up, Aurora's arms grabbed the jagged lip sliced with Sai's sword. She felt the cuts, accepted them as she pulled herself free from the creature's latest grapple. Standing in the lift, sweating, bleeding, Aurora took her first real look at the damage Sai had done.

There wasn't straight fire, not exactly. More like a blinding, suffocating heat emanating from the broken array. Flames lit the air in flashes, devouring what little oxygen made it inside the pipe's chamber.

Even with Kaia's blood, Aurora had to believe long exposure to heat like this would work, but the virus had to reach it. Would have to swarm around the pipe. Aurora glanced down through the lift as the virus began seeping through Sai's hole. She could run herself into the flame and it would follow.

Aurora would die, and the creature would burn.

Then she looked up, at the lift's top and the waiting exit hatch. Closed, torched, but viable. Aurora would give any plan that didn't involve a fiery sacrifice a second look. Maybe even a third.

Using the lift's sides as boosts, Aurora kicked herself up to the hatch and pulled the lever, popping the hatch open. The springs carried Aurora up with the opening door. She was out, she'd be free, she'd done—

A tendril grabbed her leg, wrapped itself around her foot as Aurora started climbing out. A second tendril joined, pulling as the virus surged into the lift beneath her. On the hatch's edge, Aurora yanked at her left leg, tried to free it as the virus climbed. Its stinging, biting slime infiltrated her wounds, swam into her blood.

Aurora had nothing to cut with, or she'd have sliced the leg clean, taken a risk on bleeding out then and there. Instead, she pulled, she watched as the virus climbed past her knee to her thigh. As it reached her waist, a tendril crawled for her face.

The virus shuddered. A tremor Aurora felt through its grasp. The shudder grew more violent, and a new smell filled the sweltering air, the awful stink of burning flesh. Smoke furled through the gaps in the hatch, climbing into the lift shaft. High-pitched pops, searing squeals rang out. Superheated bubbles bursting.

With another yank, Aurora broke her leg free. The virus lurched away, retreating down into the lift. Aurora leaned over, and pulled back as a fiery wave nearly torched off her hair. Orange flames filled the hatch, before descending along with their newfound food. Light filled the lift as Aurora sat, her back against the shaft's wall, and let the heat wash over her.

She'd sweat, but she would live.

That would be enough.

On An Edge

SAI WATCHED Aurora drop into the pit. His squad leader going in while he waited, butt in the sand. His right hand gripped his katana's hilt, though the sword, too, lay in the dirt. All along his body, grains and grime mingled with cuts and burns, wounds that salves and time had healed in the past, that Sai would need to heal again. He itched, his throat scratched with thirst, and his head pulsed with an exhausted ache.

So many missions ended like this, with Sai begging for a spin in the medical ward and a few long days spent doing nothing at all.

"She's a brave one," Vana said.

Sai turned his head, keeping Vana in view. The agent, seemingly unhurt, stood with her arms folded and a curious look, as if waiting to see whether Sai shared her opinion.

"We're all brave," Sai replied. "Not that an agent would understand."

"Oh, yes. We're all cowards because we don't go in with our guns out."

"No." Sai drew out the word into a stretch, pulling his tight muscles together and convincing them to stand up one more time. "You're cowards because you would rather run than own your actions."

"Is that what this looks like to you, running?"

Sai gestured his katana towards the pitted landing pad behind him, "There were agents all over here a few hours ago. You say you wanted Anaskya stopped. Any one of them could've done it."

Vana nodded, dropping her smile and reminding Sai with the lines running her face, the gray in her hair caught by starlight, that she wasn't some rookie to be scared.

"Why did Aurora keep coming back for you and Rovo?" Vana asked in a teacher's tone.

Sai, though, also wasn't some neophyte on his first trip away from home.

"You'll never convince me you care so much about these agents that you wanted to save them," Sai laughed. "What'd you do on Gillane Four? Oh yes. You injected your own team with Anaskya's poison. Did you know what would happen to them? How many died?"

"They were Renard's people, not mine," Vana said, as if that excused everything. "Aurora saves her squad. I save my agents."

"Aren't you a saint."

"The galaxy's going to understand why I did this," Vana replied. "I don't need you to."

"The galaxy's going to see you for the monster you are."

Between them, sand swirled, the wind whipped, and grumbling noise arose from the landing pad. Aurora's quest for the power station must be doing something, because Sai couldn't see the virus's red glow from the pit anymore. It'd pulled itself away after her, chasing the squad leader through the underground lab.

All because Vana gave Anaskya the opportunity.

"Is that sword all you have?" Vana asked.

Sharp with suspicion, Sai faced the agent straight, katana level. "It's more than enough."

"You're hurt. Tired and weak." Vana tapped her chin. "If I ran, could you catch me?"

"Try it and see."

The agent's eyes wandered, gauging the space to Sai's either side. Behind Vana, a dune rose up to the base's central building. A hard dash to make. Where else could she go? There weren't any ships left on the landing pad to grab, and every other part of the base seemed too far away for a straight up sprint.

Then again, this was an agent.

Vana took a single step to her left. Sai didn't budge. She took another.

Sai stayed still.

"Giving me a lead?" Vana said.

"There's nothing over there."

"That you know of."

"I'm too tired for games, Vana. If you want to run and give me an excuse to cut your life short, then do it. Otherwise, sit down and wait for Aurora to get back."

Behind Sai, the power station and its suit-making facility rumbled. Sai glanced back that way, seeing shadowy smoke rising into the sky. And no sign of Aurora.

"She might need help," Vana said. "Better go check it out."

"Then you're coming with me."

Vana didn't protest. With Sai letting the agent take the lead—always safer behind the enemy than in front—the two padded across the landing pad. Vana jogged with an effortless ease, while Sai wheezed his way through the crossing, giving the agent a chance to flash a laugh back his way.

"Going to make it, soldier?" Vana said. "Aurora might be dying right now."

Sai caught the jab, but couldn't really argue. Vana could get to the power station faster than he could, would be able to give Aurora a lift.

Or murder her if the Sever captain was wounded.

"Stay close," Sai said. "She'll survive."

For once, Vana didn't reply with open contempt. Instead, holding for a moment so Sai could catch up with her, Vana appraised him with a straight look.

"Now you're making the right choices," Vana said, matching pace with Sai, who tried and failed to get the agent to take the lead a second time. "You can't let me get away, no matter what the cost."

"You talk a lot for an agent, know that?"

Those words, at least, killed Vana's voice until the pair reached the power station and the tunnel leading inside.

The blown doors let them in, Vana sighing as she saw what Sai's mines had done to the suit assembly. The conveyer belts hung in shreds, the turning gears meant to keep them moving breaking with the sudden stop. The roof's collapsed sections flattened other parts, spraying debris around. A sweltering heat swam through everything, no breeze to be found.

"Smells like bodies are burning," Vana said as they stood at the tunnel's end looking at the mess.

"A smell you'd know," Sai replied.

"I don't see Aurora." Vana ignored Sai's slight. "Maybe she didn't make it after all."

"Come over here." Sai led the agent to the lift doors, shut closed. "Know how to get these open?"

"Without power? Isn't that supposed to be your specialty?"

"Might be. Go stand there." Sai pointed to his right, over to a corner.

Vana would have to run past Sai to get to the exit. A little added insurance. The agent, arms folded, leaned against the wall and watched. Steadying himself, Sai pushed away all his problems and hefted the katana. Lift doors weren't usually all that thick.

Here's hoping these followed the trend.

One strike threw sparks, left little more than a scratch on the surface. A second didn't get much deeper.

"Aurora's going to die of old age before you get through that door," Vana said. "Mind if I take a look?"

Sai gave the agent a good glower, but pride couldn't stand in the way of results. Standing back, he let Vana go past him. She went right for the lift's control panel, and specifically, a section beneath the badge scanner.

"Look at this," Vana said. "An emergency release. It's almost as though lifts sometimes break with people stuck inside?"

A fresher Sai might've laughed at his own mistake. Sure, being a Sever sometimes put him on a one-track mind, where every solution started and ended with destruction. Right now? Sai was hurt, tired, and paired with an agent he despised.

Logic, strategy, weren't exactly starring in his mental show.

With the lock released, Vana waved Sai forward and together the two pushed the doors aside. Like opening an oven, dry heat washed over them, putting Sai's already sweating skin into overdrive.

"And to think, all this time the base had a sauna and I

didn't even know," Vana said as they turned to look down into the shaft.

A wristlet's silver glow shown several floors down. Sai's eyes popped.

"Aurora?" Sai called.

A hacking cough answered, eventually forming into an affirmative. Sai let the katana sink to his side as he looked around for some way to get down there, to help Aurora up. No ropes, no maintenance ladders, but—

The shove came quick. A hard push, and Sai fell into the shaft. Reflex had him thrust his hands out, looking for something to grab. The katana's blade found the shaft's wall, slicing into the thin container and lighting the plummet with orange-white sparks.

Lighting, and slowing.

Doubling up his grip, Sai held onto the blade. The katana caught something hard, swinging Sai into a tough crash with the lift wall's side, hard enough to blur his vision and slip his hold. Sai fell free, only to land a second later on the lift's roof, a hearty clang ringing up through the shaft.

"Sorry about that!" Vana called. "Aurora, thanks for taking care of the virus for me. It's been a real pleasure working with you."

Without another look, the agent turned and left. An escape made without any chance of getting caught.

"Some rescue," Aurora whispered, her voice raw and tight.

Sai rolled up to a sit, looking over his captain. Together the two of them made for the filthiest, most damaged pair Sai had ever seen. Both had skinsuits that were, now, more shreds than suits. Hands and feet bore bloody scratches covered in black grime, with sweat streaking new lines across dirt-coated faces.

"I've had better," Sai replied.

The lift's roof didn't offer any obvious options for getting out. Smooth walls abounded, and Sai's katana sat up and away from his reach.

"Any ideas?" The swordsman asked Aurora. "Or are we going to melt in here?"

Aurora cracked a weak grin, her teeth a pearl counterpoint to the rest of their bodies, "I was working up the courage to try something before you came crashing in."

"Not my best work, I admit."

Without arguing Sai's assertion, Aurora motioned to the lift roof's opening, "Comm signals don't seem to work in here, so, back in?"

"Down there? Isn't that where the virus is?"

"Was, unless I'm way off in my guess," Aurora said. "I think the thing had a close encounter with your blown conduit."

Sai didn't have a better idea, as much as he hated this one. With one last look at the katana, the swordsman followed Aurora through the lift roof. If the heat had been intense up above, it stole their breath inside the lift. Sai's feet picked up new blisters touching the lift's inside as he and Aurora made their quick traversal. He didn't look at the searing orange glow: every other part of him had been torched, his eyes didn't need the treatment.

The drop to the bottom floor didn't bring them to cushions this time. Instead, a smoldering ash pile caught their fall, both Severs reacting with their training to roll away as they hit the ground. Together, with Aurora offering Sai a helping hand, the two made it from the lift shaft's pit, swatting burning bits off themselves.

Sai's wristlet had shorted in the fall, its screen a molten, melted thing. Aurora's still worked, fuzzing its way through spastic flashes.

"Worst part's over," Aurora said.

"It's all the worst," Sai replied. "Vana's escaped. I should have finished her up above."

"We'll find her, Sai. That's the mission." Aurora started down the hallway. "She can't get away every time."

"You sure about that?"

"You're not?"

Sai laughed, trudged off in Aurora's wake. The captain had a point. So long as Sever survived, the mission would continue.

And the squad hadn't failed yet.

THIRTY-THREE

Reeled In

After a certain point, after enough times on death's edge, Rovo no longer expected to cross over. With the power armor taking a beating, with the swarm all around him, Rovo held to the clear skies overhead and waited for the miracle that would come.

Admittedly, he had inside information.

Javelin's happy shouts hit Rovo's comm as soon as the rookie landed on the docking bay floor, whoops punctuated by the Twilight Ranger's ship bumping itself off the ground. The rumble paired with the diseased's grasping hands to give Rovo one more massage before his rescue, or his demise.

"Pick me up?" Rovo replied, wincing as another grime-coated fist smashed into his visor.

"Sure thing," Javelin said. "Where are you?"

"Look for the frenzy and you'll find me."

"Man, this whole thing's a frenzy. Do better."

Rovo gave the command to his armor, turned on the shoulder lights. Even with the mobbing mass, the rays shot up towards the sky. Their golden beacons lingered for a second, with Rovo calling them out to Javelin, before the swarm smothered the lights. Before they smothered Rovo too, blanking out the stars and everything else.

"You have a grip ready?" Javelin asked.

"I can't see anything."

"That a no?"

The visor punched up an alarm. Something had torn off a shoulder pad. Other fingers hooked into Rovo's chest plates, tugging at them. These things didn't seem too smart, but they'd figured out the meat lay inside the shell.

"I'm saying you need to get me out the hard way."

"You want the works? Then close your eyes."

Rovo didn't follow directions. The visor compensated for the flashes as the Twilight Rangers turned their ship into a weapon. The dark around Rovo went hot white and orange, followed by flames as the lasers scorched a line around the fighter. Bits of slime and wriggling virus pools clung to Rovo as the rookie sat up, looking at the burning circle around him.

"Effective," Rovo said.

"Glad you're happy. Grab the cable and let's get outta here," Javelin replied.

The ship's boarding door hung open above Rovo as the orange-lit gourd hovered over the bay. As Javelin spoke, a long rescue rope, a slashed black and steel combo designed for drop-in raids as much as rescues, unspooled Rovo's way.

"Hold that thought," Rovo said. "I didn't come here alone."

"What?"

"Meet me outside the entrance, you'll be happy you did." Rovo turned, saw the mass congealing around him. "And, uh, if you'd clear a path?"

The angle wasn't perfect, but the target wasn't small.

Sanje or Javelin—Rovo didn't know who did the shooting —sent blazing bolts from their ship's turrets into the mass beneath the entrance hall. Like the creatures attacking Rovo, like Felix way back on Dynas, the hits struck and ignited the things, sending them shrieking away or torching them to ash.

Taking off, Rovo lurched through the fiery gap. Every step came harder now, sparks spitting from the rookie's boots as he moved. Apparently those creatures could do some damage. A chill emerged at the idea of what Rovo would've faced without a rescue.

Well, he knew what. The evidence shifted all around him, growling and hissing and shouting as the creatures fled the turret fire.

Running along the entrance hall, Rovo saw a flash. His scythe, having fallen from its ceiling tile hook, lay on the ground. Without pausing, the rookie bent down and scooped it up, splitting it apart and slipping the halves into his holsters as he moved. Sai might've won the weapon for Rovo on Wexer, but the rookie had come to like the scythe.

One day, he might even learn how to use it properly.

Bursting through the bay's ground-level doors, Rovo saw Perro right where the rookie had left him. Both comforting and worrying—was Perro still alive?—Rovo stomped over and lifted the man up, striking a hero's pose. Behind him, the creatures advanced, snarling their way into the bay's entry as the Twilight Rangers flew their ship overhead.

"Who is that?" Javelin asked when the ship cruised overhead, sinking down and twisting its turrets to blanket the entrance hall in hot fire. "Doesn't look so hot."

"He's not," Rovo replied, watching the cable drop down. "Tell me you have some medical equipment on that tumor you call a ship."

"You be nice to her, or I might not let you onboard."

Rovo rolled his eyes, slung Perro over his left shoulder, and snagged the coil with his right hand. Javelin did the honors, retracting the coil, and after a few lovely seconds spent leaving the creatures behind, Rovo had Perro on the cold deck of his squad's ship.

Javelin and Sanje, leaving the ship hovering in place, broke into action when they saw their squadmate. While Rovo sat off to the side, taking off his damaged power armor one piece at a time—the ejection sequence had been damaged by the damn creatures—the two Rangers slathered Perro in healing salves, near drowned the man with drug-blessed water, and carried him to his quarters.

Freed from his suit, Rovo ventured into the ship's cockpit while the other two Rangers worked on Perro. Outside the windshield, Rovo saw the creatures spilling out from the bay. Some, not yet entangled, broke in random directions, sprinting across the dunes in search of food. Others, enmeshed with each other, stumbled and lurched at random.

How long would the things survive, with nothing but each other and sand to eat?

Rovo watched the outflow, absently spreading salve over some of his own cuts. He'd have infections to deal with, but for the moment, the rookie enjoyed taking breaths without fearing they'd be his last. They'd tried, all those monsters. They'd tried to get Rovo, and they'd failed.

Now they were running, lost, and . . ..

The thought faded as Rovo blinked, took a longer look. At first, the creatures had been going in all directions. Now, though, the things seemed to be chasing one another. The bigger masses pursued the smaller ones, all heading off to the east, to what seemed like open desert. Rovo would've looked for more, but the ship's windshield didn't give him a full view.

Glancing at the flight stick, Rovo listened for Javelin and Sanje. Neither seemed close, so the rookie leaned over and gave the stick a nudge. He wasn't a pilot, but any DefenseCorp soldier had enough training to land a drop shuttle in a crisis. The nudge sent the Ranger's ship turning left, giving Rovo a better view.

The creatures chased someone, a running figure—the long hair snapping out gave a hint it might be a woman—scrambling over a dune. She headed away from the base, apparently into the desert. A suicidal direction, given the tireless things chasing after her.

"Sanje!" Rovo called. He'd made the nudge, but any rescue attempt would be stressing his non-skills to the limit. "I need a pilot!"

"Need a pilot for what?" Sanje said, running back in. "What're you doing with my ship?"

"See her?" Rovo pointed. "She's in trouble."

One of the creatures reached the woman at the dune's crest. Expecting a swift demise, Rovo's eyes popped when the woman dropped into a fighter's stance and delivered a snapping kick sending the creature tumbling down the sand. Without waiting to see the result, she took off again, disappearing down the dune's other side.

"She doesn't look in trouble," Sanje said.

"Yeah, one down, a million to go," Rovo replied. "Let's help her."

"If she wanted help, she could've called," Sanje said, but he slid into the pilot's chair anyway. "It's not good business to rescue strangers. Particularly today."

"Treat it as a favor then, for Perro."

Sanje didn't argue that transaction. He goosed the flying gourd forward, over the creature parade and the dune's crest. On the other side, where Rovo expected to see an endless sand array, sat a squat hanger nestled into several other dunes. Big enough for a fighter, or a small transport the *Prisa*'s size. The woman ran towards it, more creatures tumbling down the dunes after her.

"This place has too many secrets," Sanje muttered as they coasted towards the hanger. "What's this doing here?"

"If you were doing terrible things to people who might want revenge," Rovo said, "might not be a bad idea to have a secret getaway."

"What're you saying?"

"I think I know who that might be."

Rovo didn't want to wonder about what seeing Vana way out here might mean for Aurora. The Sever captain would never let the agent go, so either Aurora died, or something had forced her off course. Either way, Sever had a mission, and its objective pounded sand right beneath them.

"Is that Vana?" Sanje said, leaning into the windshield. "She's still alive?"

"Blow up the hanger," Rovo said. "I don't know what's waiting in there, but she can't get to it."

"Tarla said to help you all, she didn't say anything about shooting our former employer."

"Let me put it this way," Rovo said as Vana finally took real notice of the ship above her, shooting a confused look their way. "DefenseCorp's going to be pissed after today. They'll want someone to pin all this on, and Vana's that person. Guess who they'll pay for delivering their excuse into their hands?"

"I get you, buddy," Sanje nodded. "I get you."

The Ranger punched away on his console, and the gourd lanced out with its twin turrets, grinding lasers into the hanger. The shots bit into and through the thin structure, hitting whatever lay behind and obliterating it in a lovely fireball.

At the sight, Rovo went back to the gourd's center and opened the boarding door. Sanje brought the ship down low enough for Rovo to unspool the coil, but instead he looked out and down at the woman who'd held him hostage for far too long.

Vana stood on the sand, wind whipping her dark hair across her face. The creatures and their hissing roars piled closer, hunting their stuck prey. The agent had seconds to make a choice, one Rovo didn't even have to articulate.

"I'm not going with you," Vana shouted up. "They'll kill me anyway. DefenseCorp deserves to die for what they've done."

Leaving Vana to get devoured by creatures of her own making did sound pretty damn appealing, but the agent might know where Aurora had ended up. Might know something that could stop these creatures, or prevent future attacks. All Vana's agents had scattered, some might have the virus with them, waiting to spring it on an unsuspecting planet.

The rookie owed it to the galaxy to reel Vana in alive, much as he might hate the idea.

"You think being dead's going to stop them?" Rovo called back. "DefenseCorp's just going to use you, and if you're dead, you won't be able to talk back. They'll suppress what happened here, and you'll be nothing."

"I planned for that," Vana slipped a look towards the oncoming creatures, frowned, then forced back her determination. "I have drives, I sent out recordings. The galaxy will know the truth!"

"Because you're going to tell it!"

Instead, Vana only smiled, then closed her eyes. Rovo

knew a death pose when he saw one—thanks again, movies—and cursed.

"Sanje, cover me!" Rovo shouted towards the cockpit.

Holding the coil in his hands, Rovo jumped from the boarding door. Around him, the gourd opened up its turrets again, laying down a firing line. Unlike the bay, though, the creatures weren't corralled here, and they spread out and around, coming in from all angles.

Rovo slammed into the sand next to Vana, ruining her serene moment. She turned, stared at him in stunned surprise, a look that took on a wholly different vibe when Rovo socked her in the face. The punch sent Vana slumping, Rovo catching the fall. With another shout up to Sanje, the coil retracted, yanking Rovo up for the second time in too few minutes as a viral tide swarmed his sandy footprints.

And Tarla had called him useless.

THIRTY-FOUR

Up And Away

Aurora and Sai followed the embers, their feet soaking up the hot remnants as the pair walked through the decimated underground lab. Ash littered Anaskya's home, the retreating virus bringing flames with it, a force even hungrier than itself that lapped up the grime on the walls, the pools in the rooms. The pair took hard turns several times, finding the direct route back to the stairs impassable thanks to still-raging infernos.

"Kaia's blood wasn't as strong as we thought," Sai mused as they crossed another spark-strewn intersection, his voice withered and dry.

"It worked with people," Aurora replied, wincing at the scratches her own words made as they came out. They both needed an express trip to, and a long stay at, a med bay. "Whatever Anaskya created might not have the same composition."

"Or maybe Aurum Three's just too damn hot."

"That too."

When the flames dwindled, Sai used his wristlet to guide them onward. After all the beatings, the burns,

Aurora felt like the silver-lit wander through torched passageways could've been their own walk to some dismal afterlife. Her body creaked and groaned, while what was left of her mind struggled to keep its composure. A feeling that often came after a mission's end, one Aurora preferred to tackle with a drink in hand and a long sleep in her future.

"We can't leave my sword," Sai said.

"It's not going anywhere," Aurora replied. "There's nobody left to take it."

"I'm realizing now how lucky it is I've kept that blade this long. How many times did we lose our power armor? Our rifles?"

"Gregor always seems to wind up with his hammer."

Sai didn't have a ready reply, which made Aurora wonder if the man wanted her to engage in some dialogue about the katana. Frankly, Aurora was amazed. She was amazed Sever had made it through all this crap with any of them alive, much less with any gear intact. If speaking didn't make Aurora feel like she had knives stuffed inside her neck, like her lungs hadn't been charbroiled, she might've given Sai the words he wanted.

For now, though, Sever's captain just wanted to walk.

They emerged into the deep night after climbing those metal stairs, steps that were blessedly cool on their burned feet. Above, the star smattered sky seemed devoid of lasers, a sign the fleet had either all been taken over by Vana's invaders, or her DefenseCorp friends had survived. She didn't have the energy to invest in either outcome.

Instead, she followed Sai as he started back towards the power station. Together, they padded across the pitted landing pad, avoiding the holes caused by the marauding virus.

"Think Vana escaped?" Sai asked.

"She tried to rocket me up to space on her old ship," Aurora replied.

"What?"

Aurora ran through the chase, the fight, and the drive still in her pocket. She felt for the little stick, its cold plastic and the metal inside hopefully workable after the fiery encounter.

"What a ridiculous plan," Sai said as they neared the power station's entry. "How many steps had to go right?"

"She pulled it off, though. And got away."

"We'll find her, like you said," Sai replied. "Next time she won't have a bunch of infected civilians screening her either."

"That she won't."

Orange lights interrupted their entry into the power station, a bulbous ship rising over the nearby dune and coasting their way. Its boarding door stood open, a familiar face waving in it.

"Is that Rovo?" Aurora asked.

"I did send him for help," Sai said, shaking his head. "Apparently he found some."

"You'll never believe who I've got in here!" Rovo called as the ship settled into a hover near the power station. "Also, there's a whole bunch of awful things coming this way, so you should get on board. I'm too tired to fight anymore."

Sai refused to leave without the katana, but with Rovo's help and the coil on the Twilight Ranger ship, the trio retrieved the blade and made it back on board before the infected masses found them. While Sai went for the medical kit, Aurora followed Rovo to the crew cabin he'd turned into a cell for Vana.

The woman had glares aplenty, but after confirming the stun cuffs were on right, that the door sealed tight and no other device beyond the agent's own wristlet waited in the room, Aurora left Vana to her own protests.

"Nice work, rookie," Aurora said to Rovo in the hallway outside, flashing a grin when Rovo started to protest the nickname.

From there, Aurora salved up, took a much needed shower, and found some of Tarla's clothes that'd fit her. Sai did the same while Sanje took the ship up to space, finding the DefenseCorp fleet in dwindling disarray.

Vana's shuttles and their crews had been dispatched, albeit with more than a dozen ships lost. Small ones, mainly, but with severe casualties nonetheless. Worse, Aurora had barely begun to feel like a human again before Deepak reached out to her and declared her presence necessary, with Vana, at an emergency meeting on the *Nautilus*.

Aurora waved away the idea, instead stealing the comm control from Sanje. She had higher priorities than sitting in a room while DefenseCorp's newest officers tried to take control.

First came the call across Sever's band, a shout directed to the *Prisa*, a ship thus far not showing on Sanje's scanners. Enough debris floated among the fleet that Sever's craft might be among the junk, but Aurora refused to believe Eponi would've fallen victim to some drop shuttle lasers.

"Captain!" Eponi's voice pumped through, crackling both with weak signal strength and delight. "Wasn't sure I'd hear from you again."

"Why weren't you there to pick us up?" Aurora said, suppressing her relief at Eponi's apparent survival.

"The *Prisa* isn't exactly good for atmospheric flight right now," Eponi said, and Aurora wondered why zero embarrassment came across with the admission. "We've been through a lot up here, and it's going to need some work."

"You let our ship—"

"My ship," a new voice interrupted, sounding very close to Eponi's. "My ship, Aurora. That was the price. We helped you, saved all your Sever lives, and in return, we get this ship."

"Tarla, if you touch a single thing on the *Prisa* . . . " Aurora warned.

"Chill, captain," Eponi came back on. "She's right. They really did help. After, I mean, almost killing us, but sometimes that's how it goes, you know?"

Did Aurora know?

"Eponi, you don't let her take that ship until we have a proper discussion about who saved who, and which of us decided to take a contract from a criminal," Aurora said.

"You got it, captain."

"'Til later, Aurora," Tarla added. "It's so good knowing you survived. I don't know what I'd do without you to despise."

"Likewise, Tarla. Likewise."

Sitting back, cutting the call, Aurora glanced Sanje's way. The Twilight Ranger pilot shrugged back at Aurora. Before she could start interrogating Sanje for more details, another call came in. This one from a nearby frigate. A captain who's face suggested far better days than this one fizzled into the console screen.

"Admiral Deepak said this was the right frequency for Sever squad?" The captain began, and when Aurora nodded, the man picked up some confidence. "We have a member of your team on board, and, well, he could use some help."

The Twilight Ranger's ship turned into a medical transport. Docking on the frigate, Aurora, Sai, and Rovo—

Javelin and Sanje stayed behind to keep an eye on Vana—met up with Briana and a clinging-to-life Gregor. The big man looked so alien in the bed, skin gray and plastered with sweat, his eyes closed and barrel chest barely rising and falling.

Together, with Rovo carrying Gregor's hammer, they loaded Sever's biggest member onto the gourd ship and set course for the *Nautilus*. There, they all joined him in the med bay. Each one stayed their own length, with new information from Gillane Four serving to help the treatment for the viral infections.

Rovo and Eponi, with the *Prisa* fixed up enough to fly over to the *Nautilus*, were the first freed to wander the ship. Aurora filled her recovery days with Deepak's requests to join the continued meetings between DefenseCorp talking heads, everyone jockeying to keep their new commands and the contracts they entailed.

Deepak tried to suppress Vana's tale, a move that failed when she found some willing surrogate to leak her story. The drive she'd given Aurora disappeared from the Sever captain's belongings, too—Aurora suspected Javelin, maybe Tarla herself as the thief—and its contents blasted out across the galaxy. The resulting media firestorm did more damage to DefenseCorp than any of Vana's suited killers. Aurora stayed on the periphery there, not wanting and not caring how DefenseCorp's factions dealt with the sudden suspicion of every civilized planet.

Instead, Aurora pulled Sever squad together a week after the events on Aurum Three. Everyone had new scars, and Gregor had a special patch over his abdomen designed to keep his guts in place while they healed. Still, the whole crew looked mostly like themselves as they all sat on the *Nautilus*'s viewing deck, watching the sandy planet and its white star shine. DefenseCorp clean-up crews scoured the base down there, making sure no infected remained.

Aurora wasn't one for tears, but she felt a couple rim up the edge of her eyes as the five of them gathered around a table. Rovo ordered the drinks for everyone, catching all their favorites and dishing them to the bar bot without missing a beat. The banter started, then slowly died as Sever's eyes turned Aurora's way.

"You have a speech for us, Aurora?" Sai asked, the father wearing an easy smile. "Something about how Sever's going to continue turning the galaxy into its personal piggy bank?"

"Actually," Aurora said, letting her own quiet grin fade, "I don't think that's what we're going to do, and I think all of you know it."

The sheer lack of surprise on all those faces, with Eponi even nodding, confirmed Aurora's own conversations with them all over the last few days.

"Sever started as an elite squad for an organization that," Aurora looked around them, "doesn't look like it's going to survive much longer. At least, not in the way we knew it. Not too long ago, the five of us voted to leave DefenseCorp and strike out on our own. We know how well that went."

"Not our fault," Rovo interjected, and Gregor added a nod of his own.

"Even so," Aurora continued, "we put our cash accounts at risk and earned, instead, a lot of danger for little reward. The mercenary game isn't as easy as we thought it would be." She went for her drink, thinking to take a long sip, but stopped. Aurora didn't need a squaddie interrupting here. "Deepak's asked me to come back. With everything that's happening, he wants someone he can trust in charge of his soldiers."

This time, at least, surprise kissed a few faces. Only Sai kept his knowing look unfazed.

"I'm accepting, and not just because Deepak's going to pay me damn well," Aurora put up the grin again, fierce this time. "I learned a lot from all of you, lessons that the soldiers on this ship ought to learn themselves. It might save some lives."

Another breath, the speech coming now to the part she hated most.

"Deepak asked me to extend offers to each of you as well. If you're interested, we'll find you a spot," Aurora continued. "But I have a feeling that's not going to be a problem."

Sever looked at each other. Rovo coughed. Then Gregor leaned forward, picked up his drink and held it high.

"A toast," Gregor growled, "to the best damn squad the galaxy has ever seen."

Five glasses clinked an end to an adventure, and started a long night swapping stories everyone had already heard, and that everyone relished hearing again.

The Trade

THE TAXI SLOWED to a hover at a lane's end, the blue grass giving cushion to Sai as he stepped off. The air nipped at his nose beneath a sea green sky. Modest homes, giant compared to crew cabins on the *Nautilus* or the *Prisa,* decorated the landscape in the swirling layouts designed to capture rainfall. His target?

Three doors down and on the right. A yellow home, with toys scattered around the wide front yard. Sai, one bag over his shoulder, the katana over his other, sporting an itchy civilian sweater, stared for a long second at the kiddie pool and the animal toys scattered around it. He'd left when his children were already too old for this stuff. Did he have the wrong address?

He checked his wristlet, compared it to the number plastered above the home's doorway, framed in faux flowers. Nope, definitely the right one.

Sai's daughter wouldn't make a mistake like that.

As Sai went towards the door, he fought to keep his eyes on the entry rather than scanning for threats. Being outside without a working visor sent twitches through his hands and legs, and Sai found his palms drifting towards holstered pistols that didn't exist.

The DefenseCorp official tasked with processing Sai's discharge said Sai's term of service would bring with it baggage that time would have to unravel. He loaded up Sai's wristlet with subscriptions to programs designed to ease Sai back into a life not filled with lasers, with missions, with random acts of violence.

Time, the man kept repeating, would solve any problem, so long as Sai let it.

At the door, Sai reached for the bell, a soft blue button inset against the pastel lemon home, then noticed the door sat slightly ajar. Sai set his bag down and listened. Out and around, Sai heard the calm background noise ever present in places like this—running machines, people calling to one another—but inside the house came a decisive sound.

The last time he'd heard a child laugh, Sai had been with Sever. After Dynas and on their way to Wexer, Kaia playing on Anaskya's ship. Faith restored, Sai pushed the door open all the way and stepped inside.

The child's giggling continued, drawing Sai back through a wide hallway, one with pictures clustered along the walls. He recognized the faces in those frames, his family growing through the years. It'd been a while since Sai had watched a new video—transmission times across the stars were so slow—but the father didn't forget his children.

Didn't forget his wife either.

She'd gone from a scrappy partner to a regal leader, matching and exceeding Sai's own role in keeping the family afloat. Given the house around him, her soft smile in all these photos, she'd continued right on in that role.

The hallway ended in a glass expanse opening into a broad backyard. Sai caught a long and wide table, set for ten, atop a cobblestoned patio. It all felt, looked so domestic. Sai felt dizzy, felt like an interloper in some life so far from his own.

But the child's laugh, a high squeal this time, pushed Sai forward one more step. The patio door opened without fuss, sliding aside. Going through, Sai tracked the child's now-muffled sounds to the left.

Standing there, arrayed as if from one of the pictures in the hall, were the people Sai loved more than anything else in the galaxy. The people he'd left behind looking for his real home. A home Sai knew, now, was right here.

"Hey dad," Sai's daughter said, holding the young one in her arms. "Want to meet your grandson?"

"I'll trade you," Sai replied, shifting his shoulder to swing the sheathed blade into his grip. "Katana for the kiddo."

Who knew if he'd ever trade back.

New Contract

THEY'D FOLLOWED the cash back to a planet Gregor never wanted to see again. Wexer's black-gray bulk loomed outside the *Prisa*'s windshield, a view Gregor held for a long minute before returning the central space to tweak his hammer and belt on his vest, leg and wrist pads.

"Bet you didn't see this one coming," Briana said, plugging in the battery packs to her cannon. The weapon made a tight fit getting on and off the *Prisa*, but the woman refused to leave it behind. "Calico Max and the Talpa on the same side?"

She laughed, a glorious gutbuster that had Gregor joining in. When Tarla announced the contract, mere days after departing the *Nautilus* in the Twilight Ranger's two-ship fleet, Gregor and Briana had laughed in much the same way. Calico Max and his mine-operating alien friends needed some security after the old DefenseCorp office closed up, its former official declaring himself owner of the planet and demanding his due.

Sounded like a prime target for Gregor's hammer.

"Eponi," Gregor called. "Put us down right on their base. I want this man to see how doomed he is."

"That's not Tarla's plan," Eponi replied, holding down the pilot's chair. Sanje flew the gourd ship—it had a name, just one Gregor never bothered to remember—and, as expected, the slower craft forced the Rangers into tedious strategies. "You want to go against her orders?"

"The faster we take this guy out, the sooner we get paid," Briana said. "Do that, and Tarla will love you forever."

"You better be right." The *Prisa* shuddered as Eponi kicked energy into the engines, launching the *Prisa* ahead of its counterpart. "Cause I'm blaming you if she gets upset."

"Uh huh," Briana replied, "like she could ever be mad at her golden girl."

Eponi had no counter to that, and the two in the back shared another laugh. Watching his friend navigate a wholly new challenge with Tarla had given Gregor more entertainment than anything since bashing through those suits above Aurum Three. Eponi, so far, seemed to be winning: she kept the right to fly the *Prisa*, and had Aurora transfer the ship's official title into her name, not Tarla's. Apparently Deepak agreed to find and compensate the craft's former owners, preventing any future nastiness.

A just reward for stopping that rogue cruiser.

Finishing with his hammer, Gregor sat back against the *Prisa*'s wall. He glanced at his wristlet, found the latest message beamed into his tag, coming in quick after Gregor sent out his own overdue hello. Long, meandering, and in every way amazing, Gregor indulged in the paragraphs his parents had sent along detailing their latest project, now supervising instead of blasting rock on a new comet.

That the messages had come and gone so fast meant

something even more fantastic: the comet, and his parents, were close by. Near enough that after they reduced this annoyance to nothing, Gregor might get Tarla to do a pass-by on the rock.

Briana whistled as she patted her laser cannon, a casual prep that had Gregor marveling at the moment. Without Aurora's meticulous briefings, the power armor, or the unspoken ranks throughout, the Twilight Rangers represented something new, something different.

"Told you this would be fun," Briana said, throwing Gregor a wink.

Gregor could only agree.

Career Change

THE KNOCK DREW Rovo's eyes away from the window and the ever-flowing sea beyond and below it. Another beautiful blue sky graced Gillane Four, the daylight pouring into Rovo's office and highlighting its blank walls, a sparse desk.

"Getting comfortable?" Raquel asked, opening the door and beaming in with a radiant smile.

"You could say that," Rovo replied, gesturing at the desk and the workstation, dark, on it. "It's a bit like going back in time."

"I thought we kept up with technology?" Raquel said.

"Not the components," Rovo said, then looked down at himself, "but the work. Last time I sat in an office like this, I wanted to be anywhere else."

Raquel crossed her arms, leaned against the wall. Without the constant stress of an agent attack, Salinity's security chief had a new life to her, a drive that showed in her sparkling eyes and clothes meant for a day spent getting things done with whomever she could wrangle. She and Aurora had a lot in common: all Raquel needed was a rifle and some power armor and Rovo would feel right at home.

"You're not going to be pushing papers," Raquel said. "After lunch, we're starting the interviews. You get to pick your own squad."

"That's what you're calling it? A squad?"

"Unless you'd prefer something else?"

Would he?

With DefenseCorp splintering into tiny fleets and mercenary contractors, Salinity decided to take further charge of their own security. Rovo would get to lead part of that effort, specifically training new and old officers how to actually defend a ship, a platform, a people. First up, Rovo had to find the crew who'd help him do that across a wide galaxy.

"A squad works, though now I've gotta think up a name," Rovo said.

"You can do that over lunch," Raquel said.

"Think I have time?"

"You most definitely do. Come on."

Not that Rovo would say no to Raquel anyway. A job hadn't been the only reason the rookie wanted to return to Gillane Four.

Salinity's office tower cafeteria lacked the *Nautilus*'s steel-and-sober setting, reminding Rovo once again he now worked for an organization that didn't throw its members into harms way day in and day out. Casual beat music floated overhead while happy noontime chatter bounced around the wide space, side wall skylights giving a refreshing glow.

All that, though, faded when a single sparkling shout rose above the noise. Rovo, three steps off the lift, crouched down to receive Kaia's rushing hug. Behind her, for once not showing open frustration on his face, came

Kashmal. The girl seemed happy, glowing with health, and when Rovo said she could see him any day she wanted, Kaia's light washed away any doubts about ditching DefenseCorp.

No, the job definitely wasn't the only reason.

THIRTY-EIGHT

Penance

Despite spending most of her nights on the observation deck, the views had yet to tire Aurora. With the *Nautilus* on the move back towards the fringe—Deepak's preferred place to play—looking towards the galactic core presented popping colors across the spectrum, interstellar beauty sliding through an infinite sky.

"Her story squares," Deepak said, the admiral joining Aurora with two drinks in his hands. "Everything we've been able to find matches up."

"She's not keeping secrets."

"I can't figure out what game Vana's playing," Deepak said, matching Aurora's look towards the sky. "I kept her here with a promise that I'd find out what she wanted, and I still don't know."

The beverage trickled a saucy spice with the bourbon. A good mix with the deck's cool temp.

"You've been obsessing over her," Aurora said. "You're looking for ghosts that aren't there."

"Could be." Deepak raised the glass to his lips, didn't take a drink. "You think I'm chasing nothing?"

Aurora had listened to Vana's straightforward story along with everyone else. The agent, tired and victorious, delivered every answer without hesitation, without calculation. That Deepak and his own team found Vana spoke the truth came with no surprise.

"She lost her home because the wrong side bought our services," Aurora said. "There's millions like her out there, Vana just had the guts to do something about it."

"Tear us apart from the inside out of spite?"

"And scare the galaxy away from creating mindless monsters." Aurora didn't play games with her drink, enjoying the burn. "I'd call it noble if she hadn't killed so many to do it."

Silence filled the gap while a purple-white nebula took centerstage overhead. Streaks burst across, silver lines showcasing passing comets, debris, even other ships.

"You think she was right?" Deepak asked.

"No," Aurora said. "But she thinks she is, and that's all it takes."

"The families who lost people to Dynas and Anaskya's experiments want blood," Deepak said. "They want her dead, and dead the old fashioned way."

"No airlock for Vana?"

"I can't. She still has agents out there in the wild, ones that may have the virus. Until we find them, I can't gamble more lives on her."

"Guess it's hard being in command."

Deepak sighed, glanced Aurora's way, "When you left for Aurum Three's surface, did you intend to kill her?"

"We thought she was going to unleash an invincible, invisible army. The goal was stopping her," Aurora matched Deepak's look. "If ending Vana's life brought that about, I would have pulled the trigger. No hesitation.

When it became clear putting her in the dirt wouldn't stop what'd happened, we changed the mission."

"And left me with a big headache."

"Poor you." Aurora waved her glass around. "Such a hard life you lead."

Deepak laughed, "No easier with you in it."

"No easier? Your ranks were a mess! Your—"

"Stop." Deepak held up his hands in mock surrender. "You'll tell me all about it in the morning, I'm sure. And Vana will still be there too. Let me have one peaceful moment."

That one moment went by. The stars outside indulged.

"I have one idea for Vana," Aurora said, slow, feeling out the intuition as it came.

"Do tell."

"DefenseCorp's breaking up. It's going to be the *Nautilus* and friends fighting with so many other factions for contracts," Aurora said. "You're going to need goodwill after what's happened, some way to get planets on your side."

"I already said we won't do a public execution."

"No, different." Aurora set her glass down, gave Deepak the squad leader stare. "Vana makes memorials. Tells the stories of everyone that died on Dynas, on Aurum Three. We give them polish, send them out. Vana's agents can help her get the information she needs to put them together, and we get some much needed love whenever a planet, a city, a family gets to say goodbye."

Deepak's wheels turned. Unlike Rovo, or even Sai, the admiral never bowed straight to Aurora's words. Frustrating, at times.

"Vana would do this because . . .?" Deepak asked.

"Because it's what she wants," Aurora replied. "This

lets her tell her story again and again, which means the galaxy's never going to forget what happened here. The factions can't wait a few years for people to move on and reform DefenseCorp. It's Vana's legacy as much as anything."

They chewed on that for a drink and a half. The purple nebula shone brighter with every sip. Aurora kept replaying her words, kept finding little holes that might need addressing, but nothing that'd collapse the whole idea. Deepak brought the musing into the open, and they traded thoughts, building a plan like colleagues, like friends, like lovers did.

"Is that what you want?" Deepak said finally, when they'd gone back and forth enough that the lines blurred as much as their vision. "Vana to stick around, make all these things?"

The moment or the mission.

"We kick her into a star, we get a satisfying second," Aurora said. "We honor all those lost lives, we achieve what we sent out to do in the beginning: rescue the people on Dynas."

"That mission was for one person and, if I recall your debrief, he was a drunk looking to make some quick cash."

Aurora grinned, "Don't let perfect be the enemy of good, admiral. You need cash to pay your people, Vana needs penance, and I need something to inspire my soldiers. This hits all three."

Deepak settled into the words, shook his head and raised his glass to clink against Aurora's.

"Know what this means?" Deepak said.

"What?"

"I'm never sending you on a mission again. You're too valuable."

Aurora laughed, "You know, I think I could use a break."

Besides, it'd be weeks before the *Nautilus* reached its destination, a swamp-covered world in need of a clean-up. Looking out at the stars, the nebula, and even Deepak's bourbon-flushed face, Aurora figured she'd enjoy the ride.

An Excerpt from PARAGON'S FALL

THE HERO'S CODE BOOK ONE

From the snow-slicked street, Aegis saw the lights, heard the sounds of his targets. Voices didn't carry the sixty-some floors down the sole lit span in the tall, wide building dominating the abandoned business park, but the shots did; rattle-cracks from old model guns, tattled on their owners with their rat-a-tats. The noise proved Aegis had a reason to be out here at a time of night known for villains, and perfect for those hunting them.

The pod behind him gave a warm beep as it began rolling towards its next request. The sound triggered a quick inventory check: gloves, a plated vest over a thick dark wool sweater to keep Aegis warm, a pair of Paragon-uniform pants belted over with accessories, including everything Aegis would need to disable, kill, or call for help. Nestled over his nose and cupping his eyes sat black-and-blue goggles that kept incoming light optimal for anything.

No helmet. Aegis wouldn't go that far. News crews would chase his pod signature, and they would be here. The Paragons ran the world. Their mascot couldn't hide.

His boots, with soft pads built into the heels to keep old feet comfortable, did a fine job conquering the concrete walk towards the building's entry. Snow piled up on the sides, plowed with precision by automated labor so cheap the cities could keep it running for ghosted buildings like this one. A pair of tall, shock-white columns flanked the entrance, bearing an etched logo not quite strong enough to overcome decades of irrelevance to find a trigger in Aegis's memories.

Between rounds of cracking fire from above, Aegis crunched snow to the thrum of New York. Trains pulsed beneath him, the rushing keeping pace with his steps, while a vague scent of decay seeped through the breeze into every breath. A lot of these broken business parks surrounded the compacting city, now, and they all smelled like this. Felt like this while they waited for someone to save them.

A set of double-doors provoked a majesty marred by shattered glass, by the bent handle showing reckless force applied to the opening. Aegis used his predecessor's handiwork and stepped over the shards. He'd send a rep offer out tomorrow, get someone to clean it up. Image mattered, even out here.

"You're there?" Celice came through his earpiece. She chewed something, teeth gnashing thick.

Eggplant. One of the reasons Aegis had taken this call personally. He looked forward to dinners with his daughter, but now she kept insisting on recipes meant for old men and goats. Aegis would eat the leftovers when he came back, though. After he'd had a bit of aggression to work up his appetite, when he could justify some sort of protein to go with the veg-tastic dish.

"I'm here," Aegis said. "They broke in. Not subtle about it."

"Do you need back-up? I can send the call," Celice paused, except for her chewing. "A couple drones aren't too far. Ten minutes."

"I'll be fine."

"Dad."

The lobby had held up better than the door, possibly owing to its barren blandness. A long desk stretched in front of an empty wall the same white as the columns outside. Space for chairs, a line of receptionists and, where Aegis stood now, a constant flood of customers and employees. Working so hard for money at the cost of family and friends. While the Paragons had much left to do, they had at least ended the mad scramble for cash.

"Call the drones then," Aegis said, "but I'm not waiting."

The elevators posed a problem. If the criminals up top had any sense, they would have someone watching the only reasonable entry to their floor, and elevators like these displayed their location in white numbers on black bars atop their slate-gray doors. The moment Aegis punched a number, his imminent arrival would be clear to anyone paying attention. Stairs lingered as a possibility, but for sixty flights, not a sane one.

The drones would beat Aegis to the targets if he took that route.

"Going in," Aegis said, both for his daughter and the recording.

Every mission, every word the Paragons spoke in action sat in their vaults. Ready and waiting to counter the dual threats of hyper-inflated media and the myth-making enterprises involved in painting the Paragons like arbitrary gods. Recruit anomalies, keep the normals from getting scared. Two birds, one stone, etc. The more the Paragons were seen not only as the world's guardians, but its friends, the less trouble would be thrown their way. For that matter, it'd been too long since Aegis had sent out a release of his own, proof that the Champion himself still performed out here, still chased down evil.

Inspiration came from the top, and if providing it required a few hits, then Aegis could take them.

The elevators matched the front entrance, one suffering violence extreme enough to leave its door hanging while the other waited for passengers, though its sharp squeals signified good looks wouldn't keep the elevator long from forced retirement. Aegis ought to survive if the thing fell apart with him in it, but those people already up top likely would not. Which means they were both brave and stupid, or they'd made the safe, slow call and climbed the stairs. Knowing the sorts of people who would take potshots with weapons in an abandoned tower at night, Aegis bet the former.

The elevator's speed preached new definitions of the word *slow*, which gave Aegis another chance to stretch out. Feel his shoulders crack and test the limits of his lungs with a few deep breaths. His stun gun had a loaded dart, and he kept the weapon ready in his right hand as the numbers on the panel climbed. He shifted to the left side of the elevator, minimizing his profile. Years ago, Aegis would have stood stock center, hands on hips and ready to win through cocky intimidation alone.

That time ended when the bruises started following him home, haunting him the day after. When the concern in Celice's eyes stole away his macho grin.

The elevator announced its arrival with the sound of a dying balloon instead of a cheery ding, but the lift made it to the sixtieth floor. The doors began their same, slow crawl and the *blam blam blam* of heavy weapons fire poured through. Not at Aegis, though. The morons continued their party. They'd had every opportunity to prepare, to set an ambush, and instead they'd opted for more champagne.

The opened door cleared the way to a smaller, nicer lobby, as though its height preserved the glass-lined white furniture from the seeping decay down below. A circular desk sat off to the right side, required chair and anything on it gone, ransacked for what could be carried. The lobby's sole occupant leaned against the desk now: a man holding an old-model handgun down at his hip and staring at his Tama and the image it projected above the man's forearm.

Aegis lowered his own gun and walked out of the elevator, making it halfway across the lobby before the man bothered to look up. At the sight of the armed and armored head of the Paragons, the world's most famous Champion, the man's head cocked to a side, eyebrow raised. Questioning the impossible. Aegis decided to prove it.

A long stride, a good stretch of Aegis's right quad leading into a solid right hook, took the man's just-opened mouth before he could make a sound. With his left arm, Aegis caught the fallen guard and set the suited figure onto the pearl-white tile.

"Trig blink neutral," Aegis said, following a hunch.

His goggles took the command and shut off their processing for a solid second, giving Aegis a true look at where he operated. Line lights, with their bright trails, filled the gaps between the ceiling tiles and sprayed such a harsh glow that the lobby seemed like a snow-covered mountain at noon. No wonder the guard had trouble reacting to Aegis—keeping the floor this washed out would make identification impossible without goggles like his.

The lobby played security for a single path, one locked by a walnut-wood door whose key card seal stood out on the wall with a small speck of red showing power. A look behind the reception desk showed any bypass that might have existed had gone the way of the chair and the monitor.

"Trig P-Lock," Aegis said to the room, then held his left, Tama-bearing wrist against the card reader.

Paragon technology worked again and the reader beeped its submission to Aegis's rank, jutting open the lock and allowing Aegis to open the heavy door via the chrome-metal bar on its front.

Another ambush opportunity came and went as Aegis, with the door opened just enough to see around, looked into an empty hallway. At the far end, past a number of secondary split-offs, the hallway opened into the sort of broad, overlooking space so favored by the high floors in these buildings. A chance to look down upon all those you'd managed to rise above.

The weapons-fire had stopped, and from the door, Aegis could see why. Some of the windows of that overlook were shattered, and the intact pair that Aegis could see sported the telltale star-burst of bullets streaking through. Bullets that likely came from the big, turreted gun in the center of the room, facing outside.

"Are you seeing that?" Aegis said.

"Looks like we've found our target," Celice replied.

"They could take out the drones with a weapon that size," Aegis said. "Tell them to keep off."

"I'll tell them to watch out. Mynx can always make more."

Aegis wanted to say that Mynx made enough of the things already, but stopped. These jerks might not have an ambush ready now, but they could change their mind any second. Better to take advantage of surprise while you have it, than lose it arguing about things that didn't matter.

Besides, Aegis knew the real reason he didn't want the drones around: they'd take away the glow. That oh-so-sweet vindication Aegis would get when he stood in the courtyard below, speaking to the media about another successful Paragon operation. Sharing the spotlight with a pair of Mynx's mechanical monsters would mean . . . sharing.

Aegis slipped through the door into the hallway, hugging the right wall and watching the far glass for any sign of motion. Every step came with a roll of the heel, his hands holding his stun gun forward and ready. He crept closer to the first cross-section, quick-stepped up to the bisecting hallway and leaned to give himself a view without exposing his back.

Empty. Aegis reversed to the other side of the hallway, stun gun aimed along the opposite direction. Nothing there either. Closed office doors. Empty white walls with brighter, square blotches exposing art's former home.

Aegis took a breath. Slow, shallow. Listened.

Laughter. Towards the windowed room. The sound of liquid hitting glass. Not laying a trap, then, but celebrating.

He'd spent too much time going after hardened criminals. Enemies who knew full well what Aegis and the Paragons could do and prepped to fight them. These, these were the kinds of bottom-barrel criminals you fought when all the others were gone. Who filled the void left when you'd eliminated the truly terrifying.

Aegis shook his head at nothing. He'd be surprised to get a single interview after this one. Who cared if a bunch of low-level bums shot up some abandoned buildings? He slipped the stun gun back into its holster. The least he could get from this would be some fun.

Aegis wheeled left, into the side hallway whose end revealed another cross-section. He moved quicker now, padding his feet to the sounds of chatter, talk of weapons moved and weapons made. New deals struck. Despite all efforts, the Paragons could never get rid of every under-the-table transaction, couldn't quite cleanse the world of its muck, but Aegis felt they'd at least made sure to punish the main offenders. You could swim in the swamp, but you would pay a price.

At the end of the new hallway, Aegis peeked right and saw the party. A quartet of chuckling nobodies, who wore a mix of drifter-style gear that confirmed Aegis's assessment of their neophyte status in the criminal game. Two cylinders occupied the center space on a pop-up plastic table otherwise covered in the remnants of a garbage dinner; synth food Aegis wouldn't touch. One cylinder bore the telltale brown of bourbon or whiskey, the other looked like water. No surprise which held less.

The real shock, for one of the four, a capped man whose eyes floated past his friends in mid-drink, was Aegis making his way in long strides down the final stretch of hallway. The man paused his swig, his bloodshot stare struggling to make sense of what came towards him, before his hand lost grip on the glass entirely and the man stumbled back, uttering some form of warning shout that drove his partners to confusion.

Aegis connected his first swing with the sound of the capped man's glass hitting the tiled floor and shattering. Not that his target, whose puffy, pale cheeks took Aegis's blow with a satisfying squelch, appreciated the timing. Nor, Aegis figured, did the man enjoy having his face collide with the remnants of dinner and the pop-up table, but the life of a criminal was often one of disappointment, especially when Paragons were around.

The next one in line, a gibbering, shorter man whose legion of coats and sweaters belied a tropical ancestry, didn't get enough distance on his scrambling back-step to escape Aegis's reach. With both hands gripping the short man's coat, Aegis whipped him to the right, into and through the thin, decaying wall into what was once a high-profile office. Now, in a far cry from the monetary mountains once moved in its confines, the short criminal laid unconscious and covered in drywall on the office's floor. One more injustice leveled in the building, and not the last to come.

Two left. The capped man, who'd made it as far as the glass windows on the level, who's hands were reaching for a gun somewhere on his person, and a lanky, suit-sporting specialist. Aegis had seen enough fighters in his time to know the leader, to know who posed the greatest threat, and he could dissemble any of a thousand clues to find that one person in a group of enemies. This time, it didn't take much: the specialist's eyes were narrow, his hands weren't twitching, and he didn't appear to be praying to some deity for salvation. In other words, the specialist was everything the capped man wasn't.

Aegis broke for the specialist with a barreling charge, using the sheer spectacle of the Paragon leader in full battle array for intimidation. This tended to result in the cowering collapse of most enemies, with the occasional outright turn and flee for the true cowards. The specialist, though, reached into his jacket, pulled out a handgun the likes of which the Paragons had banned decades ago, like the one the elevator guard had held, and fired.

For most of his life, Aegis had a cordial relationship with bullets. They would greet him with their usual ferocity, and Aegis would disarm their damage with the very thing that made him the Paragon's icon: an invulnerable skin. The shots would sort of sink against Aegis, and then fall away to the ground, leaving nothing so much as a mark for their trouble. Missions had gone by where hundreds or thousands of rounds had poured into the Paragon and found themselves rendered useless, whether they struck his arms, legs, eyes, teeth or anywhere else. As though a divine cloak covered Aegis and kept him safe from harm.

That cloak did its job again now, catching the bullet as it struck Aegis's left shoulder, outside the reaches of the vest where the shot tore through Aegis's clothes and rendered its ineffectual verdict against the Paragon's body. The specialist managed to snap off a second round that went directly into the vacuum hole of Aegis's vest, causing nothing so much as a microsecond's pause in the Paragon's momentum.

There was no third shot.

The capped man, having seen his partners laid to waste, took the safer road and awaited his arrest with the simpering pleas of the over-matched and guilty. Any thoughts of further escape vanished when Mynx's drones arrived, shattering the remaining glass and hovering inside the room, stun guns at the ready, lethal options awaiting an algorithm's calculation.

"Late, as always," Aegis said to the machines, standing near the capped man with the unconscious body of the specialist hanging from his right arm.

Aegis took the specialist down himself, leaving the drones to watch over the other three. By now, at the base of the building, a few pods had arrived and disgorged news crews looking to feed the ravenous beast of popular content. And the media found nothing more popular than a Champion conducting a raid. Aegis strode out to meet the flashes, the cameras, the pouring of questions from reporters and fans alike.

Before answering a single one, though, Aegis directed the other late arrivals, the lower Paragons whose job included this district, who had asked Aegis to cover for them. Who would have taken the bullets he bore instead. The trio of motley anomalies, wearing their Paragon blues, swept by Aegis towards the tower. They'd take the other three, plus this one, and divine the proper punishment. The cost in reps owed, and the best methods of repayment.

"Are you all right?" Celice's voice, coming through the ear piece, cut through the calls from the press.

"I'll live," Aegis gave his classic comeback, then dumped the specialist on the ground in front of the cameras as snow began to fall between the lights.

He had a speech for this, a modified version of the stock Paragon set of warnings, lessons, and calls for a better tomorrow. The difference this time, what made Aegis's words come slower, and forced him to focus to keep standing tall, was the spreading pain in his left shoulder. An aching, deep, bone-crunching pain that he'd never felt before.

Continue the adventure in PARAGON'S FALL, available now!

Acknowledgments

This novel is the product of my family and friends refusing to let a dream die. My wife Nicole, for letting me write in the early mornings and making sure I don't starve. My brothers and parents for their continual comments, support, and enthusiasm.

Evan Aaseng, for being a constant sounding board and reeling me back in whenever my ideas went too far.

And, of course, you, the reader, for giving me a reason to write.

About the Author

A.R. Knight spins stories in a frosty house in Madison, WI, primarily owned by a pair of cats. After getting sucked into the working grind in the economic crash of the 2008, he found himself spending boring meetings soaring through space and going on grand adventures.

Eventually, spending time with podcasting, screenplays, short stories and other novels, he found a story he could fall into and a cast of characters both entertaining and full of heart.

After Sever Squad, A.R. Knight plans on jumping through to other worlds and finding new stories to tell in the limitless borders of our imagination.

Thanks, as always, for reading!

For more information:
www.adamrknight.com

To Peter